MYTH-FORTUNES

ROBERT ASPRIN
and JODY LYNN NYE

ACE BOOKS, NEW YORK

THE BERKLEY PUBLISHING GROUP
Published by the Penguin Group
Penguin Group (USA) Inc.
375 Hudson Street, New York, New York 10014, USA
Penguin Group (Canada), 90 Eglinton Avenue East, Suite 700, Toronto, Ontario M4P 2Y3, Canada
(a division of Pearson Penguin Canada Inc.)
Penguin Books Ltd., 80 Strand, London WC2R 0RL, England
Penguin Books Ireland, 25 St. Stephen's Green, Dublin 2, Ireland (a division of Penguin Books Ltd.)
Penguin Group (Australia), 250 Camberwell Road, Camberwell, Victoria 3124, Australia
(a division of Pearson Australia Group Pty. Ltd.)
Penguin Books India Pvt. Ltd., 11 Community Centre, Panchsheel Park, New Delhi—110 017, India
Penguin Group (NZ), 67 Apollo Drive, Rosedale, Auckland 0632, New Zealand
(a division of Pearson New Zealand Ltd.)
Penguin Books (South Africa) (Pty.) Ltd., 24 Sturdee Avenue, Rosebank, Johannesburg 2196,
South Africa

Penguin Books Ltd., Registered Offices: 80 Strand, London WC2R 0RL, England

MYTH-FORTUNES

An Ace Book / published by arrangement with Bill Fawcett & Associates

PRINTING HISTORY
Wildside Press trade paperback edition / December 2008
Ace mass-market edition / December 2011

ISBN: 978-1-937007-07-2

ACE
Ace Books are published by The Berkley Publishing Group,
a division of Penguin Group (USA) Inc.,
375 Hudson Street, New York, New York 10014.
ACE and the "A" design are trademarks of Penguin Group (USA) Inc.

PRINTED IN THE UNITED STATES OF AMERICA

10   9   8   7   6   5   4   3   2   1

ONE

"Immortality is a once-in-a-lifetime deal!"
—L. LONG

I sat back in my chair with my feet propped up on Aahz's desk. My baby dragon, Gleep, lay curled underneath the bridge of my legs. Whenever Samwise, a pink-faced Imp with blunt little horns on his bald head, in a hideous checked black-and-yellow suit too wide across the shoulders for anyone but a Troll, made one of his frequent exclamations, Gleep would raise his green head sleepily, checking to see what the fuss was. When it turned out to be another bombastic sales pitch, he went back to sleep. I wished I could do the same, but I had promised Aahz I would sit in on this one. I didn't mind. There was no place in any dimension I would rather have been.

It had been a couple of weeks since M.Y.T.H., Inc., had put itself back together. Oh, there were changes. Everyone had some getting used to it to do, especially me. And Aahz. But I thought and still think that it was for the best. Trying to come out of my self-imposed retirement had not been the booming success I had hoped it would be. Try as I might, I kept stepping on the toes of the people I most cared about. Still, in the end, I was back in M.Y.T.H., Inc., with my friends and trusted colleagues, though not as its president. I'd lost that privilege, but I found that I was happier in my current, and I hoped permanent, position as partner. The others seemed as glad to have me back as I was to be there. They had chosen a new president: my former assistant, Bunny. I couldn't argue with the decision; I had relied on her intelligence, tact, and organization for a long time. M.Y.T.H., Inc., would benefit from her talents. Bunny had some new ideas that she was putting into operation, most of them received without argument from the other partners. On the whole, it had been a good reconciliation.

We had opened a second office a few miles from this one, our original location. When the lease on the remote site was up in a few months, we'd vote on what to do with it. At the moment, it was used for private meetings with clients who didn't want to be seen entering the narrow tent in the Bazaar at Deva that was well known as the home of M.Y.T.H., Inc. It also was a home away from home for Buttercup, my war unicorn. In the Bazaar, owing to cramped conditions, a lot of establishments opened out at the rear into extradimensional space, extending them as far as the host dimension would allow. This tent backed onto a gloomy, low-magik dimension called Limbo. By contrast, the secondary office occupied a piece of Ombud, a pleasant and pastoral dimension mostly populated by farmers and low-technology craftsmen, not unlike Klah, where I grew up. Buttercup occupied a field behind the farmhouse that was our small tent's presence in Ombud. I almost wished I was there at that moment, lying in the sun in the grass, with Buttercup here in my place, prodding the Imp with his single, well-sharpened horn to make him get to the point.

"So what kind of business proposition is it?" I asked, no longer bothering to be subtle.

"Profitable," Samwise declared, with the lift of an arched black eyebrow. If a red-skinned Deveel—Deveels were the natives of the dimension in which M.Y.T.H., Inc., operated—made the same gesture it might have come across as elegant or menacing. In Imps, a smaller, lighter-hued race, it came across as supercilious. Even their horns and pointed tails didn't hold any menace. "But I wouldn't expect a Klahd like you to understand an intricate arrangement like this one."

I glanced at Aahz. His yellow eyes were half-lidded with unconcealed boredom.

"Pal," he said, in a low, genial tone that I recognized as the one he used just before he ripped someone's head off, "as a salesman, you're a washout. Did you ever make a successful deal by insulting the partner of the guy you're trying to sell to? Didn't you listen when I introduced you? This is Skeeve the Magnificent, the most famous Klahd magician of all time."

The Imp turned from hot pink to pale ecru. "No offense intended!" he said hastily. "I mean, Mr. Aahz, it is you Perverts who are masters of the complex scheme."

"That's Per-vect!" Aahz snarled. Samwise blanched to off-white.

"Of course. I misspoke. Sorry. No intent to offend. Klahds are usually, er, more *straightforward*, if you get my drift."

"I've heard enough," Aahz said lazily. "Skeeve, does your dragon want an Imp for lunch? Or a snack?"

"I don't like him to eat too many Imps," I said, patting Gleep on the head. Gleep blinked his big blue eyes at me. "They give him gas. I don't want him blowing out the back of the tent."

"Too bad." Aahz grinned, showing a mouthful of four-inch pointed teeth. "Think Guido could use a little target practice?"

"Maybe," I replied, keeping one eye on the Imp. "He's getting rusty without live targets to shoot at."

"You can't do that!" Samwise exclaimed. "What will people say if I don't leave here?"

"I don't know," Aahz said, leaning back and flexing his talons which were, if not as impressive as his teeth, imposing when compared with the minor claws of an Imp. "Did you leave any advance directives? Or a note saying where you went? I doubt anyone's going to miss you much, the way you manage to make friends everywhere you go." He grinned.

The Imp swallowed heavily. I tried to look innocent, good Klahd versus bad Pervect, but it's tough to be an innocuous presence with a live dragon snoring under your chair. Samwise sputtered.

"Look, all I want to do is make you a deal. A great deal! A once-in-a-lifetime deal!"

Aahz yawned. "You have a hundred words or less to make your pitch, or you can take a walk. I'm a busy man, and I don't hear any bulldogs being fed—or dragons."

"What's a bulldog?" I asked. The picture that appeared in my head was intriguing, but almost guaranteed to be wrong based upon my experience with Aahz and his colloquial expressions.

Aahz turned toward me with an expression of irritation that slowly relaxed into a grin. "Kid, I gotta tell you, I missed that. Show you later. Samwise, your hundred words starts *now*."

The Imp took a deep breath. "Mr. Aahz, when I said that this was a once-in-a-lifetime deal, I meant just that: only once in a lifetime does something this fantastic come along! Have you ever thought what your contribution to the future was going to be? I come to you today with an offer—no, two offers. One's a straight business deal. I need the help of an organization like M.Y.T.H., Inc., to watch over the day-to-day operations of my little company. The other offer *is* immortality, or the next best thing. You might not have thought about your legacy, but I want to offer you. . . ." He clamped his mouth shut.

"What legacy?" Aahz roared, lunging forward. I was pretty curious about it myself. "You're just going to stop there?"

"Sorry, but you only gave me a hundred words!" the Imp squeaked, trying to pull his tie out of Aahz's grip. Aahz let go and thrust the Imp back into his seat.

"Okay, you can finish, but with the minimum verbiage. Talk. What *kind* of immortality? Are we talking about eternal life? Because I've talked to some immortals, and believe me, it's not all it's cracked up to be."

"Well, unfortunately, it's not within my power to provide anyone with eternal life," Samwise said, straightening his tie. "I'm more in the monument business. But they're monumental monuments!"

"Describe them in concrete terms," Aahz said. "No excess verbiage. We're going to have to have the place vacuumed as it is. What do the monuments look like?"

"Why, what they are."

"And what are they?"

"Pyramids!" Samwise announced proudly. "The Eternal Garden in the Valley of Zyx. That's in the kingdom of Aegis, Ghordon. Second phase opening this month."

"Pyramids?" I asked. "Are they buildings?"

"They are, my friend," Samwise said.

"Forget it," Aahz said, waving a hand. "I'm not getting involved in any pyramid schemes. Just because they're not illegal in some dimensions doesn't mean the legislation doesn't have a point. You've had half an hour of my valuable time. Enough. I've got other clients waiting. Take a walk."

"Mr. Aahz, please!" Samwise begged. "I admit I'd like you involved personally, because it's a product I truly believe in, but it's more than that. I need help. My people are suffering a lot of on-site accidents. Too many to be just bad luck. People are getting hurt. I have Cobra, but even *he's* getting overwhelmed by the claims. Someone or something is sabotaging my project."

Aahz raised an eyebrow. "Did you bribe the local officials?"

"Every one of them!"

"Trade unions?"

"It's a union project."

"You hire enough prominent politicians' nephews?"

"Enough to hold a family reunion," Samwise assured him. "I can't figure out who's doing it. It's deliberate. It has to be. So many incidents couldn't occur just by chance. I don't believe in coincidence."

"That's the first thing you've said that I agree with," Aahz said. "What do you want from us?"

"Well, M.Y.T.H., Inc., is famous for figuring things out. That's what I need. I have to find the source of the trouble and put an end to it. It's interfering with construction. All I want to do is make people happy."

"By selling them a monument?"

Samwise shook his head. "They're more than monuments, Mr. Aahz. They're a part of future history!"

He reached into the inner pocket of his suitcoat. I whipped up a glittering handful of magikal force. He shook his head to reassure me and came out with an irregular-shaped piece of rock with a flat bottom. It looked like a miniature landscape. A toy?

"Scale model," he explained.

"What's that mean?" I asked curiously.

"For comparison," Aahz replied. "The model's in proportion to a single scale of a dragon that would approximate the size of the actual object."

"In this case, the dragon would be about sixteen miles long," Samwise explained.

I gulped at the notion. He set the scale model on Aahz's desk and held both hands over it. It started to glow. Suddenly I could see every detail.

"The stone you choose will be part of an edifice that will last throughout the ages! Each one is unique, one in a million. In fact, each pyramid is made of a *million and one* stones! From the top you can see the whole Plain of Zyx. including the River Null, the only major waterway in the dimensions that flows backwards!" The image of the river gleamed brilliant blue with hot white twinkles of reflection from an unseen sun. At the opposite edge of the model lay a mighty mountain ridge the color of bread crust. In between those two features square-based shapes rising to points dotted the plain—pyramids. I felt dizzy as my sense of perspective zoomed from one to another. In the center of the plain, one edifice rose higher than all the others, a mountain made by living beings instead of by nature.

Aahz's eyes glittered like the river water.

"How many stones are on top of each pyramid?" Aahz asked.

"Just one," Samwise replied. "The most exclusive location is the most expensive, of course—but as a special added bonus for the buyer, you get to name the pyramid after yourself."

Aahz's eyebrows perked up again. "The whole thing?"

"The whole thing," Samwise said. "It's only right. It's the most expensive site on each pyramid, so I'm offering a perk to attract just the right buyer. Of course, we can't build the top until all the sites below it are sold. It's a great location, Mr. Aahz. It is absolutely peaceful—except for designated mourner sessions."

"Mourner sessions?" Aahz had a dreamy look on his face.

"Uh, Aahz," I began, "you told me never to get involved in a project at its outset. You said . . ."

"Never mind, kid," he interrupted me. "What about mourners?"

Samwise was all business. "All part of the service. Every customer can decide what kind of moaning and wailing he wants, how much praise and how many accomplishments he wants attributed to him. And this is where the legacy I spoke of comes in: we have a team of scribes who will chisel the details of your great deeds so that they are never forgotten."

"Never?" Aahz asked. "Never's a long time."

"Absolutely never. When I say written in stone, I mean written in stone!"

"About how much would the peak stone cost?" Aahz inquired, aiming an idle talon at the centermost pyramid.

"Not a copper coin less than ten thousand."

Aahz pursed his lips. "Ten thousand copper?"

"You malign me, Mr. Aahz! Ten thousand *gold pieces*. But for a distinguished citizen like yourself, of course, all prices are negotiable. It is the most exclusive site available. I know such a connoisseur as you would appreciate it. And I like the idea of a business partner having a tangible stake in the project. Shall we say . . . eight thousand?"

Aahz grunted thoughtfully.

To my horror, Aahz looked like he was buying into the Imp's sales patter. I jumped up and put myself between them.

"Hold on, Samwise," I said. "You said there are problems here that are preventing you from building this pyramid at all."

"Right," Samwise said, with a peeved look at me. "That's why I need M.Y.T.H., Inc., to help me. Besides, I'm worried about cost overruns. What about it? Will you come to Ghordon and give me a hand?"

"Well . . ." I could tell that Aahz was just waiting for a direct question like that. He shook his head. "We're not accountants. We don't do line item analysis."

"Just make sure I'm not being cheated blind by my staff," Samwise pleaded. "The main thing is to find the source of the sabotage and stop it. I'll make you a great deal on a stone."

"I don't buy a pig in a poke, buddy," Aahz said. "But I might take a look at a penthouse location, if you knock fifty percent off the price."

"Fifty!" Samwise yelped. "That's my whole profit margin!"

"If you don't stop the bleeding, you won't have any profits to marginalize," Aahz pointed out.

"Let's discuss it after you agree to take the job, Mr. Aahz. How about it?"

"Aahz, you always told me the ideal job was one in which you didn't have to do anything . . ."

"Hold the phone, kid, I'm just listening to a proposal."

"It's just a *rock*, Aahz!"

"It's a legacy," Samwise insisted.

"A tomb!" I yelped. "You have to be dead to enjoy it."

"Not at all," Samwise interceded smoothly. "We guarantee total access for your enjoyment from now until one, er, takes up permanent residence. Some of our clients hold picnics on their site. It's always sunny in Ghordon."

"See, kid?" Aahz said. "It's not just a one-time thing.

Besides, all I agreed was that we'd take a look at the job.
That's what Sam here came to ask."

I saw something in his eyes that I had seldom seen before:
wistfulness. Whatever he felt he could get out of a piece of
the rock wasn't something I could define.

"We have to run the deal past our president," I pointed
out lamely. While we could take jobs as independent con-
tractors, I still had a funny feeling about Samwise and his
construction project. We could afford to turn down his jobs.
Each of us and the partnership had plenty of money. Except
for the commodity for sale, this sounded like a hundred
other corruption-sniffing projects we turned down every
day. "Bunny gets the final vote on whether we take a job or
not."

Aahz waved a hand. "We'll let her know after we see the
place, partner," he said.

I could see that he was hooked. All I could do was tag
along and hope I could spot pitfalls before we both fell in
them.

"Watch the office," I told my dragon.

"Gleep!" he said. It was both farewell and warning.

TWO

"You always have to read the fine print."
—E. A. WALLIS BUDGE

We transferred silently from the dusty, sunlit office into instant and total blackness. In my mind's eye, I could see plenty of force lines arching overhead and deep underground, below my feet. They were all shapes and sizes, from thin and spindly threads of lilac up to a surging, shining black torrents. I reached tentatively toward a long, snaky blue force line. When it didn't burn me, I drew some power from it. I had learned through bitter experience that if you didn't grab every opportunity to refill your internal magikal supply, you'd find yourself short at the most inconvenient moment. I took some of the power into my hand and formed it into a ball of light. I held up my impromptu torch and looked around.

We were in a narrow chamber of pale tan stone with a flat tan ceiling. Each wall had been deeply carved with tiny pictures that seemed to dance in the wavering light of my spell. The air smelled musty but cool.

"Where are we?" Aahz asked.

"This is the tomb of Waycross," Samwise explained, pointing to a large image incised into the wall just above our heads. "All visitors have to come through here the first time. And . . . they like me to enter the dimension this way. I don't exactly know why.—There's the old boy himself."

I lifted the light to illuminate the portrait. Waycross had the face of a turtle. The beady eyes looked disapproving. When I shifted to get away from its gaze, the eyes seemed to follow me, even though they were pointed toward each other.

"He originated that phrase about looking at someone cross-eyed," Samwise explained. "He's reputed to have had a really bad temper, so no one ever did anything without his oversight. And he overlooked a lot, I gotta tell you. Shoddy construction in most of his projects, especially this one. This was supposed to be on a gridwork pattern, six storeys high, but it isn't. Don't worry. We'll get out eventually."

"Don't you have a map?" I asked.

Samwise shrugged. "It doesn't help. The rooms move around by themselves. No one anchored them where they were. Cost-cutting. You won't find that on *my* projects. You just keep on walking toward the light." That startled me. Samwise waved a hand. "It's not like a near-death experience. If you see the light, you're actually getting closer to the outside. When you find an open window or a door, hang onto it. That's the easiest way out. No one ever died in here unless they panicked. Well, almost no one. Come on. There's almost always an opening off the Grand Gallery."

Just a few feet beyond the looming portrait, a long corridor stretched off into blackness. The walls here, too, were covered with incised designs.

"What's all this?" I pointed to the carvings.

"Tourist rules," Samwise explained. "Ghordon has strict regulations. 'Don't cheat the Ghords, lest you suffer a dire curse. Don't spit on public roads, or a dire curse will follow you. Do not make unwelcome advances to fellow guests in drinking establishments, under pain of dire curse.' You know. Don't worry about reading them. I've been here for years, and no one has ever tried to enforce any of them on me. I get along great with everybody. Come on."

I peered closely at the minute figures of men in skirts, birds, dogs, lions, and deer, and frowned. My facility with spoken languages didn't stretch to written lingo. If I had to, we could hire a local interpreter to translate the rules.

We trudged along. The corridor was wide enough for us to walk abreast. The smell of cool stone and ancient sweat made my nostrils twitch.

"Say, Samwise, where'd you get the name?" Aahz asked suddenly.

The Imp waved a hand. "My mother read the classics."

"Tough break," Aahz said sympathetically, but there was a big grin on his face. "Hope you don't feel *hobbited* by it." I didn't know why the name struck him as funny. I made a mental note to ask later.

"There's one," Samwise said, ignoring Aahz's jibe. I looked up. A square of brilliant blue light beckoned. "Hurry. It's already shifting sideways."

Indeed it was. The blue square started to narrow as the room to which it was attached ground to the left. I rushed toward it, my long legs eating up the distance faster than my two shorter companions.

By the time I reached it, the portal had narrowed to a rectangle.

"What do I do?" I shouted.

"Hang onto it!" Samwise shouted back.

I braced my hands against either side of the open window. The heat from outside slammed into me like a charging bull. I gasped. The wall continued to shift sideways, carrying the window and the room with it toward the corner. I hopped up into the casement and shoved my feet against the oncoming wall. The room didn't like having an obstruction in its way. It slammed against the bottoms of my feet a few times, trying to dislodge me so it could move. Samwise and Aahz hurried toward me.

"Hurry!" I yelled.

"Hang in there, partner," Aahz called.

I summoned up all the magik force I was carrying, but I wasn't strong enough to argue with an ancient stone wall. It kicked me loose. I landed on the ground, groaning. The room shifted out of sight, leaving us in darkness. I summoned up another ball of light.

"Well, you know what they say," Samwise said gamely. "Where a window closes, a door opens."

"If I find one, I'll throw you out of it first," Aahz said. "Do you have to go through that every time?"

"It's where my transference spell lands me," Samwise said. "So, yes."

Aahz looked disgusted. "I knew we should have let the kid here do the transporting. He'd have popped us right into the middle of the action."

"Why not you?" Samwise asked, with a curious look at my partner. "Or are the rumors about the great Aahz losing his powers true?"

Aahz waved a hand airily. "C'mon, I've been in the business for centuries. I don't do the penny-ante stuff. That's for apprentices and, er, junior partners."

I was still so glad to be back with M.Y.T.H., Inc., that I didn't mind Aahz saving face in front of clients—once, anyhow. At least this time he didn't suggest he would step in if I couldn't handle things.

"I'm pretty good now," I said modestly. "Aahz taught me everything I know."

"Well, that and a two copper pieces will get you a can of warm ale," Samwise said. Just before Aahz grunted out a retort, we spotted another opening, a door, as the Imp had predicted. Almost as soon as it appeared, it started to head for the floor, and the ceiling of the new room with it.

My wits were back where they belonged. Instead of running for the gap, I gathered up a large quantity of magik from the deep-rooted black force line and built a nice little frame inside the bright square. It was as strong as I could manage. I could hear the groaning of the stones as they fought against the obstruction. Sparks of magik broke away from the master spell with a *ping!* I threw more and more force into the gap. Waycross must have been one powerful magician. We ran for the opening, I nursing my bruises and the others panting behind me.

"It's going to break," I said, gritting my teeth as I rebuilt the spell one more time. I ran toward the hole.

With a loud report, the spell shattered, sending hot splinters of light shooting outward. I averted them from us with a quick flick of my wrist, but it meant that I wasn't doing anything to prevent the rapid descent of the ceiling of the next room toward the floor of this one. The gap had closed to four feet. I could just make it. Three.

"Come on, partner, let's fly!" Aahz said. He held out his arms as if he was lifting off. I scooped him up with a hank of magik and dove to join him.

"Hey, wait for me!" Samwise pleaded. He flapped his arms as he ran to catch up.

I didn't have time to look behind us. The stone slab of the ceiling was just knee height from the floor. If we misjudged our speed, it could chop our legs off. I didn't want to start off in Ghordon two feet shorter. I threw out a hook of power and wedged it into the doorway at the far end of the shrinking room, tied the other end around Aahz and me, and *pulled*.

The magikal cord contracted faster than a Deveel's good will. Aahz and I not only reached the door, but catapulted through it. I hit the sand-dusted flagstones outside Waycross's tomb and rolled to a halt twenty feet beyond. I blinked up at the hot yellow sun. Aahz struck just behind me, bounced and ended up landing across my legs.

A shadow cut off the blinding sunlight. A face surrounded by a draped cloth headdress peered down at me. The face had the long nose and floppy ears of a hound, but the bare chest and arms of a Klahd. It extended a normal-looking hand to me. I took it, and he helped me to my feet. A lion-faced Klahd helped Aahz up.

"Welcome to Ghordon, wayfarers," the dog-faced man said. He and his lion-headed companion wore pleated white skirts and sandals, but nothing else except their headdresses. "Receive the eight greetings of the Pharaoh Suzal, the eternal hospitality of her people, and the warm regard of the land of the Ghords be always upon . . . oh, no, not *you* again!"

I frowned at the unfriendly tone, then relaxed.

It was not addressed to me or Aahz, but rather to Samwise. The Imp crawled out of the porticoed door through which we had just been propelled.

The Imp dusted off his loud suit and stumped over to slap the two males on the back. "Hey, Fisal and Chopri, good to see you!" They accepted the gesture with resignation and returned to the posts they had occupied beside the doorway. He turned to us. "I told you I get along great with everybody here."

Ghordon's climate was similar to Deva's, a dry desert with a hot sun and wispy breezes that did nothing but stir up the dust, but there was something subtly different. At first I couldn't put my finger on it. Then I realized that there was little more noise outside Waycross's tomb than there had been inside it. The sprawling Bazaar at Deva, which covered much of its dimension, was never quiet. During the day, it was filled with the shouts, cries, bellows, and ululations of the Deveel traders who liked to argue at the top of their voices. Adding to the din were street performers, friends and soon-to-be-friends greeting each other, musicians, the entourages of important visitors announcing the name and business of the person they were escorting, the roar of dragons and other beasts for sale, and just the endless audible tumult of thousands of beings all talking at the same time. By extreme contrast, Ghordon was almost silent. I could *hear* the wind. It reminded me of the bucolic isolation of my parents' farm on Klah. It was unnerving. I felt like singing or shouting just to remind myself what noise sounded like.

My footsteps made a hushed, shushing noise as I trudged along in the drifting sand behind Samwise and Aahz.

"Come on, we'll catch a Camel," Samwise said.

"As long as we don't have to walk a mile for one," Aahz said, and waited for applause. None was forthcoming, since I didn't know what he was talking about.

Ahead, I spotted long, oval heads bobbing on narrow necks. I couldn't tell what they were, but the humped shapes behind the heads suggested gigantic serpents.

"What are they?" I asked as we got closer. The heads turned toward us, and large brown eyes with long lashes fluttered at me. They didn't look like snakes, but the necks connected to a lumpy body that lay flat on the desert.

"Camel, sir, Camel?" the first one, a creature with dark brown fur, inquired in a loud, hoarse voice. "Take you sightseeing around the grand pyramid, Hobokis, the city of Suzal, may she live forever, the Pharoah Isles, or the terrific shopping in the Khazbah? Your choice, reasonable rates! I will give you a most mild ride. You will think you are sailing a sheep."

"Ship?" I asked, curiously.

"Sheep," the Camel said. "I am not a boat, I am a living being. Come with me, come, hurry!"

"I saw them first," exclaimed a pale tan Camel, trying to bump the first one out of the way. "I will convey you safely and well, O tourists . . . oh, Samwise." The Camels' enthusiasm petered out.

I was beginning to realize that our potential employer, if not actually disliked, had worn out his welcome with the people of Ghordon.

"We'll walk," Aahz said.

"You'd never make it," Samwise said. "The quicksands will drag you down in no time. The slowsands are even more dangerous because they have a firmer grip."

"We could just fly."

"Er, I prefer to patronize the local businesses," Samwise said hastily.

"Hmmph!" The local businesspeople—all right, Camels—didn't seem that grateful for his custom. I suspected he wasn't good at keeping up with his bills.

"It's okay," I said, jingling my belt pouch to show that one of us had money. "My name's Skeeve. Will you take us to . . . ?" I looked at Samwise.

"To the And Company main office," the Imp said.

"And Company?" I asked.

"Well, everyone knows *me*," the Imp said. We stepped gingerly onto the humps behind the Camel's head and settled in between them. There was barely room for the three of us. I got wedged between Samwise and the rear hump. "But I have partners in some of my projects, so I named the enterprise after them. That way they get the credit they deserve, too."

Once I was on the Camel's back, I realized that it wasn't a snake or serpent. The beast had limbs at the four corners of its body, but they were submerged beneath the surface of the sand. Instead of running, it swam, gliding as smoothly as a water bird. I looked behind us. Our passage left a V-shaped wake that swirled and settled again into gentle peaks.

"The hump keeps them afloat in the quicksand," Samwise explained.

"Hold on, please. No jumping up and down, no music, no photographs," the Camel said, as he swam away from the stand. "Spitting is allowed." As if to demonstrate, he let go of a gob of brown goo that plopped onto the surface of the sand and sank. I felt my stomach turn. "I am Dromad, your driver for today."

He paddled a distance out from Waycross's tomb and began to circle around to the right. No matter what criticism Samwise had for the ancient architect, I admired the monument's construction and how well it fit into its setting. It looked as if it had just risen out of the desert at the beginning of time and would be there forever. The admonitions and curses I had seen inside continued on around the building in endless rows.

Waycross sure had a lot of rules.

THREE

"I don't want this monument thing to get out of hand."
—ZOSER

As we cleared the massive square edifice, I goggled in wonder at a new, marvelous structure ahead of us.

"You didn't tell us that you'd already built one pyramid," Aahz said.

And an impressive sight it was, too. I had never seen anything like it outside of the storybook or history books in my mother's study. A perfect, smooth triangle of pearlescent white, it loomed above the wide desert floor like a mathematical absolute. It didn't look so large from a distance, but as we glided toward it, I realized what I thought were insects walking on the stones were people my size and larger. As we paddled closer, I studied them. Their bodies were similar to denizens of my dimension, Klah, but their heads and feet resembled those of animals.

A narrow staircase led up the center of one side of the pyramid to a tiny doorway, a startling rectangle of black in the gleaming white side. The people trudged up and down the steps bearing cloth bundles, jars of colored paints, and rolls of thick parchment.

"Er, well, that one's not mine," Samwise said, fingering

his collar. "That's Diksen's. He built it. I used to work for him."

"You mean you're copying his blueprints?" Aahz asked suspiciously.

"Not at all! Not at all! I'll show you my plans as soon as we get to the office. They're *completely* different. That one's mine."

Ahead, I could see a pier made of plain slabs of stone. Beyond it was a small square building that looked like an outhouse for Waycross's tomb. Above that were three incomplete rows of enormous, rough rectangular blocks arranged on top of one another.

Compared with the completed pyramid, Samwise's project was a deep disappointment. On every side, plain blank cubes of pinkish-gray rock were piled higher than the completed portion. Many of these were surrounded by Ghords busy with hammer and chisel. Small objects that caught the light flitted back and forth between them on wisps of magik. I thought this pyramid looked more like the aftermath of a demolition than a building site. Still, more blocks were rolling upwards to the empty spaces on ramps that had been piled up against the outer edge on each side of the building.

I peered at the stones, but I couldn't see anyone moving them. It wouldn't surprise me if Samwise's people were using magik to do the construction; there was an unbelievable amount of raw power available both above and below ground. I glanced around for wizards. I saw no one whose demeanor said to me "professional magician at work." Instead, at the corners of every level and in prominent stations among the workers, stood large, husky locals. Each held a short whip and a narrow, striped stick with a curled-over top like a shepherd's crook crossed on his chest. These Ghords glared at the tourists on Camel-back who paddled around in the sand at a safe distance to watch the work in progress.

I paid our Camel when we arrived at the pier and made a mental note to add the small silver coin to the invoice when Samwise started paying M.Y.T.H., Inc., for its expertise. We disembarked. The Camel swam away, muttering and spitting.

"I thought you said this was a union job," Aahz said, watching one of the massive slabs arrange itself in place and settle down.

"Absolutely," Samwise said. "No choice, really. I just took the path of least resistance."

"But these stones are moving all by themselves. Magik!"

"No magik," Samwise said, wincing. "Scarabs. The Universal Sacred Hegira of the Everlasting Brotherhood, Teamsters Interdimensional."

"USHEBTIS?" Aahz whistled. "Powerful group. Tough workers."

"They've pretty much got a stranglehold on this dimension," Samwise admitted. "I have an ongoing argument with their chief negotiator and shop steward, Beltasar. You'll meet her later. She's always coming by with a complaint."

"You think they might be causing the problems?" I asked.

"I don't think so," Samwise said doubtfully. "I hope not. They've had more than their share of accidents. They keep babbling about an ancient curse."

I raised my eyebrows. It was time for the other shoe to drop. Here it was. I exchanged glances with Aahz. "And is there an ancient curse?"

Samwise flinched defensively. "No! Or I wouldn't have started this project in the first place."

"What about the curses in Waycross's tomb?" I asked. "There are probably thousands of them listed on that building."

"No!" Samwise was adamant. "Those have nothing to do with me. I've kept this enterprise honest . . . well, as honest as any real estate development," he admitted.

Now that I knew Scarabs were carrying the stones, I could see the tiny black dots as they swarmed toward the next block in line. Amazingly, the massive object rose about an inch, then glided as if under its own power toward the ramps. The overseers stood aside. No need to harry Scarabs with the whip. They were all hustle and go.

Aahz did some calculations in his head.

"So, there's three hundred of them per block? How much can one of them carry on its own?"

Samwise made a dismissive gesture. "Are you kidding? If union rules didn't forbid it, a Scarab would carry a whole block by itself. The only reason there's a crowd under each stone is for safety. If it tips, a Scarab can break a leg or crack a shell, and you don't want to know what my insurance bills are like already."

"Then, what are all the muscle-men for?" Aahz asked.

"Security," Samwise said. "Come on in. I'll show you the list of things that have gone wrong. Here's the office." He led us toward the small stone hut on the edge of the building site.

I should have guessed that the Deveels' trick of using extradimensional space had spread to other places. What we walked into was a small stone hut, but inside Samwise had spared no expense. An atrium with a triangular skylight soared above us. On the gleaming gray marble wall ahead, the words "And Company" stood out in high bronze letters. A girl with a wonderful, curvaceous figure but small, round ears, a thick snout, and beady, piglike eyes occupied the reception desk. Like all the other Ghords we had seen, she wore a white linen headdress; a thin, pleated robe; and a fancy beaded necklace. She was dealing with a large, angry Gorgon woman who held onto a smaller male by his forearm. Snakes whipped around the woman's head in fury.

"You're kidding! Oh, I don't believe it." The Gorgon pushed away from the desk and stormed toward us, dragging her small and apologetic husband along. The few snakes left on his head waved feebly. "Can you imagine?" the Gorgon fumed at us. "Can you *imagine*? I wanted to buy one of these tombs for my husband—but they say he has to be dead before I put him in it! Of all the *nerve*. Come on!" She dragged her husband away. He stumbled behind her like a toddler.

"Reminds me of one of my girlfriends," Aahz said fondly, watching her go. "Yeah, those were the days."

I knew from experience how formidable Pervect women could be. I didn't want to generalize, but I couldn't imagine dating one myself.

"This is my receptionist," Samwise said, leading us to a gray-faced girl at the desk. "Any calls?"

"No, sir," the girl said. She glanced at Aahz and primped the edge of her headdress with an upturned hand.

"Hey, gorgeous," Aahz purred, leaning over the desk to gaze into her eyes. "Howya doin'?"

She beamed at him, showing peg-shaped teeth at the corners of her jaws.

"Miss Tauret, these are the people from M.Y.T.H., Inc. Will you have refreshments brought into the main conference room?"

"Certainly, sir." When she rose from her desk, I saw that her shapely legs ended in thick, cylindrical gray feet.

Samwise led us down a wide corridor. On the walls, images of buildings had been incised and painted. I read a couple of the labels as I went by. A very gaudy, high-rise building was marked "Carnival Warehouse, Vaygus." A white, almost featureless cylinder said, ".Info Ctr ☺, Kobol." A tiny canvas tent was named as "Shaharwadi Empire Headquarters, Deva."

"I think I've seen that one," I said, pointing at the third image. "I bought some stuff-sacks there. The place is huge!"

Aahz glanced back at it. "Yeah, I've been there, too. Nice place. Your work, Samwise?"

The Imp shrugged, a little embarrassed. "Uh, no. These were done by the last architect to own this office, Ahmahotel. He retired a couple of years ago. Here we are. Have a seat."

We perched on stools around a high, white tabletop. Samwise unrolled a huge yellow parchment. He did his best to smooth it, but its wrinkles wouldn't let it lay flat. The plans looked like they had been deliberately crumpled up, then flattened out.

"This looks exactly like the building next door," Aahz said, frowning. "If this is a scam, it's a pretty inept one."

"No scam, Aahz, I swear to you!" Samwise turned the paper around so we could both see it. "It's really different."

"It looks the same to me," I said.

"Well . . . it was designed by Diksen, too," Samwise admitted. "But he discarded it! He had a lot of good ideas. He's a very creative guy. I knew he wouldn't mind."

"Uh-huh," Aahz said. "Does he know you're using a plan that you plucked out of his waste-papyrus basket?"

"Oh, yeah, no problem," Samwise said. I thought he was talking just a little bit too fast. "He drew it up. It didn't work for him. He threw it away. I rescued it and adapted it. He didn't say I couldn't. What's the problem with that?"

"I don't know yet," Aahz said. "Tell us and save us all a lot of time."

"You said you worked for him," I pressed. "Why aren't you with him any longer?"

"I had big ideas of my own," the Imp said, describing arcs in the air. "Plenty of big ideas."

"Such as?" Aahz asked.

"Financing," the Imp said, with his arms spread triumphantly. "Diksen had to stump up for that whole thing out there by himself. I came up with a much better idea to build my dream pyramid. It's a cooperative venture. Every buyer helps find more buyers. The more they bring in, the lower their buy-in becomes. It's a win-win proposition."

Aahz groaned. "That's just what I was afraid of. Why didn't you tell us that in our office in the Bazaar and let me say 'no' then? C'mon, kid, we're leaving." He stood up.

"Aahz, just listen!" Samwise begged.

BOOM! The floor lurched out from under me. I pushed away from it with a handful of magik and retrieved Aahz before he hit the ground. Samwise was tossed sideways. He grabbed onto a hank of air and steadied himself.

"What was that?" Aahz demanded as soon as his feet were back on the ground. "An explosion?"

"No, nothing like that, I'm sure," the Imp said. He hurried out into the hallway. A Ghord with the face of a bull rushed toward him. He whispered in Samwise's ear.

"Oh, no," Samwise said. He strode toward the doorway, but it was too late. A fist-sized knob of black buzzed in the door and hit him smack in the chest. It backed up a handspan and zipped up to the Imp's eye level. It shook a tiny finger in his face.

"Have I not told you a thousand times? It has happened again!"

Samwise took a pace back and rubbed the point of impact. "Beltasar," he said weakly.

I regarded the newcomer curiously. Since my first visit to the Bazaar at Deva, I had made friends and acquaintances that ranged from the size of a building down to the size of my thumb. I had thought at long distance that Scarabs were all black, but Beltasar was an iridescent blue with complicated designs incised on her shell in bright coral, turquoise, and gold. Her large, round eyes were also turquoise, and they were fixed with disapproval on the Imp.

"Another stone came right off our backs!" she exclaimed. "Unauthorized use of an unregistered magician on a union site will get you fined ten gold pieces per incident."

"There aren't any magicians working today," Samwise squawked. "It has to be your fault. You dropped a stone? Whose was it? What will my clients say?"

"They'll say you run a dangerous operation," Beltasar said, firmly. "It landed on your building."

"What?" Samwise yelped. He hurried outside, the Scarab flying next to him. We followed.

FOUR

"All that matters in real estate is location, location, location."
—IMHOTEP

Outside, the air was full of flitting Scarabs, all humming with alarm. The Ghord laborers, too, had all stopped working. They had gathered around the building to look at the accident. I turned to gawk. One of the carved blocks lay at an angle on top of the And Company office building, flattening a corner of the structure to rubble. I couldn't believe how large it was up close. Klah was full of family cottages smaller than this single piece of rock. It must have weighed tons. Nothing short of a major cataclysm or magik could have tossed it from the top of the partly built pyramid. It would take heavy lifting equipment to move.

I peered inside the office. It was unaffected, since it didn't exist in this dimension. The secretaries and clerks continued about their business with only an occasional glance out the door at us. Miss Tauret gave me a broad wink and went back to her papyri.

"Could've thrown it over here themselves," Aahz said suspiciously, looking the accident up and down with an expert's eye. "Pretty nifty action. No way to tell what direction it came from. Take a look at the power lines."

I shook my head. "No fluctuations that I can see, but those lines are strong. Any magik that was dipped out of one wouldn't leave a trace. Or it could be an overload. That black line just under our feet is bucking like a bull goat."

"We could have been killed!" exclaimed a Ghord with a long bird beak. "It is one of the ancient curses! Someone must have left gum on the paving stones!"

The rest of the crew joined in with their panicked suggestions of the cause of the disaster.

"What are you doing?" Samwise screamed at his staff, waving his arms. "Go back to work! Beltasar, get this rock off my office!"

"Sign a work order," Beltasar said, crossing her upper two sets of arms. "My people get regular hourly pay plus hazard pay plus off-site supplement."

Samwise groaned and smacked his forehead with his palm. "All right, all right! Get the paperwork ready. I'll sign it. What choice do I have?"

I didn't notice any satisfaction, smug or otherwise, on the Scarab's little face as she whipped a document from under one wing, flicked it open, and handed it to him. "Sign here. We'll have it off your building in two wags of a Sphinx's tail."

The Imp resignedly took the pen she proffered.

"Not so fast." Aahz pushed in between them. "You brought me here to check for holes in your operation." He turned to the Scarab. "He signs nothing from this day forward unless it goes past me first."

"Fine," Beltasar said.

Aahz scanned the page. He grunted and shoved it toward Samwise. The Imp signed it.

Tucking the document back under her wing, Beltasar flitted away.

"You see what I'm dealing with?" Samwise appealed to us. "Thanks for agreeing to help."

"I'm not committing," Aahz said. "But if we *do* take you as a client, I can't watch you make bad decisions in front of me."

Aahz and I stood back as a swarm of USHEBTI workers poured down from the worksite and ascended the side of the small stone building. If I hadn't seen them do it before, I wouldn't have believed it possible. As Beltasar shrieked out orders, the wave of black dots spread out around the fallen slab. Slowly, as if under its own volition, it moved away from the broken side of the building. I looked closely, both with my open eyes and my mind's eye, and I didn't see a trace of magik. The Scarabs were just that strong.

"I could help them," I offered.

"No!" Samwise exclaimed, palms out in alarm. "Thanks, but no thanks. If you interfere with the Scarabs, they'll strike, and I'm already months behind schedule. Look, come out with me and see the rest of the site. I think you'll like it."

We passed in through a narrow gate. Beside it was a large sign.

This is an And Company Construction!
We Pride Ourselves on Providing a Safe Working
Environment. Days Since Last Accident . . .

There was a blank underneath. The number "43" had been written there at one time, but it had been scratched out. The numbers that had replaced it over time included eight, five, two, one, one, one-half, and at the moment the sign proclaimed "Eight hours since our last accident!" As I passed, a hawk-faced Ghord came over and dejectedly drew a line through it with a pencil. I looked uneasily at Samwise. He ignored the Ghord, me, the sign, and anything except the existing construction work.

"Isn't it wonderful?" he exclaimed, waving his arms at the heap of rocks.

I was unimpressed.

The guards and the other employees regarded us with suspicion as we followed Samwise to the foot of the pyramid.

"This is Phase One," he said. "It's already eighty percent

sold. We're starting Phase Two pretty soon. It'll be even more exciting than this one!"

Aahz looked up at it, his fists on his hips.

"What a tower of junk," he said.

"No, it isn't!" Samwise protested. "You have to let it grow on you, Aahz."

"If anything like that grew on me, I'd have it removed," Aahz retorted.

"You just need to see it from a better angle," the Imp said. "This way."

I followed him to the left, past heaps of sand and gravel, small bundles of personal items, and a Ghord with a monkey's face grilling vegetables over a smoking fire. The three layers of carved stones didn't strike me as exciting—far from it. To me, it was just an upright graveyard. Still, there was something I couldn't define. As we got closer, the unprepossessing chunks of incised stone took on a new glamour. I reached out to touch the carvings on one of the monoliths that even on its side rose above my head. It tingled under my fingers. Alone, they were just inanimate hunks of mineral. Together, though, they created their own magik. I took a deep breath. I felt almost as if I could hear voices from the past, tingling bells, the call of horns, the bray of animals and voices, voices, voices. I took my hand away, and the sounds and tingling stopped.

"That's amazing," I said.

Aahz didn't seem to find any wonder in it.

"It's just a heap of rocks," he said flatly. "Why would anyone invest a silver coin in it, let alone thousands?"

"Ah, but this isn't the best way to view it," Samwise insisted. He beamed at Aahz. The crisis was over, and he was a salesman again. "Now, follow me. Please stay out of the way of the workers. I have to pay them an interruption fee if they have to pause more than 1.5 seconds to let someone by who is not on the payroll."

"You sure have to put up with a lot of regulations," I commented.

"The Deveel is in the details," Samwise said with plaintive resignation.

"In other words, some Deveel wrote your employment contracts," Aahz growled. "That'll cost you extra if we have to untangle it."

"Whatever it takes, Aahz," Samwise said. He patted the stone I had touched. "See, down here are the economy stones. A whole family can have the eternity of their dreams for not much more than a year's income in Imper. Engraving and other services are extra, but can be arranged for in perpetuity. I think you will find we don't have a single unhappy customer."

"Uh, what's your . . . occupancy rate?" I asked. In Klah, stepping on someone's grave was punishable by a curse.

Samwise turned to me. "Do you mean, has anyone taken up permanent residence here yet? No, young sir, not yet. Barring accidents, I doubt that will happen for many years. By then, I hope the Valley of Zyx will take its place among the dimensions' greatest destinations! Now come with me. This always wows the customers."

He felt around with one foot, then began to climb, step by step, up an apparently invisible set of stairs. I looked more closely with my mind's eye and saw that a staircase had been constructed of magik. It reached upward at a diagonal, leading to a point high above us where it intersected with three other tiers of steps.

Aahz stumped upward, unfazed by stairs he couldn't see. I kept some magik available in case I needed to keep myself from falling. I was good at flying, after years of practice, but I hated having the floor drop out from under me.

"You can see what a great location we have here. We're positioned in the heart of the western portion of the valley. Over the hills to the east is the city of Aser, the seat of the empire. It comprises a marriage of old and new, a city of millennia with a new outlook. Why, the Pharaoh herself is a big fan . . ."

"Just the facts, pal," Aahz interrupted him.

"That is a fact, good sir!" Samwise exclaimed. "Why, all the best people are going to be interred here. Only the best. They are the most forward-thinking of consumers, wholehearted supporters of the cooperative scheme. Dying is the new living!"

Supported on the invisible steps, we walked right over the heads of the Ghord stonecarvers. I'd always been fascinated by artisans who used skill instead of magik. Dressed in the same kilt and headcloth I had seen on everyone in Ghordon, they knelt before the slabs in place, hammer and chisel in hand, tapping away. I thought there was already plenty of ornamentation on each of the stones, but the craftsmen and-women worked away at minute details, almost bringing the images to life. In fact, a hawk-headed female incised on a nearby stone turned to look at me. When it did, the two female Ghord carvers kneeling at the rockface glanced over their shoulders. They giggled. One leaned forward and tapped something on the stone wall with her hammer and chisel. The other bent to read it, then hammered out a small carving, which her friend read. They giggled again. So did the image of the hawk-faced woman. I grinned at them awkwardly. What was so funny? I'm told I'm not bad looking. I had run a company. I had faced insane wizards. I had made friends and enemies across the dimensions. So what they were laughing about?

I *really* didn't understand women. All my choices in the dating field thus far had been bad ones.

"*C'mon*, kid," Aahz called. I hurried to catch up.

FIVE

"You can take it with you."
—TUTANKHAMEN

Samwise was still talking. ". . . So I said to myself, who wouldn't want their very own monumental tomb? Everyone has to die sometime. So why not find like-minded individuals, with money, of course, to create that fantastic piece of real estate in time for . . . in time for . . ." The Imp sought a suitable euphemism.

". . . Their permanent nap?" Aahz supplied.

"Mister Aahz!" Samwise said, shocked. "I have the greatest respect for my clientele. It's something that everyone's going to need eventually, even Vampires; and Ghordon is a dimension at easy access to Limbo as well as Klah and Deva. It can't miss!"

Aahz gave Samwise a wary eye, but I put it down more to his dislike for Limbo than the idea of a *modest* commission per sale. We could do well financially out of the deal. I just kept thinking there had to be a catch.

We passed the top tier of guards. They bowed to Samwise and looked us over pretty carefully. Though most of them were Ghords, I was surprised to see a Titan, a Troll, and a few other surprising species represented.

"You do a little hiring from outside the dimension," I mentioned casually, tilting my head toward the Titan. Aahz's eyebrows rose when he saw him. Titans—gigantic, well-muscled and silver-skinned—had notoriously bad tempers. They disliked working for anyone but themselves. Rumor had it that they even ate their own children if they were displeased. I took that last with a grain of salt. After all, I had heard some pretty disgusting rumors about Pervects. Most of them weren't true, no matter how much Perv spent on P.R.

"Oh, yeah," Samwise said. "They are here to work off the cost of their own pyramid tombs—their piece of the rock, so to speak."

"Speaking of that, let's talk about financial specifics," Aahz suggested smoothly. I could tell he wanted the top spot on the pyramid being built.

"Fine." Samwise rubbed his palms together. "What can I do for you, my friend?"

"Well," Aahz said, looking unimpressed as he watched the Scarabs manhandle—or should I say, beetle-handle?—another massive slab up the ramps and into place on the current level below us, "I think maybe you have something going on here—maybe. It's not great yet—but with our help it could be bigger than Diksen's place."

Samwise's eye summed Aahz up. I think he knew exactly where Aahz was going. An Imp making a deal is a weakling compared with a Deveel, but they can usually hold their own against a Pervect. Still, he'd never dealt with Aahz before. I stood back to enjoy the bargaining.

"Well, my friend—I can call you my friend, can't I?"

"No," Aahz said. "M.Y.T.H., Inc., can be your business partner or your paid consultants. Depends on how devoted you want us to your enterprise."

"I've always believed in letting enterprise go where it wants to. Exploring strange new worlds, you know," Samwise said.

Aahz grinned.

"Huh?" I asked.

"Tell you later, kid. So, Sam, what's it going to be? Your construction project has a long way to go before it equals the magnificence of the guy next door."

"What do you have in mind?" Samwise asked. "I don't really need you, but you would be a great help."

"That's not what it sounded like in our office," Aahz countered. "You would have sold us the whole farm if we had asked."

"I was just using my powers of persuasion on you, Aahz," Samwise counter-countered. "It worked, didn't it? You're here!"

"This was all a fake?" Aahz bellowed. "I suppose you set up the accident to make it look good!"

"You impugn my honor?" Samwise demanded.

"Imps don't have any!"

"And Perverts do?"

"That's Per-vect!"

"Where I come from, it's pronounced Per-vert!"

I stumped upward, letting nature take its course. As the two of them hammered out a price for M.Y.T.H., Inc.'s services, I concentrated on feeling my way along the invisible steps.

"Ten percent! We wouldn't get out of bed for ten percent!" Aahz shouted. "You should have offered us twenty-five!"

"If I give you twenty-five, my profit is gone! Twelve! That's my highest offer!"

A Ghord salesman with a lion's face and a thick mane peeking out from under his headcloth mounted the steps on the opposite face of the pyramid to ours. With him was a family of Kobolds, denizens of a dimension that relied on technology rather than magik. I recognized them by their gray skin, domed heads and large, almost black eyes. The adults were almost identically skinny and small. I could tell the wife from the husband only because she had a bun of black hair coiled up on the top of her head, and she was carrying a pink Perfectly Darling Assistant instead of a steel-blue one as the other one had. They were talking in symbols that were nearly readable in spite of the distance. The Ghord halted them at the top level of stones, pointing out some feature I couldn't see. The male Kobold shook his head, and pointed upward. The Ghord pointed to his clipboard. The female Kobold countered, angling the screen of her PDA so he could see it. They were negotiating, too. The Ghord led them upward a level at a time until the Kobolds began to look happy. They started exchanging symbols again. They soon were far above us, still gesturing back and forth. The children looked bored, but they tagged along behind, sending messages to one another with fruit-colored devices. The cloud of symbols got more complex the higher the party ascended. When they were about fifty feet above me, the Ghord stopped and offered the adults his stone clipboard. The Kobolds became excited and shook hands with him several times. At least they had come to a mutually satisfactory conclusion. I glanced back. Not like Aahz and Samwise. The Imp blustered.

"Fifteen percent! Not a copper coin more."

"Twenty-three," Aahz said. "We're worth twice that. You came to us because of our reputation. We'll make it worth your while."

"Twenty-three! My children will starve!" the Imp pleaded, wringing his hands.

"Do you have any children?" I asked.

"What has that got to do with anything?" Samwise demanded. "What happens when I do? They won't have any food, thanks to your greedy partner."

"Pal, if you haven't worked in a twenty percent fudge factor, then you'd better turn in your horns," Aahz said dryly.

"Are you calling me stupid?"

"How about naïve? Is naïve better?"

"We Imps were running successful businesses before Perverts stopped contemplating each others' navels! Sixteen, or nothing!"

"I don't know why I bother," Aahz snarled. "Sounds like you don't value our services. It would serve you right if we walk out and your entire project comes crashing down on your head!"

A wild yell interrupted us. We looked up. The Kobold had backed up along the invisible platform with his PDA held up to his eye. He missed a step and fell. He plummeted toward the open layer of stones far below.

Samwise squawked. With a disgusted look, Aahz leaned out over the edge and held out a hand. The Kobold reached out for it, but missed by inches. His wife and children shrieked, filling the air with exclamation points.

I threw myself flat on the stairs and tossed a handful of magik woven into a rope toward the Kobold. It flew down, easily outdistancing the falling body. It wrapped around his waist like a snake. His weight yanked me close to the edge, but I anchored myself with more magik. On my command, the rope retracted slowly. When he came within reach, I grabbed the Kobold and helped him up onto our steps.

The little male recovered his wits swiftly. He shook hands with us several times, and emitted a stream of unintelligible symbols.

"Are you all right?" I asked.

"#$*&;@!" he exclaimed, his face a darker shade of gray. He waved angrily toward the Ghord, then turned to me. " . . . ☺."

"Gee, am I glad to hear that," I said.

As soon as he was free of my spell, the Kobold opened his small device and tapped the keys with one finger. A handful of sparkling points rose into the air. They lengthened into lines, then spread out into geometric shapes. At his command, the shapes collected themselves into a narrow platform supported by a framework of wedges.

"Mathematical construct," Aahz said, approvingly. The Kobold gave us a cheery wave and walked across to the other staircase.

His wailing spouse and family surrounded him as soon as he arrived on the other side. The Ghord politely dusted him off. Small symbols filled the air as the Kobold gave his guide a piece of his mind. The female turned toward me. Her mouth moved. A single symbol appeared over her head. It looked like a pair of puckered lips. They blew me a kiss.

"My pleasure!" I shouted and waved. I glanced down again. In the middle of the expanse, a single Ghord stood staring up at us. He looked so tiny in the distance that my stomach did a double roll. I gathered up more magik from the force lines, just to be sure. Then I picked myself up and dusted myself off.

"I suppose," Samwise said, weakly, "that I could squeeze out twenty percent of net profits."

"Ten percent . . ." Aahz said.

Samwise looked astonished, but he grabbed Aahz's hand and shook it.

"Ten percent? Done!"

". . . Of gross," Aahz finished, firmly. Samwise gawked at him.

"Gross! Not a chance!"

Aahz looked unconcerned. "Gross. Or the kid and I find the nearest inn and drink it dry. You can deal with your own problems. We wouldn't be around for the next potential customer to take an unscheduled dive."

Samwise swallowed hard.

"Gross," he said, weakly. "I suppose . . . your expertise would be worth it."

"Right," Aahz said. He stalked uphill. I followed. Aahz was still up to something.

Samwise hurried on his shorter legs to catch up with us.

"So," Aahz said, "that's my partners taken care of. What can you do to make *me* happy?"

"Ah, yes! You showed some interest in joining our little community here." Samwise rubbed his hands. "Well, then, you understood the cooperative nature of my business here. I don't have to draw a picture for you, do I? If you want to secure a spot on this fine edifice, you just have to say the word. I'd be delighted to have you involved—delighted! I have locations on almost every level. Your indoor locations are, of course, much more modest in price than your outdoor locations, but the spells provided by our magicians make certain that you and your loved ones will have permanent access. Furnish it with whatever goods you choose. Decorate

it! Our artists and artisans are the finest to be found anywhere in Ghordon. The neighbors are all quiet. And you'll
never find a better deal in your life. Or death. Ha ha ha."

I was not amused.

"What about theft?" I asked. "You said you had a
problem?"

Samwise grinned, showing a mouthful of pointed teeth
that would once have daunted me, but I'd seen lots bigger
and worse since I started working with Aahz. "I hired the
most notorious bandit chiefs from the three biggest bands as
my consultants to prevent shrinkage. Nothing that has been
left by the owners for safekeeping in any of the tombs has
been stolen."

"Yet," Aahz said.

Samwise hurried past me until he was only a step behind
Aahz.

"And that's something I expect you will advise me on,
now that we have agreed as to terms. I can even offer you
an advantageous price for a stone."

"How advantageous?" Aahz asked.

Samwise puffed after him. "In the name of good will, to
my new consultant, a generous offer is in order."

Aahz waved a dismissive hand. "And how much is that
translated from Imp-speak?"

"Oh, twenty percent off," Samwise said. "If you take a
look down, you can see our model tombs. The tops have
been made transparent so you can see the dimensions and
the workmanship."

"Twenty percent off how much?" I asked. I peered down
at the rectangular cases. They looked like identical shoe
boxes fitted together side by side. "They all look the same
to me."

"Naturally, the price is different for identical repositories
depending upon how high up the pyramid you buy, my
friend," he said. "And there are other amenities we can discuss once you decide on your location." He stopped and bent
over with his hands on his knees.

Aahz continued upward, ignoring both of us. When it

felt like we had been climbing for an hour, he touched the
air with his foot, then stopped where he was. I looked down
again, and realized that we were almost at the center of the
massive square formed by the sides of the pyramid. Aahz
must be standing on the apex.

"What about this one?" Aahz asked.

SIX

> *"I knew it was too good a deal to be true."*
> —DR. FAUSTUS

I looked at it with my mind's eye. Under Aahz's feet was a tiny square platform, just big enough for one person to stand on. Samwise elbowed past me, gushing.

"Oh, that is our very best, the bestbest benben. There's only one of those. It is the capper of the whole project. The top. A fitting memorial to a well-lived, not to say well-recompensed life. And, as I said, the person who purchases the top location will have the pyramid named after him, giving him a place in history."

We gazed around us. The Valley of Zyx spread out beneath us like a giant's sandbox. In the distance, winged creatures I couldn't identify dipped and swooped, but the most numerous living things out on the surface of the pale golden quicksands were Camels. Here and there, Ghords paddled tiny, one-being boats just large enough to sit in with their knees bent. Otherwise, the desert looked lifeless.

Humble, flat-roofed buildings like the And Company office clustered here and there, and against the eastern foothills colorful tents were spread out like an armload of discarded handkerchiefs. I could just see the corner of

Waycross's tomb. There were no other edifices of impor-
tance in this desert landscape except Diksen's monumental
structure. The whiteness of its sides picked up a tinge of
pink now that the sun was starting to dip toward the mountains to the west. Behind it, I noticed a shimmering, pale
blue sphere that floated yards over the surface of the sand.

"What's that?" I asked.

"Oh, that's Diksen's office suite," Samwise said dismissively. "Such a showoff."

"What is it? It looks like a bubble."

Samwise snorted derisively. "It's a ball of water. The guy
just has to flaunt his wealth."

"Wealth?" I echoed. "Water is free."

"Not in a desert, my good man," the Imp said. "It hasn't
rained in Ghordon for centuries. The cities maintain magical
wells or they irrigate from the Zyx. Wealthy Ghords have a
bathtub. The really rich ones have showers."

I admired the finished pyramid again. "Gee," I said,
shaking my head.

"Your place really suffers by comparison," Aahz added.

"One day, this pyramid will look like Diksen's," Samwise
said, defensively. "Better! It won't have that boring white
covering. This one will be faced with clear crystal so that
all the work my stonecutters are doing on each tomb can be
seen by visitors. It's also thirty feet *taller* than Diksen's. It
will be the tallest thing in the Valley of Zyx!"

For a moment, Aahz's face grew dreamy, but he regained
control over himself in a moment. "So . . . if I invested in
the top spot, the pyramid would be named after me?"

"Of course!" Samwise said. "It's the very least I could
do to indicate that location is special—beyond special. Not
that its location isn't the most important aspect of it. No one
would ever look down on you, in any way, shape or form.
Even the steps end at the base of that level, as you see. The
top stone itself will form the peak."

"And how much does a penthouse like that cost?" Aahz
inquired.

"Only one hundred thousand gold pieces."

I was shocked, but the effect on a Pervect who hated to turn loose an extra copper was dramatic.

"Forget it," Aahz snapped. "I can't think of anything that I'd spend a hundred thousand pieces on." He stopped, and his face softened. A huge, wicked grin spread across it. All his teeth showed. He let out a low-throated guffaw. I wished I could see what he was thinking, but glanced at his smile again and was glad I couldn't. "*Almost* nothing. But on a hunk of rock?"

Samwise tapped him on the arm. "Ah, but sir, you can't take it with you. What else are you going to do with it?"

"Do?" Aahz echoed. "The moment I find out that my time is up, I'm gonna start whooping it up with all my buddies, and with luck, drop dead the next day without a plugged nickel to my name."

Samwise wasn't giving up. I could see how he had attained an eighty percent sell-through on a stretch of empty desert. "A most admirable goal, my friend. But before you go, you surely want to make provisions for your . . . legacy."

"*What* legacy?"

Samwise waved descriptive arms. "This will become the valley of the celebrities.

"These monuments will ensure that your name is remembered for all eternity. Those who have questions can read the legend that is you in the very stone. Your legacy. Your value to the future. As you want it told." He reached into a pocket and came out with a scroll. "Here. Let me show you a few samples that some of my customers have ordered for their own inscriptions." He unspooled it, and it grew lengthwise and widthwise until it was larger than the Imp himself. I peered over Aahz's shoulder at the rows of eagles, dogs, cats, dancing girls, men in headcloths, musicians, suns, moons, stars, and many more esoteric symbols that would not have been out of place in a grimoire. "See here? Denby's a second under-stonemason from Bolder." Samwise perused the symbols and cackled to himself. "Oh, yes, he pulled out all the stops. Yes, you would think from reading this that he ruled half a dimension and had a dozen wives and a fortune the size of the Gnomes!"

Aahz frowned at the rows of pictographs.

"I can't read that."

Samwise reached into the other pocket and came out with a small, handsomely bound leather book for each one of us. "Here's a lexicon to the Ghordish language. Each sign can stand for a letter, a word or even a whole paragraph. You write out the text of what you want on the sides of your stone, and my scribes will render it into glyphs. You can say whatever you want. And most people do."

I looked at the first symbol, the image of a kneeling Ghord wearing a short kilt on one side of its body and a long dress on the other, one hand waving in the air, the other making a fist. On the top of its head was a spindly-legged chair. The translation next to it read, "In the name of Oris, the Ghordess Who is Her Own Brother, I commend to you this male or female who is as lofty above all fellow beings as the clouds are in the sky. How strong and mighty is this male or female, as powerful as the earth!"

The next image was of a Ghord female with a cow's head topped by a wild coiffure.

"Hail to the reader of these precepts in the name of Hat-Hed, She Who Looks As if She Slept in a Field, who commends to you the heroic soul known as (Your Name Here), whose doughty deeds must be proclaimed throughout the land as the finest of all (Your Profession Here) who ever practiced this honorable skill."

I skimmed a few more of the glyphs, but found them to be more of the same, some longer, some shorter. I admired the way the Ghords had managed to get all that information into a single symbol. Since their primary means of noting down information was hammer and chisel on stone, I supposed it was a necessary timesaver. I glanced between the lexicon and Denby's autobiography. On a quick study, I observed that Samwise wasn't telling us the half of what Denby had to say about himself, but in an impressive economy of space.

"You should certainly have this one on your stone, Aahz," Samwise said, pointing to a hawk in a loincloth with one wing extended. "The god Chorus is the Ghord of acclaim. Having that in your inscription really tells people what an important guy you were . . . I mean, are."

That reminded me all over again what the purpose of the pyramid was. As astonishing as the view was, I still felt uneasy about being around dead people all the time.

"Aahz, this doesn't really sound like a good idea. . . ."

But Aahz wasn't listening to me. "What about an offer in cash? Will that bring the price down a little? How much?"

"Well, you know how my operation works, Aahz," Samwise said. "I can arrange for the artisans to begin work on your stone immediately, but I can't build a penthouse until the rest of the pyramid is filled in below it. No matter how much magik I use, the least cataclysm will bring the whole thing down on our heads. So, are you willing to help me find clients?"

"For a commission?" Aahz asked, one eyebrow up.

"Naturally."

"How much?"

"Oh, we don't need to discuss that now."

"You don't think I'm going to buy a Pegasus in a poke, do you? Twenty percent? Fifteen?"

"The standard commission."

Aahz sneered. "Oh, ten percent. Why didn't you say that? It's an insult."

"Too little?" Samwise screeched. "When I'm giving you the chance of a lifetime?"

I tapped him on the shoulder. "Uh, Aahz, you said you didn't want to be involved in any pyramid schemes. You said . . ."

"Save it, kid," Aahz said sharply, throwing off my hand.

"But, Aahz, look at it from my point of view. There are over a million stones in a pyramid. If I allow you a ten percent commission on each one, you could end up *making* money. Plenty of it." Samwise smiled as my friend stopped to think. "In no time at all, you would have a free stone plus a weekly paycheck on top of your share of M.Y.T.H., Inc.'s fee. Now, how does that sound?"

Aahz hated to give up without a fight even when he was getting everything he wanted. He glowered for a moment. "What's the catch?"

"No catch! Twenty-five thousand gold pieces for the top stone in Phase Two, reduced by a percentage for each new prospect you bring me who buys in." Samwise held out a hand. Aahz clasped it.

"It's a deal. I think I'm gonna like spending eternity in your little penthouse, pal," Aahz said, with a huge grin. "Yeah, I like the view. Right here, you get the best of the sunset, and probably the sunrise, too. You ought to get a magician to cast illusions of the stones in place. I can't wait to see mine right here." He held up his hands, fingers forming a frame. "Of course, four sides isn't going to be big enough to contain all of my accomplishments, but I can abridge them. Kid, which ones should I have illuminated by the light of the setting sun with those mountains framing them right here?"

"There's only one wee little teensy problem with that, Aahz," Samwise said, edging around carefully so that he was standing behind me. "You can't have this one."

"What?" Aahz roared. He lunged in Samwise's direction. The Imp ducked and sidestepped further. The only way at him was through me. I lifted my hands helplessly. Aahz backpedaled. His eyes glowed yellow. "Why the hell not?"

Samwise's voice was small and apologetic. "I'm sorry, Aahz, but this place is already spoken for."

"By *you?*"

The Imp waved his hands. "No, no, mine will be a much more humble place. Besides, I couldn't afford the write-down. This one is earmarked for the Pharaoh Suzal, she who rules this fair land."

Aahz's shoulders slumped visibly. "Why didn't you say that in the first place?"

Samwise sighed. "Between you, me and the benben, Aahz, it was the only way I could get permission to build on this half of the Zyx Valley. After getting snubbed by Diksen, she wasn't in the mood to grant any more licenses. I had to come up with some serious bribes, let me tell you, but when I talked to the great lady herself, there was absolutely only one thing that I could offer that would even keep her from having me pitched out of the palace on my tail, and you're standing on it."

"Deal's off," Aahz said, turning to stomp down the invisible staircase. I could feel the magical structure shake under the force of his footsteps. He was really upset. "I don't settle for second best. I doubt M.Y.T.H., Inc., can help you, pal. Good luck. C'mon, kid."

I have to admit I was relieved. I followed Aahz willingly, readying the spell to take us home.

Samwise, seeing twenty-five thousand gold pieces and his business consultants departing on a pair of green-scaled feet, hurried to head us off.

"Don't despair, my good friend. Don't go! This is only Phase One of my grand project. Phase Two will be even *larger*. In fact," he drew close to us and dropped his voice to a near-whisper, "it will be substantially taller than the Pharoah Suzal's pyramid."

Aahz narrowed his eyes. "How much taller?"

"Sixty feet," Samwise said. He pulled a papyrus out of his pocket and glanced around hastily before opening it. "It will be the biggest one in the project. The location is slightly less ideal. I had to give this one the finest site since it was scaled down from my original plans. Cost overruns, you know. But the next one—oh, yes, the next one will be the most impressive. Watch this." He took a small wand out of his pocket and waved it. At once, the bleak desert filled with buildings. I counted about twenty pyramids. Each one was constructed of the blocks we saw being made below us. A skin of smooth, clear crystal covered them creating the four-sided façade I had admired in Diksen's pyramid. In fact, Diksen's was still visible beyond the points of two of the buildings to the east. It didn't look that impressive by comparison.

Between the pyramids were smaller buildings with colorful fronts which I guessed to be shops and guest-houses. Camels swam over the surface of the sand, bearing visitors in what looked like expensive clothing. I could hear faint, mournful voices chanting dirges.

"That's the one I am talking about," Samwise's voice came from behind the image of the completed uppermost tomb. On its side was the image of a swan wearing a crown. A pink hand protruded through the illusion and pointed. Just to the west of the structure on which we now stood, another point aimed toward the sky. Even at this distance it dwarfed the first pyramid and all the other ones close to it. "That could be yours, Aahz. You, at the top of the highest point in the Valley of Zyx. Think of it!"

Aahz was not mollified. "And how do I know you won't build a bigger one in Phase Three?"

"Footprint, Aahz," Samwise said, emerging from the benben with a smile on his face. "You can only put so many square feet in a yard. Tell you what: you can register my plans with the Pharaoh's clerk—but only after Phase One is complete. I don't want Suzal pulling my license before I'm through. I've had enough problems. You will start tomorrow, won't you?"

"We-eel . . ." Aahz was letting himself be persuaded. "Maybe I won't tell the Pharaoh what kind of scam you're pulling. . . ."

"The local beer's very good. I'll make sure you have your own barrel."

"I don't know," Aahz said. "I don't want to break any local laws. I bet if I read through the regulations in that tomb—what was its name, Skeeve?"

"Waycross."

"I bet there'll be dozens of rules we're violating."

"Daily barrels of beer?" Samwise offered, looking increasingly desperate.

"Two," Aahz said. "It's a hot climate. You don't want me dehydrating on you. I might start to lose my equilibrium, and you know what happens when a master magician loses his equilibrium. What do you think, kid?"

"Catastrophic," I agreed. "Better make it three barrels."

Samwise gulped. "W-w-why not? I'm sure you'll help me save more than you're costing me. I hope."

"Double, at least," Aahz said, with a casual wave.

"Well, then," Samwise said, pulling two more papyri out of his pocket, "let's formalize our agreement." The first one was between M.Y.T.H., Inc., and And Company. The second, which Aahz read over twice as carefully, was a personal contract for Aahz. I noticed that the terms had been written in exactly as discussed. It puzzled me, until I saw the Pyxie peering out of the Imp's pocket. It looked exhausted. Those miniature beings were the fastest scribes in all the dimensions. Samwise probably figured he couldn't lose a minute when signing a prospect. He flicked a talon at a series of dotted lines. "Sign there, there, there, and there."

That was when I stepped in. "We'll take that first one back with us tonight and bring it back tomorrow," I said, taking it from Samwise. "Aahz will want to read it over first."

Meaning it had to go up before the partners to agree if we took it. Bunny had made us start checking to be sure that we didn't have conflicts of interest after Guido and Chumley had ended up on opposite sides of what had sounded like a pretty good deal. Aahz shrugged.

"No problem, no problem!" Samwise said. "Do you want to take the second one home with you, too? The only way to make sure that everything is the way you like it is to sign right now. Because I warn you, the terms will go up every few hours. Standard Deveel contracts."

I opened my mouth to suggest that Aahz do just that, but he was too impatient. He grabbed the second document and put his name on the dotted line.

"Thank you," Samwise said. He snatched it away as if he was afraid that Aahz might change his mind and tear it up on the spot.

I heard a loud rip.

"Ow!" Aahz bellowed. "What did you just do to me? I wasn't going to sign it in blood!"

I looked at his finger. A narrow slit had opened up in the pad just under the talon. Yellow-green blood welled up.

"That's strange," I said. I didn't know Pervects could get paper cuts. Their scaly skin was too thick and tough. I'd known Aahz to squeeze handfuls of broken glass without cutting himself.

"Just bad luck," Samwise said and then looked guilty.

SEVEN

> "Well, you don't know everything about me."
> —M. BUTTERFLY

Once out of the Imp's sight, I popped us back to Deva. We appeared in the president's office in M.Y.T.H., Inc.'s headquarters in the Bazaar with an explosion of displaced air. Everyone looked up.

"Hi, everyone!" I said. At her desk, Bunny was poring over a sheaf of papers, looking concerned. "What's wrong?"

"Nothing much," Bunny said. She smiled up at us. She wore her thick red hair cut very short at the nape of her neck, like a Pyxie. The hairdo and her large blue eyes made her look cute and vulnerable. The former was true, the latter absolutely not. She was no more unprepared than my dragon, whose big blue eyes also misled people as to the brains behind the stare. No one made the mistake of crossing either one twice. "My Uncle Bruce just sent over some paperwork. I didn't really expect it . . . but, hey, forget it. Let's start the meeting. I'm going home to visit my mother tonight, and she'll skin me if I'm late for dinner."

"No problem," Aahz said, settling back in the armchair in the corner of the president's office. "There's not much to report on our end."

It was Bunny's new custom to have a group meeting once a week in the M.Y.T.H., Inc., headquarters. Partners and associates working on projects—if it was possible to get away from them—to compare notes and give everyone else a run-down on their progress. Guido and Nunzio, a pair of Mob enforcers who had been sent to me by Don Bruce, had also initially protested the idea of a weekly confab, but only out of loyalty to me and the way I used to run things. I thought it was an intelligent idea and had said so.

Apart from that, I hadn't seen any real moments when the others showed difficulty accepting Bunny as the president. She was, after all, the niece of their former employer. Still, she didn't take their respect for granted, any more than I had. But some of our clients had to adjust their expectations, being shown in to the knockout redhead whom other firms might have had taking appointments behind the front desk. She had only acted as my public interface while I was attempting to be a sole practitioner, and even now I feel foolish having given such a menial job to such a talented person. Bunny had a degree in accounting, a knack for figuring out how things worked, and an eye for style. I appreciated that she didn't hold it against me, and hadn't made me take on a subordinate role once she took charge. I owed her, as I owed all of my friends and partners.

I settled back in the chair that she had picked out for me and tried not to feel jealous as she sat down behind the desk that had been mine for so long. Bunny gave me a look of understanding but without apology. However, I hated her new chair. The back was made of thin wire woven into a big oval and molded so that it stuck forward into the sitter's lower spine. The seat cradled the rear end like a basket. We'd all tried it when the Deveel salesman brought a sample buy. I liked to sit with my legs comfortably splayed. This chair was made to keep a lady's knees together. Bunny claimed she was very comfortable.

The rest of her—formerly my—office had been redecorated to suit her tastes, sleek and subtle. I admit that my style is more the "finding it out on the curb" chic, or "it felt good to sit on." The walls were a pale shade between tan and pink, with white trim like whipped cream sprayed into curlicues. An oval mirror on a stand opened through extradimensional space Bunny's personal wardrobe, which was extensive, to say the least. It meant she could change into something more formidable if an upcoming meeting demanded it. *Objets d'art* hung on the walls or stood on plain little pedestals that were elegant in themselves. Her files occupied a tiny box on top of the pristine, pale wood desktop. Usually she kept it cleared of everything but the box, her coffee cup, and Bytina, her PDA, or Perfectly Darling Assistant, a flat roundel of red metal about the size of her palm that kept her notes and sent letters for her.

Across from the desk were a sleek couch and a carved bloodwood chair with needlepoint cushions on the seat and back. Neither piece of furniture invited a long stay, to get clients to come to the point of their visit as swiftly as possible. Her partners weren't expected to use those. On meeting day, Bunny opened yet another hidden closet in which she concealed our personal furniture, each item chosen especially by her for us. My chair, as comfortable as a hammock, was covered in a loosely woven cocoa-colored fabric that looked like old sacks but felt soft to the touch. Guido favored a seat that kept him upright, in case he had to spring into action. His chair, made of heavy wood, would have been a great weapon in a fight. It rolled on puffs of magik that allowed it to scoot across the floor. Nunzio liked shiny leather padding. His upholstered chair was the color of oxblood and smelled like money. Tananda's, like Tananda herself, was silken to the touch and tougher than it looked. She sat cradled in its gleaming, golden depths, like an emerald in a ring. I glanced around for the heavy, steel-framed seat with the shaggy brown cover favored by her brother, the Troll. It wasn't against the wall where it usually stood during meetings.

"Where's Chumley?" I asked.

"Big Brother's on a private assignment," Tananda said, filing her nails.

"Where?" I asked.

The file paused. "It's confidential," Tananda admitted. "He started the contract a long time before M.Y.T.H., Inc., went into operation."

I didn't push further. When Chumley came back, I could always ask him. Some missions were only confidential throughout their duration. We'd often been called on to provide security for a wizard working on a new invention he didn't want to see duplicated all over the Bazaar or some other marketplace before he was finished with it.

"Pookie's not coming, either," Bunny added. "She and Spider are working for mercenaries in Dromolind."

"Which side are they on?" Guido asked.

"The Dromoderries," Bunny said.

Guido grunted. "My sympathies for the other side. Should we send flowers to the losers?"

"I doubt they'd appreciate the gesture," Bunny said. "But it's sweet of you to suggest it."

Guido's cheeks reddened.

Gleep didn't have a chair. He curled around mine and rested his head on my feet. Buttercup, my war unicorn, was also absent but voting.

"So, how'd the prisoner transfer go in Diberot?" Bunny asked Nunzio.

"It went fine, Miss Bunny," Nunzio said, uneasily. "Look, I know we agreed to do it, but isn't there a less brutal way to make sure a guy shows up for his wedding?"

Bunny was not without sympathy. "It was the sixth time he'd tried to leave Lady Tumult at the altar. She was just making sure. Guido, you checked in with the Merchants' Association for my uncle?"

The big man in the wide-shouldered, pin-striped suit straightened at her address. "Yes, Miss Bunny. Everybody was reportin' no problems at all. I made the collection. Our cut has been deposited as accordin' to our usual custom. Nobody tried to stint us, so no one required any excess persuasion. It's all there." Guido aimed a thumb at another delicate little box on a tiny shelf of black, polished wood.

When you dropped pieces into it, they landed in our safe-room at the Gnome's Bank and Trust in Zoorik. This was another new change. While I had favored keeping our money in a strongbox here in the tent, Bunny had decided it was too much of a temptation to thieves. She let it be known that we only had expense money on hand.

Not that 'expense money' for us was a few coppers. My favorite old strongbox still stood about half full of gold, silver and jewels. It wasn't hard to find, either. At the moment it was propping up one end of the table in our atrium next to the mermaid fountain. If we needed money, we just needed to pry up the tabletop and take a handful of pieces.

Bunny smiled at me.

"Skeeve, what are you working on?"

"I'm between assignments," I said. "That Werewolf who wanted to talk to me at lunchtime didn't show up, so I went with Aahz this afternoon."

Bunny turned to Aahz, who had kicked back in his reclining armchair. At his elbow was a specially made drink holder with a diameter the size of a dinner plate. It held a wine cup deeper than a well bucket. "How'd it work out with Samwise? Should we take him on as a client?"

"Yes, I think so," he replied. None of the enthusiasm he had shown in Ghordon registered in his voice. I gave him a puzzled glance, and he shot a look at me that told me to keep quiet. "All the guy needs is someone to fix up the books and oversee the spending. And he's got some problems with on-the-job accidents."

"A lot of them?" Guido inquired. He twined his fingers and extended his arms outward. His knuckles exploded with a loud *crack!* While working exclusively for Don Bruce, he and Nunzio had been called on to arrange similar "accidents."

"Plenty," Aahz said. He waved a diffident hand. "But I figure it's a disgruntled employee causing trouble. I'll find the guy and get him to knock it off."

"You goin' to need some backup?" Guido cracked his knuckles deafeningly. "I got some time free."

"I've got the kid with me," Aahz said, aiming a thumb my way. "If we need some muscle, I can ring the bell."

Bunny asked, "What's your recommendation?"

"I say go for it. It's an interesting project. Massive construction, not quite unique but with the possibility of becoming historic. I think it'd be good to be connected with it. Samwise's business is slow at the moment, but if it picks up as I think it could, with a little expert guidance, we could be in for a nice profit. In fact," he added, in a casual manner, "I decided to invest in it myself."

Bunny nodded, a question in her eyes. "You believe in it that much?"

"I figure it makes it a little more worthwhile to me if I have a piece of the action," Aahz said. That much was true. I always took more interest in businesses in which we had a share. The Even-Odds had become a frequent hangout for a friendly game of cards.[1]

"All right," Bunny said. "Since it's the only piece of new business at hand, let's take a vote on it. Everyone in favor of Aahz and Skeeve consulting for Samwise And Company, raise your hand."

Without hesitation, I threw up my arm. Everybody else voted in the positive, including Bunny, though her hand went up more slowly than the others. Why?

"Carried," Bunny said, tapping a bright red nail down on Bytina's surface. The little PDA warbled, indicating that it had made the note. "So, what will you do next?"

"You know, fix up the books, help organize the finances, oversee the spending, and make sure M.Y.T.H., Inc., gets its cut."

"Find a solution to the accidents as early as you can. It might just be some people trying to get the day off."

"Not the guys who almost got squashed by a stone. They'd be taking more than the day off. Or the Kobold who took a dive off the high platform," Aahz pointed out.

---

1. To learn about Skeeve's connection with the casino in question, read *Little Myth Marker*.

Bunny raised her eyebrows. "Industrial sabotage? Who else is interested in the site?"

The scales on Aahz's forehead went down. "I already made a note to check around," he snarled. "I didn't get into this business yesterday."

Bunny smiled sweetly. "No one suggested you had. I assumed that was your first step. That would have been mine. But our styles are different. What will *you* do after that?"

Aahz grinned, the bad temper dissipating as swiftly as it had come. Bunny was a natural at managing people, even cranky Pervects.

"Depends on what I find out about Samwise's business rivals. The guy across the way, for example. He and the Imp seem to have split the Zyx Valley between them, but maybe Diksen wants the whole place to himself. I don't think it'll be that big a deal. The biggest problem will be convincing the employees that there's no curse on the place." Aahz reached for his wine cup, or rather, bucket, and lifted it to his lips.

The bottom fell out of it.

Wine gushed out all over his clothes. Aahz jumped up, swearing. Pervect cursing creates its own miasma. All the potted plants in the room suddenly turned brown and wilted. Aahz squeezed a rainshower of red liquid out of his natty tunic. He picked up his cup, now in two pieces, and glared around the room.

"Who did that?" he demanded.

"No one," I said. Tananda and I both checked. No outside magik had touched the cup. I couldn't detect anything special about it. Just in case, we examined our own goblets closely. Mine seemed to be intact. I pulled up some magik to dry Aahz off, but I wasn't that good at stain removal. The more I tried, the more of the shirt the purple blotch covered. I frowned and readied another spell.

"Stop that!" he bellowed, backing away from me. "You're making it worse. I'll take it to Zafnir the tailor three doors down." He turned to Bunny. "Are we done wasting time here? I've got a lot to do before I go back to Ghordon in the morning!"

Bunny glanced at Bytina and let out a squeal. "Ooh, I'd better get going. My mother is going to scream! If there isn't any further business?"

"No," we chorused.

"Good! Meeting adjourned." Bunny stood and adjusted her dainty jacket. "Tananda, can you give me a lift home?"

"Why not?" Tananda said. "There's a shop I want to visit near her house. The manager's really adorable." She gave a wicked smile. The two of them laughed loudly as Tananda waved a hand. They vanished with a loud *bamf!*

Aahz didn't say another word. He stalked off through the door of the tent, wringing out his clothes and growling to himself. I thought about catching up, but all I could do was draw attention to the accident and my part in it.

"Hey, Boss?" Guido asked. I turned to find him and Nunzio at my elbow.

"Hi, guys," I said. "Want to get some dinner? I hear there's a new Wyvern restaurant down by the grand promenade."

"Uh, maybe later, Boss."

I smiled. "You know, you don't have to call me that anymore. I appreciate it, but Bunny's the boss now."

"We have infinite respect for Miss Bunny," Guido said. "However, if you would do us the favor of acceptin' our ongoin' respect, it would be a favor to us."

I was touched. "Gee, guys, I don't feel as if I really deserve it."

"You do," Nunzio said. "It isn't as if we throw our support around to just anyone. It has and continues to be a pleasure to work with you."

"I feel the same way, guys. Thank you." They both still looked concerned. "Is there something wrong?" I asked.

"We was goin' to ask you just the same thing," Guido said. "Is there somethin' the *rest* of us ought to know?"

I wrinkled my forehead. "What do you mean? About what?"

Guido tilted his massive head to look at me sideways.

"Okay, Boss, you don't have to go all innocent on us. Far be it from me to poke my nose into somethin' that I shouldn't. We're not tryin' to snoop into personal business. Right, Nunzio?"

"Just as you say, cousin," Nunzio agreed.

I blinked.

"I think I missed something, Guido," I said, trying to force my brain to make sense of what he had just said. "Let's start over. Ask me what you want to know. I've never held back anything from you fellows. You know that."

"Dat's why we trust you," Guido agreed. "Okay, I will be more directly blunt than I originally was. For what reason did Aahz just buy himself a tomb?"

"Well, he really liked the site," I said. "You can't believe how amazing the view was from the top of that pyramid, and the workmanship that the Ghords put into each one is absolutely unbelievable. I admit, I almost got swept up in the hype, too; but I wouldn't get any real use out of one for a long time. . . ." My voice trailed off. I felt as if I had just been hit by an oncoming Gargoyle. "I have no idea at all. Aahz seems fine. He never said a word to me about feeling . . . under the weather," I said weakly. "He'd tell me if he was sick, wouldn't he?"

"Maybe you're the last one," Guido said, "seein' as how you are the closest person to him that we know of, nephews and cousins notwithstandin'. I might trust Pookie, but not that Rupert, and Pookie don't exactly invite confidences from us, not even Aahz."

"That's true." I sat heavily on the footstool of one of the armchairs in the tent's vast atrium. Gleep understood my distress and came to insinuate his head underneath my palm. I stroked him. "I don't know. He didn't say anything. I mean, I haven't seen him for months. Anything could have happened in that time. When I first got back to the Bazaar not long ago, he had been home seeing his mother."

"Or so he said," Guido pointed out. "A visit to a medical professional might be somethin' he wanted to keep to himself."

My brain felt as if it was spinning. It was a lot to take in.

Aahz had always been more than healthy, or so he seemed. Maybe I wouldn't know what to look for. Pervects had little in common physically with Klahds, and I was no doctor. I would have to ask around and see if he had been consulting a doctor. Chances were that he wouldn't use a physician anywhere in the notoriously porous Bazaar, where everything was for sale, even information about conversations and treatments that should remain private between a doctor and patient.

But if Aahz didn't confide in me, considering that I had been out of sight, if not out of reach, there was one person he might have. Then and there I made up my mind to do something that I had meant to do for a very long time. Now I had two reasons instead of one. I turned to the cousins.

"You've given me a lot to think about. In the meanwhile, I've got a favor to ask."

"Anythin', Boss," Guido said. "You don't even haveta ask."

"It's just a little piece of information. Nunzio, you know more about the inns and restaurants in the Bazaar. Let me get your opinion. . . ."

I left Gleep in the office with very specific instructions and ran out to take care of two errands.

When I returned, my dragon was on his back in the middle of the floor, eyes slitted, crooning, as Tananda ran her fingertips up and down his belly.

"Hi, tiger," Tananda said. "I jumped back here after I dropped Bunny in Klah. Gleep kept circling around me every time I headed for the door. He didn't want me to leave. I've got to check in with a client in the Fleeced Customer Inn."

"Sorry," I said. "That was my doing. I wanted just a minute to speak with you without any of the others around. Do you mind?"

"Not at all," the Trollop said, smiling up at me. Gleep let

out a moan redolent with sulfur fumes that made us both
cough. "What's on your mind?"

"I, uh . . ." Now that the moment was upon me, I could
hardly force myself to talk. "Can I ask you something?"

"Anything," she said. She leaned forward. The action
shifted her generous décolleté forward against the low-cut
green deerskin top she was wearing, causing a change in
the garment's geometry that made my blood pressure shoot
through the roof. "What can I do for you?"

"Well . . ." I swallowed nervously and ran a finger around
the inside of my collar. Before I could corral them and let
them out of the paddock one at a time, my words rushed out
of my mouth all at once. "I was wondering if you would go
out to dinner with me. Tomorrow. Or the day after. Whenever. I mean, if you would like to."

Tananda looked taken aback, as I was afraid she might
be. Then she realized she might have hurt my feelings and
brought her face under control.

"You'd like me to go out with you?"

"I really would," I said. I pulled myself together and
remembered the speech I had memorized. "I mean, if you
would do me the honor of having dinner with me, I'd consider it a big favor."

She tilted her head as if trying to figure out if I was joking. I gave her my most sincere, open expression. She smiled
at me. "It would be a pleasure. Tomorrow evening is fine."

"That's great!" I said. "Okay. I've heard of this great
restaurant about six miles from here on the edge of the
Home Entertainment zone. Say about seven o'clock or so?
I'll make a reservation."

"Great," Tananda said. "Formal? Informal? What's the
dress code?"

I was the wrong person to ask about clothes, no matter
how long Bunny had been teaching me the ins and outs of
fashion. "Uh, kind of nice, I guess. Not wedding-reception
nice, but not just drop in off the street nice. That's what it
looked like when I checked the place out."

"Seven o'clock, then," she said. "I'd better get back to this. The client's expecting it by close of business. It's an unexpected invitation, tiger, but it'll be nice. Thanks." She clamped me in a solid kiss, then undulated out the door.

I recovered enough to say thanks as the tent flap dropped.

Gleep popped up and laved my face with his tongue. I nearly gagged at the smell of his slime, though I appreciated the gesture.

"Good . . . idea," he said.

Did I mention that my dragon can talk? When I told Guido that I don't hold back anything from my colleagues, that wasn't completely true. Gleep's ability to speak was one thing that he and I kept between us. I hadn't even known at first how long it took baby dragons to become verbal, and considering how often he was underfoot, it might become awkward if I let it be known now. Someday, though, we'd let everyone know.

But I'd done it! I'd finally worked up the nerve. Inordinately pleased, I gave Gleep a vigorous scratch between the ears and went out to confirm a reservation for the next evening.

EIGHT

"The gods won't really mind."
—PROMETHEUS

"Hand me volume three of lies and deception, willya, kid?"
Aahz said, holding out a hand.

I ran my finger down the pile of ledgers sticking out of
the mouth of the gigantic Crocofile and found the one he
wanted. I passed it to him. He flipped it open and looked
from the papyrus sheet he was reading to the book and back
again.

He shook his head. "I don't think I'd ever want to go into
a fifty-fifty partnership with this guy. I'd end up owning his
underwear."

"Why?" I asked. The Crocofile yawned. I patted its nose.
Samwise kept his books protected by the ultimate security
system, a toothy beast the size of a house. When its jaws
closed, nothing could get at what was inside. "Has he cooked
the books that much?"

"No," Aahz said, with disgust evident. He sat back on
the stone seat that served as an office chair in this dimension. "In fact, they are not as crooked as I thought they
would be. He must be too dumb to cheat. There's the usual
amount of larceny and bribes, but that's just the cost of doing

business. He's using a magikal accounting system that automatically reconciles input and outgo. As far as I can tell, he
didn't work in any fancy wrinkles to hide money. Well,
figuring out the cost overruns just got that much easier. Want
some beer?" He held up a sloshing stone pitcher. The gray-
skinned secretary spent a lot of time running back and forth
between the reception desk and our office three doors down
the hall to refill it. I think she liked waiting on Aahz, and
he certainly looked as if he appreciated her.

"No, thanks." I held up a mug of ice-cold fruit juice. The
beer was as good as Samwise had promised, but I watched
my alcohol intake. I'd made too many mistakes when I
thought I was still sober, and it had cost me.

Aahz had turned up in the company tent later the previous
evening. He'd had time to mellow out once the wine had been
bespelled from his tunic. By tacit agreement, we hadn't mentioned anything. A stain here or there was not a significant
event between two people who had saved each other's lives
several times. He was more irate about the destruction of his
favorite wine cup. The next morning, before we departed for
Ghordon, we went looking for the silversmith who had made
it. Practical jokes and delayed-reaction spells were big business
in the Bazaar (considering the tremendous success of Genuine
Fake Doggie Doodle with Genuine Odor That Really Sticks
to Your Hands) and it wasn't beyond reasonable thought that
someone had decided Aahz deserved the dimension's biggest
dribble glass. The silversmith pleaded innocence and offered
to repair the cup for a fee that amounted to half of its value.
A loud screaming match, uh, bargaining session later, Aahz
had strutted out, with me in his wake, leaving the silversmith
to undertake the repair for a much more reasonable price.

As promised, Samwise had provided us with an office
and beer. We were on our own for everything else, but that
was pretty much what we expected.

A loud rumbling shook me out of my studies about mid-
morning. Aahz patted his belly. "Sorry about that. We cut
out of Deva before I could eat a decent breakfast. I smell
food out there. You want to see what you can turn up?"

"Sure," I said, putting aside the ledgers. Bookkeeping was my second least favorite duty when I was management.

After talking with Guido and Nunzio after the staff meeting, I was worried about Aahz's health. If he was suffering from some kind of fatal condition, I intended to do what I could to help him live a healthier life. Who knew? If the condition didn't progress too fast, a magikal cure could be found. In the meanwhile, I'd find something healthy for him to eat.

As I left the office, I was nearly hit in the nose by a small chunk of stone whizzing by. It zipped into the hands of one of the clerks working at a desk behind me. I glanced back and the Ghord with the sheep's face looked, well, sheepishly at me. I had become used to Ghords constantly sending glyphs back and forth to one another all day long. With the easy availability of power in all the force lines, it was no trouble for Ghords to drop notes to one another, chiseled on a small piece of stone or scribed on a scrap of papyrus. Scarabs carried a few of them, but they mostly went by magik. I picked up from my brief examination of the glossary the fact that the open mouth meant O My Ghordess. It began many of the short glyphs from young workers to one another. But I also noticed some glyphs incised on the big blocks of stone in place of the pictographs that they were supposed to be carving. Chief scribes, wearing sour expressions, had to check the work of some of their employees to make certain that they were chiseling what the customer wanted, not some remark about a hot date or a cute guy. The glyphs also talked about the frequent accidents. I would speak to some of the stonemasons later on to get full details.

I headed out in search of a snack. Naturally, wherever people work, a support system grows up around them, offering services that busy workers don't have time to do for themselves. Near the rear of the pyramid's base, a long walk from the office at the front of the site, snake-faced laundresses knelt over wash tubs. Dozens of dripping kilts hung on lines. They wouldn't take long to dry in the parched air. Barbers wielding long shears gave haircuts to Ghords sitting on backless stools with their headcloths wrapped around their necks like towels. A slick-looking individual in expensive and brassy robes oversaw a trio of gambling tables where bored stonemasons might try their luck at dice or cards. Nearby, curvaceous lovelies beckoned to passersby, inviting them to try for a different kind of luck. Prosperous women in aprons poured beer at a semi-permanent bar counter mounted on two carved pillars. I recognized the seal on their barrels as the same one on the excellent beer Aahz was being supplied. I gave them a friendly wave and followed my nose to the food sellers.

The variety of edibles in the makeshift cookshops told me that Ghordon was used to dimensional travelers. Next to staples like mixed beans and sausages, Imperial specialties were plentiful and, judging by the crowds, popular. I walked past vendors shouting the virtues of their fried bread, oiled meat with greasy sauces, thick stews, and pastries dripping with honey, all of which smelled delicious. Ghords crowded around, clamoring for service. Shopkeepers bantered with their customers as they hurried to fill clay bowls with orders. I stopped at the booth of a forlorn female with a short-beaked face who had plain, baked crispbreads for sale. Knowing Aahz had a substantial appetite, I bought a basketful for a few coppers. I left her shouting blessings after me.

A few tables down, I was able to get a large selection of sliced vegetables and a quantity of smooth dipping sauce made of ground legumes, the kind of thing Bunny had always been trying to get me to eat instead of roast meats and cream sauces.

I brought my offerings back to Aahz.

"What's this?" Aahz demanded.

"A snack," I said. "Look. This bread was baked fresh this morning. And these vegetables were all home grown."

Aahz looked at me as if I had gone out of my mind. "You call this food? If I eat this wallpaper paste and rabbit food I'll die of boredom! You could use these crackers for roofing tiles! What made you buy them?"

This wasn't working out the way I had hoped. "Well, you

seemed as if you weren't . . . feeling well," I began. "I didn't want to bring you anything that would upset your stomach." Even as I said it, I knew how foolish it sounded. I wasn't supposed to know anything was the matter.

Aahz blew a raspberry. "That was nothing, kid. I was ticked off at an incompetent craftsman, that's all. I'm fine. In fact, blowing off steam made me feel pretty good. I'll pop back to Deva and stop in at the Pervish restaurant near the dump."

I brightened. If he felt he was up to his native cuisine, then he couldn't be very ill, not yet. No weakling ever attempted to eat Pervish food. Half the time you had to wrestle it back in the bowl before it escaped.

"No, don't bother," I said hastily, heading for the door. "I'll get something better."

Samwise's books didn't take much longer to review. That left the main puzzle to investigate: the accidents. The first variable to consider was the people involved. Aahz and I split up to interview the workforce.

The workers on site were generally cheerful. Many had come directly out of school. I had seen the ads for Glyph Art College ("If you can carve Ra-nem-het, you could be an artist!") in the local daily papyrus left around the necessary. They were overseen by long-time veterans of projects around the dimensions, including Deva and a few other places I had visited. Even the team of professional mourners were upbeat people. They only sounded sad when they were rehearsing.

Except for the accidents, they felt Samwise's pyramid wasn't that bad a place to work. I got some of the stonecarvers talking over the communal water jug about where they came from and what they thought. It was a convivial location, presided over by a shrine dedicated to the Ghord of the water cooler, Hapi-Ar, He Who Makes Others Merry Through Drink.

Very casually, I introduced the idea that the accidents and mishaps might be deliberately caused.

"Oh, no, Skeeve, no," Ba-Boon, a monkey-faced Ghord assured me. He bared his teeth. "Saboteurs? No, not at all. We are proud to be part of this operation. It is not every day you work on something that will become part of history."

I recognized some of Samwise's pep talk and grinned.

"Does everyone feel like that?" I asked.

"I am not so sure about the commitment of the Scarabs," sniffed Pe-Kid, a male who resembled a Klahd except that his skin was dark green. "You notice that none of them ever seem to get hurt."

"O My Ghordess, but that is not true," piped up Lol-Kit, a kitten-faced young female. "I was on the second mastaba when those four stones fell all at once from above. Many Scarabs were killed, and all of them were destined to be buried here!"

"I forgot about that," said the green Ghord. "But, when you are working with heavy stone, some mishaps are to be expected. It is the will of the Ancients. They must not have placated the sacred ones in the correct manner."

"You believe that's the reason?" I asked.

"Sincerely," said Pe-Kid. "The Ancients control every aspect of our life. Who is to say they are not responsible for the departure from it?"

"How can that be?" I asked. "I mean, they're not around anymore."

"Did not your parents not order your comings and goings when you were a child?" Lol-Kit asked.

"I guess so." I thought of how it was before I left home. I defied a number of rules my parents laid down, but I was always aware of them. And I was punished when they caught me.

"Think, then, of the power that your fiftieth-times great grandfather will have over you, then. That is why we pay attention to their will and desires."

That the Ghords did their best to obey those desires I knew to be the truth. Shrines abounded on every level and in the most unexpected places of the construction site. All the Ghords performed little rituals prized by whichever ancestor they wished to honor or placate, such as blowing a whistle, ringing a bell, tossing a pinch of tiny leaves in the air, turning in a circle, waving an incense stick, or saying a word like "boo." They performed these ceremonies upon clocking in every morning. Aahz refused to do it, calling it nonsense, as did Samwise. Those weren't their ancestors, after all. Still, I felt a little guilty about not participating. When in Zyx, as Aahz might have told me, do as a Zyxian.

"Oh, yes," added a baritone Mourner, Bah-So. "Nonli lost his favorite chisel between two blocks and nearly was squashed between them before the Scarabs noticed him. It took several offerings of beer to placate the Ancients."

"You don't think it could just have been bad luck, do you?" I asked.

"Oh, no!" the Ghords agreed. "We don't believe in superstition!"

A loud blatting interrupted our conversation. The over-seers of the carvers, master scribes, came to urge their work-ers back to their stations.

I was impressed by the workers' eagerness to get the job done. Samwise was in a hurry for his investment to pay off, and his people reflected that sense of urgency. It didn't mean they were cutting corners, though. I had never seen such fine stonework.

Throughout the day, I noticed strangers climbing the invisible ramps overhead. Most of the time they were accom-panied by Ghord salespeople, but often they were following someone from a different race altogether. I guessed those were customers who had the same deal as Aahz; they wanted to reduce their own payments through commissions, but by their gestures I could see their enthusiasm for the project itself. I'd done some listening around the Bazaar. No one had ever proposed such an undertaking before. Many of the Deveel merchants thought Samwise was crazy, but I think they were just jealous. One look at Diksen's structure across the way, and it was hard not to want a piece of that.

Samwise was right about Beltasar, too. Several times during the day, the voluble Scarab came flitting after the

Imp, with a high-pitched complaint about something. I tried to tune her out, but her voice carried. I could hear her almost anywhere on the site.

In spite of my efforts to steer Aahz to healthier food, he invited me to join him for lunch on the far side of the pyramid at Fat Ombur's, an open-air cookshop run by a Ghord with a bird's face but a corpulent body. ("I get this way from eating my own cooking!" he assured us. We both considered it a good sign. Aahz's motto never to trust a skinny cook almost always held true.)

Like everything else we had seen in Ghordon so far, the tables and stools were made of chunks of stone. I perched at the edge of a squared-off piece that seemed to have been a practice sheet for some pretty complicated runes. My rump was going to have reverse impressions of goats, birds, shepherd's crooks, and open eyes by the time we finished eating.

Fat Ombur did good business, for good reason. The thick, flavorful stew, which we ate with our fingers or with torn pieces of fluffy flatbread, was delicious. Even Aahz went for the grilled vegetables, snatched off a low burner heated by a tiny snoring Salamander.

"Here, my good gentlemen," Ombur said. "Eat up!" He beamed proudly.

The strips were too hot for me to eat, so I chilled them with a touch of magik. Aahz, impervious to most temperatures, grinned as he ate them by the handful. As we chewed, I listened to the mourners keening on the level above us.

"Not my idea of dinner music, but it adds to the local color," Aahz commented.

"They're actually pretty good," I said. The ululations combined in six-part harmony. Then a shrill buzzing audible over the wailing and moaning made my ears contract. I winced. "There she goes again."

I turned toward the painful sound. Samwise picked his way through the tables, his eyebrows drawn down, as Beltasar harangued him from the air.

". . . And there will be five further fines for the interruption by Deveel visitors. They prevented us from seating a cornerstone. That will cost you also a secondary penalty. . . ."

"Hey, Sam!" Aahz called, waving to him. "Come and join us. Leave the bug."

Samwise hurried over. "Would that I could, Aahz," he said, aiming a thumb at the Scarab. "We'll talk later," he told her.

"We will talk now!" Beltasar shrieked. "The safety of my workers is paramount."

"What about the job?" Aahz asked.

"What?" the Scarab demanded.

"Is the job less important than your workers?"

"N-no," Beltasar said, hesitating briefly. "We wish the work to be done, but in a safe fashion!"

"Then why are you constantly leaving your own work station to harass Samwise here?" Aahz asked. "If there's no active danger, then you're pestering him unnecessarily. If there is a safety problem, then you're leaving your people in harm's way by tracking him down. That doesn't make sense to me."

"That is the way USHEBTI works! We must notify the management of violations at the time of occurrence!"

"Not cost effective," Aahz said bluntly.

"But it is the way we do things."

"*That's* a great reason," Aahz said, with a smirk.

"Are you telling us how to do our job?"

"Not how. Just when. Like now. If you're not stopping for lunch or a beer break, then you're goofing off. You just cover it by following Samwise around and haranguing him."

The Scarab blew up in outrage. "How dare you? Nine hundred generations of my family have been involved in construction. You walk in, and in one day you claim to be an expert? You must be as stupid as you are ugly!"

"Sticks and stones," Aahz said, dismissively. "I'm saying that you're wasting your employer's money. I'm limiting access to him from now on. You can say 'hello' to him in the morning, 'how was your lunch?' after the noon break, and 'goodbye' when you leave the site. Everything else will have to be a real matter of life and death."

"You're interfering with a union official!" she shrilled.

"Now, Aahz," I said, raising my hands to placate the combatants. "You can't stop her from conferring with him when she really needs to. Beltasar here is an experienced manager."

"That's right, I am!" she exclaimed, then looked puzzled.

"You're defending what she's doing?" Aahz looked dubious.

"I'm saying she's doing it for a good reason. The fines are just a way of reminding Samwise they're serious. Right?" I turned the Scarab.

"Uh, right."

"So, how can she let Sam here know what she needs him to?"

Beltasar's head went back and forth between us. "Yes! How can we?"

"Well, if was me," Aahz said in his most reasonable voice, "I'd save up all the problems and report them to him at the end of the day. I'd hit him up for all the fees then. That'll give him a chance to institute better safety measures overnight. Bel here can pass out the new policies every morning to the workforce. What about that?"

"I think that sounds like a good idea. Doesn't it, Beltasar?" I asked her.

"Yes, er, no. No!" The Scarab finally realized she was being double-teamed. She beat one tiny fist against her undercarapace. "*We* decide how we institute new orders. We do! Otherwise, And Company faces strike action!"

Aahz shook his head. "I'm the paid representative of your employer. If you'd rather shut him down than coöperate and get the job done that you're being paid to do, be my guest."

The Scarab's bright blue eyes turned red with fury. "Perhaps we will! You will see the might of the USHEBTIS!"

"Yeah, yeah," Aahz said, waving a hand. "You and what army? Throwing your weight around?"

As if on cue, I saw a shadow appear and grow larger and

larger until it covered all of us. Just in time I used all the magik force I had inside me to push Aahz back. I fell backwards on top of Samwise and Fat Ombur, who was just bringing a steaming dish to us.

A Titan guard in loincloth and headwrap crashed down on the table, splattering food in every direction. He lay moaning until Aahz helped him up.

"What happened to you?" Samwise asked.

"Scarabs," the blue-faced male puffed, pointing upward. "Under my foot. I think they did it on purpose!"

Could the green-faced Ghord have been right about the Scarabs wanting Samwise to fail?

"Impossible!" cried Beltasar indignantly. "You impugn us!"

"You tried to kill me!" the Titan bellowed, making fists. "I'll squash you like the bug you are!"

"Just you try it, big boy!" Beltasar fumed, curling her tiny forelegs into balls. I could picture steam coming out of her ear holes.

Tan-ta-ra! Tan-tan-tan! Ta-ra!

A flourish of horns drowned out the argument. A booming male voice echoed across the valley.

"Make way for the Queen!"

"Oh, no!" Samwise exclaimed. "You must not tell her what just happened! Everybody to their places! Hurry!"

All the Ghords ran out of the cookshop. They bumped into one another, running around the corners of the pyramid.

"What's going on?" Aahz asked.

"The queen! The Pharaoh Suzal. She didn't tell me she was coming. Hurry up. Follow me!"

Samwise leaped onto the ramps and flew over the top of the uppermost layer of the pyramid. Aahz shrugged. I furnished us with magik, and we took to the air after him.

NINE

"I hardly noticed her face."
—ASTERIX THE GAUL

My heightened vantage point gave me a good view of the eastern part of the valley. At first, I couldn't see what was approaching because of the massive cloud of dust that surrounded us. Suddenly, the roiling cloud dispersed.

Approaching toward us across the sand was a parade. At its head were dancing girls in sheer robes, undulating and spinning. Behind them was a covey of musicians, puffing into or strumming away at a marching song. Drummers pounded the tops of skin-covered drums in time with the beat. Magicians threw balls of flame into the air and conjured rainbows. For a moment, I thought that they were responsible, too, for the stream of knives that flew in a circle at each side of the procession, but then I realized a troupe of jugglers was throwing the knives. All of them stood on Djinn-woven carpets that conveyed them over the smooth surface of the dunes.

Behind them wafted the most impressive carriage I had ever seen. At least thirty feet high, it had a curved, gilded back like that of a chair, but as wide as a street. The sides sloped down to carved arms of black wood. At the ends were finials in the shape of red hearts. It was pulled by a team of eight creatures with the bodies of lions and the heads of Klahds and massive, golden-feathered wings.

At the center and riding high enough that her head was just below the upper edge of the chair sat a slender female Ghord. Over her headcloth, which shimmered like pure silk, she wore a golden circlet that supported a golden snake's head. Cascading from underneath her crown tumbled tresses of long, blond hair. She had high cheekbones, a slender neck, a lovely nose, large blue eyes, and a decided mouth.

I realized suddenly that I was the only one in my immediate vicinity still standing. All the Ghord workers and all the Scarabs were on their knees, foreheads touching the ground. Hastily, I did the same.

The carriage swept up and over the pier and the And Company office, then came in for a landing at the foot of the pyramid. The entourage hastened to catch up. The musicians finished their marching tune with a flourish, and launched into a regal melody. At the top of the carriage, the queen rose and descended the steps.

"What a babe," Aahz murmured.

I peeked. The fine linen of her robes outlined a figure that, while slender, was furnished with plenty of the usual female attributes. Not only that, she walked with a sway that I couldn't take my eyes from.

From the rear of the structure came girls carrying fans and Ghords of both sexes wearing chains of office around their necks.

"Hail, in the name of all the Ghords of Ghordon, Eternal Ancestors Who Give Life and Light to All Creatures. Blessings upon Suzal, daughter of Geezer, she who is Pharaoh and Queen of Aegis from the Underworld to the Overheaven. All hail!"

"All hail!" echoed the Ghords around my feet.

Samwise dashed over the paving stones to be at the foot of the carriage before Queen Suzal got to the bottom. He threw himself to one knee and bowed his head. She touched his shoulder and he rose, talking with his usual animation. Suzal listened with a regal tilt of the head.

Samwise turned and beckoned enthusiastically for us to join him. We made our way to his side. Under the Pharaoh's eye, we bowed deeply.

"These are the ones I told you about, your majesty," Samwise said. "This is the Great Skeeve and, er, Aahz."

Aahz rose and bent over her hand like the practiced courtier he was.

"Hey, doll," he said.

"Hey, yourself," Suzal said, fluttering her eyelashes at him. "You have a noble face, sir, reminiscent of our scaly river Ghord, Sober, He Whom Rivers of Drink Do Not Affect."

"He and I have a lot in common," Aahz said, modestly. "I'm on my second barrel of the day. Would you . . . care to come around to the office and knock back a couple?" He raised his eyebrows suggestively. Her ministers were shocked, but Suzal looked pleased.

"You are too kind, Sober-faced one," Suzal said. "Perhaps another time I will be able to accept your hospitality. This is just a casual visit."

Casual? I glanced at her entourage: at least thirty dancing girls, twelve musicians, a pair of conjurors, and two files of courtiers in pleated linen and fancy striped headdresses.

My mouth dropped open when I spotted one of the courtiers. He stood at least two feet taller than the rest of the nobles. His body was covered in thick purple fur, and his two, large moon-shaped eyes were different sizes.

"Big Crunch!" I exclaimed.

"I beg your pardon?" Queen Suzal asked.

Behind her, Chumley cringed. The Troll hastily patted the air with both big palms. 'Big Crunch' was his *nom de guerre* as a monosyllabic enforcer in most other dimensions, but clearly not here. I immediately tempered my statement.

"I mean, your majesty, we're on a *big crunch* for time here, trying to get the pyramid done, but I'm very pleased to have the opportunity to meet you. Samwise here has been telling me what an honor it is that you have given him permission to build such an amazing structure. I am eager to see it finished."

"As am I, O great Skeeve," she said. She smiled at Samwise, who turned brilliant pink with pleasure. "He shows honor to me that had been heretofore withheld. I, too, would see it complete."

"Who would dare refuse to give you whatever you wanted, beautiful lady?" Aahz purred.

Suzal's long lashes flicked as she eyed him up and down, but her blue eyes flashed.

"Why, that ignoble wizard across the valley from here," she said, aiming her nose toward the eastern mountains.

"You mean Diksen?" I asked, puzzled.

"Speak not his name!" Suzal snarled. "I call him accursed. And selfish." Her lip quivered. Indignantly, she put her nose in the air. Like all of her features, it was unusually pretty. Chumley realized I was staring and cleared his throat audibly. I lowered my gaze.

"But I am very pleased to give you what you want, your majesty," Samwise said. "Everyone knows that this is the Queen Suzal Pyramid. When it is finished, it will be the wonder of Ghordon and, er, many other dimensions."

"When *will* it be done?"

I jumped. This unexpected question came from somewhere around my waist. I looked down.

Another official in striped headgear stood at the queen's side. He was only half her height. He peered up at the Imp. Samwise gestured impatiently.

"When it's done, Gurn, I have told you that a thousand times."

"And I will ask you a thousand more times, on behalf of my lady. She would like to see it finished long before she needs it. So . . . when will it be ready?"

I felt my stomach churn. Gurn had a face like a handful of squashed dung. No, that didn't come close to approximating the misshapen quality of his features. Each looked as if it had been designed by a sculptor with less than no talent and who had failed to communicate what he was doing to the others. I thought I was used to ugly. After all, I hung out with Pervects. But Gurn was something above and beyond the dictionary definition, a degree past where two drunken master magicians would have kept daring one another to go. It actually hurt to look at him.

He leered at me.

"So you are on a big crunch to complete this enterprise, Klahd?" he asked. "Do you think it will be done in *your* lifetime?"

"If Samwise says it will, then it will," I stated boldly, not knowing whether or not it was true. The Imp had been notably vague on his estimate of a completion date of this or any other pyramid in his plans.

"Her majesty is not accustomed to lies and half-measures."

"So, she doesn't have anything to do with politics at all?" Aahz asked innocently.

"I don't deal with politicians, either, Pervert."

"Per-vect!"

Gurn looked up at him and wiggled his hand back and forth. "Not so much. Do *you* have an answer for her majesty?"

"Do you, Sober-faced one?" Suzal asked. "My favored Imp here is coy with his answers. I would like to see my stone erected in as little time as it took that excrescence there to the east to be completed."

"And how long was that?" I asked, curiously.

"Five years and two days," said Gurn. "How about it?"

"Well, your majesty," Samwise said, fingering his collar and sweating more than the heat might account for, "my financing is of a cooperative nature. Diksen was able to pay for his entire bloc by himself. . . ."

"Perhaps, majesty, you were not wise to give a license to an underfunded architect," Gurn said, his voice velvety with menace. "I see it—one day he will come crawling to you for alms to complete your own monument."

Aahz slapped him on the back and sent him staggering.

"I can tell we're not gonna like each other, pal. Come on back again some time. When we're not here."

"Sober-faced one, do not abuse my courtier," Suzal chided him in her soft voice.

"Looks like Mother Nature did the job for me, majesty," Aahz said. "But if that's what you want, who am I to refuse you?"

I stepped in. "I bet you'd like to see how the project is going, your majesty. May I escort you around the site?"

"You may," Suzal said. She lifted a finger, and two of the Sphinxes separated themselves from the others. They brought over a sedan chair with poles sticking out to either side. The queen stepped into it. The Sphinxes fluttered their wings, and the structure hovered three feet off the ground. Using a coil of magik, I pushed off from the ground and followed. To my dismay Gurn clambered onto the leg of the queen's mini-chair, scaled up, and made himself comfortable on her chair arm. I frowned at him. He leered at me, or perhaps that was just the way his face worked.

"You think I don't belong here, do you?" Gurn asked.

"I think your head's higher than the pharaoh," I commented mildly. "When I was last a court magician, the queen just hated that."

To my surprise, Gurn hunkered down a few inches. I decided he wasn't all bad. After all, he didn't work for me.

"You were a court magician, O Klahd?" Suzal asked. "Tell me which of my sister monarchs you served."

"Hemlock of Possiltum,"[2] I replied.

Suzal nodded. "I have met her at the Royals and Despots Convention in Zoorik."

"Uh, how did she look?"

"Imperious."

"Uh, that's good."

I fell silent, not wanting to say the wrong thing about my

---

2. To review Skeeve's job history with the notorious queen, invest in copies of *Myth Conceptions* and *Hit or Myth*.

former employer. We had since gotten on better terms than when I left the job, and Suzal might be a friend of hers.

The queen's chair headed up and I followed.

It took no time to rise above the finished layer of stones.

"Uh, as you can see, your majesty, we're up to level three." I did a quick calculation. "Only eighty-six stones to go, then we can move on to level four."

"That's nice," she said absently. She was staring over her shoulder at Diksen's pyramid and let out a heartfelt sigh of longing. Everyone reacted like that. Poor Samwise had a tough act to follow.

"I doubt that your master could ever produce anything as well-proportioned or sleek as that," Gurn said to me. "I mistrust his skills. Stolen dreams never prosper."

"His dreams aren't stolen," I said. "And it'll be great, you'll see."

"I command that we should go down," Suzal said suddenly. "I do not feel well."

Her lovely skin had taken on a green tinge, and small drops of sweat dotted her brow. Gurn shouted an order to the Sphinxes, who wheeled around and headed for the carriage.

"Make way for the royal ejecta!" Gurn bellowed as we landed. Aahz looked up from his talk with one of the Sphinxes at the cry.

The mini-chair landed as softly as a leaf falling, impressive under the circumstances. Scantily clad ladies in waiting hustled toward their mistress. One held a bejeweled golden vessel shaped like a pail. Eight others bore fans made of enormous white plumes. Suzal staggered somewhat ungracefully from the small chair toward the girl with the bucket. The others surrounded her, shielding her from view, but the sounds that issued from within the makeshift place of concealment were unmistakable. I felt sorry for her.

"Is she usually airsick?" I asked Gurn.

"Never," he said, frowning. "She has always had a magnificent head for heights."

"Rest of her's not bad, either," Aahz commented.

"It is only recently that these spells overtake her. Our court magician is baffled. I see your master's hand in this."

"He's not my master, he's a business associate," Aahz said. "Making queens sick is not in my job description."

"Then you must be freelancing."

"Look, pup, if seeing you every day doesn't make her sick, then a face like mine's not going to affect her. You heard what she called me. Noble." I could tell Aahz liked that.

Gurn wasn't convinced. "Because she's delirious."

Samwise bustled up, frantic. As soon as the queen emerged from her place of concealment, he tried to usher her into his office.

"I think not, kind Samwise," Suzal said, applying the back of her hand delicately to her forehead. "I wish to return to my palace. I thank you for the tour, Master Wizard," she added, with a wan smile at me. "You will be welcome if you should choose to visit."

"I'd be honored," I said.

The ladies helped Suzal up the golden steps to her seat and fussed over her with cold drinks and more fanning. I wanted to talk to Chumley, but he gave me a warning look. Instead, I went to join Aahz. The Sphinx lay on its belly with its tail wrapped around its haunches. Lying down, its head was still higher than my own.

"This is the partner I told you about," Aahz said to the Sphinx. "Skeeve, meet Tweety."

"Tweety?" I asked, astonished, looking at the huge creature. He outweighed me and Aahz put together. "Uh, is it an old family name?"

Tweety eyed me. "What is it that is dark in the morning, pale at noon, and gone by sunset?"

Aahz looked concerned. "You'd better answer him, kid. It's an important test. Sphinxes don't like people who can't solve their riddles."

"What happens if I can't answer him?" I asked.

"I eat you," Tweety said simply, compelling golden eyes fixed on mine. "Please answer the question."

I looked down at the curved yellow claws of his front paws curled on the flagstones just inches from my feet. I felt panic rising in my stomach. My brain couldn't fix on a single coherent word. What object fit all the qualifications in his riddle? I didn't want to be eaten. But Aahz wouldn't have introduced me to Tweety if he wasn't confident I could pass the test, of that I was certain. It sounded like a riddle that I had heard when I was a child. I ran a hand through my hair, trying to think.

That was it!

"H-hair," I stammered out, hoping I was right. I braced myself, ready to pop out of Ghordon if he came after me.

The Sphinx opened his mouth to show two rows of sharp teeth and leaned close. I cringed. Then he grinned.

"Well done!" Tweety roared. "Now you're part of the family. You can ask me anything any time. Happy to be of service. We pick up a lot of information other people might not have. By the way, Tweety was my dad's name, too." The Sphinx rose and clapped Aahz on the back with one huge lion's paw. "Good to see you, Aahz. Too bad about the Magicians' Club, huh? Tough luck."

"Yeah," Aahz said sourly. "Maybe I won't bother getting it straightened out. Who needs them?"

"No one, really," the Sphinx said. "I just like to have a place to hang out with my fellow 'users, swap spells and lies when I'm in Vaygus, that's all. Hey, come on down to my lair and have a drink, now that you're in town. You come, too, Skeeve. I live on one of the Pharaoh Islands. Ask anyone, they'll tell you how to find me."

Aahz nodded. "Don't mind if I do. See ya, Tweety."

"See you, Aahzmandius. Got to go."

The Sphinx returned to his place and attached his harness. At a signal from the flyer at the front left corner of the carriage, they all spread their wings and pulled forward. The carriage lifted off the ground.

"What about the Magicians' Club?" I asked.

"Nothing, kid," Aahz said, with the kind of expression that told me not to push it.[3] "Nothing. Dammit, what are the odds that the only Sphinx in the entire membership roster has to turn up like that? It means everyone's heard."

"Did he bring you bad news?"

"Nah. I knew already. Just reminding me of a humility lesson I didn't need." He watched the carriage depart, sailing over the sands like a shadow. "What in Crom's name is Chumley doing here?"

---

3. The details of Aahz's last visit to the Magicians' Club on Vaygus can be read in the thrilling *Myth-Gotten Gains*, a real page turner available from your local huckster of literature.

TEN

"Sometimes a dinner is just a dinner."
—T. JONES

"Ready?" I asked, extending my arm to Tananda.

"Ready," she said, smiling a little uncertainly.

I was nervous, too. I had set everything up in advance for our evening out, and I hoped the arrangements would please her. I wore an open-necked shirt in a deep slate blue that Bunny thought was my best-looking shirt, and sand-colored trousers. I had resisted the impulse to wear my favorite shoes, the ones with the toes that curled over twice before terminating in tiny bells. Instead, I had a pair of comfortable ankle-high boots in case I needed to do any fetching and carrying for her.

Speaking of fetching, Tananda wore a low-cut dress of green fabric so thin that it looked as if it had been painted on her but remained opaque. I scanned it for magik, but it must just have been a master weaver's accomplishment. The skirt was not as short as she normally wore, but it flared with each step, revealing a bewitching glimpse of knees. Tananda's were worth looking at, no matter what. The shoes were a puzzle to me, as most women's shoes were. Why anyone would bind themselves into a network of narrow straps on top of an acute slope of sole attached to a heel no wider than my little finger was a mystery I didn't understand. You couldn't run away in them. The narrow sole made it awkward to stand on one foot to use the stiletto for a weapon. Still, they made her legs look even more attractive than ever.

I escorted her out of the flap of the M.Y.T.H., Inc., tent and helped her into a chuckshaw, a local two-wheeled vehicle that was pulled by a team of Soxen, one red and one white. They trundled down the streets of the Bazaar, kicking up dust and emitting the kind of flatulence that you'd expect from large herdbeasts. I had paid them to keep from defecating until after they had dropped us off. That would spoil the mood I hoped to achieve. As evening settled over the Bazaar, the air remained stiflingly hot. It would take an hour after the sun went down before the desert cooled. Coming from the temperate climate of the dimension of my birth, I still marveled at the extremes of living in a desert.

I chatted about this observation and compared it with conditions in Ghordon.

"It's funny how alike they are," I commented. "I'm used to dimensions being really different from one another. If you'd asked me before I left Klah for the first time, I would have said there was only one way for a climate to behave, but I like the variety. What is the weather like in Trollia?"

"Different," Tananda said, unexpectedly terse.

As Tananda sat against me in the curved but not adequately padded seat, I could feel the tension in her body. For someone who came from a race of beings who enjoyed—no, actively sought out—intimate contact with others, her behavior was unnatural. I hoped by the end of the evening she would relax. Perhaps a gift would improve her mood.

"Here," I said, pulling a small box out from behind me and setting it in her lap. She looked through the clear top at the contents. White blossoms of nested oblong petals lay clustered on curling, blue-green foliage.

"Flowers?" she asked weakly.

"Squizzias," I said. "They're rare flowers from Klah. They smell really nice. My mother used to grow them in the front garden of our farm house. They're her favorite. I hoped you'd like them, too."

"I'm . . . honored," Tananda said. She opened the box and lifted the blossoms to her cheek. "Mmm. They smell delicious."

"Shall I help you pin it on?" I asked. The Deveel florist in the Bazaar had given me pretty specific instructions on how not to puncture my date with the pin. He had let me try out the lethal-looking metal skewer several times on a dummy he kept in its shop for that purpose. When it stopped saying "ouch," I found I had become pretty expert at attaching corsages. Tananda fended off my helpful hands.

"No, thanks, honey. I'll take care of it." With deft fingers, she attached the cluster of flowers to her bodice high on her shoulder. I admired the effect. She was really beautiful. I never forgot that—I'm still breathing—but sometimes it just struck me like a sack of rocks.

"That looks nice on you," I stammered out.

For the first time I could recall since I met her, Tananda blushed. Her cheeks bloomed slightly green. Instead of commenting on it, I told her about the pyramid complex, without going into a discussion of the problems or the suspicions Aahz and I had about their source. You never knew if the Soxen were in the pay of any Deveel hoping to pick up useful information from people who forgot that the cab had ears.

Before I knew it, we had arrived. Le Mouton Suprisee had a long line waiting to be seated. I handed Tananda down from the chuckshaw and escorted her boldly past the line of dapper Deveels and their dates. Some of the customers gave us dirty looks, some looks of envy, and some both. I didn't acknowledge any of them, concentrating on getting Tananda safely inside.

"Mister Skeeve! How wonderful to see you this evening! And the lovely lady!"

The maître d', who had responded to a little early bribery in the way of all good servers, seated us with effusion at the table I had chosen earlier: near the front window, in between a couple of potted plants to give us the greatest possible privacy while we watched the nightly perambulations of the Bazaar outside. He furnished us with leather-bound menus and bowed himself away to wait on the next good client. I smiled. So far, everything was working out as I had planned it.

Over the top of her menu, Tanda raised an eyebrow at me.

"Is there anything you think I should choose?"

"Nope," I said expansively. "Try whatever you like." I read down the list to make my own selection. The prices made my inner farm-boy choke, but my modern, executive magician self had plenty of money and a willingness to give enjoyment to my guest. The menu of Le Mouton Surprisee listed every kind of elegant dish I had ever heard of, plus hundreds of things I hadn't, in its crisp parchment pages.

Next in the line of employees who would expect tips was the wine steward, a female Deveel wearing her badge of office, a silver tasting cup on a chain around her neck. In the past, my knowledge of wine was limited to what didn't taste bad enough to spit out. I had since learned to pay more attention to quality, as I limited myself to one glass per night. That, I promised myself, would be the case this evening, no matter how nervous I was.

And I was nervous. I was controlling myself from shaking with a solid dollop of magik. I wondered if Tananda could tell. She knew me better than almost anyone. It mattered to me to make this evening special.

"What do you recommend?" I asked.

That was the wrong question.

"Well, sir," the sommelier said, beaming, "I am so glad you asked." She launched into a lecture on grapes, slopes, sun, brix—which I had always thought of as an uncomfortable operation—age, barrels and a whole lot of other esoteric information that would have been more useful had I planned to go into wine-making instead of wine-drinking. I needed to take control of the situation. Tananda couldn't help grinning mischievously at the expression on my face.

I held up my hands to stem the outburst.

"Hold on!" I said. "If you offer classes, I'll come and take one someday. In the meanwhile, what's the least I need to know to order something that will taste good with the food here?"

"Are you planning to order meat, fish, reptile, fowl, insect or other?" the Deveel woman asked. "That's the least *I* need to know to recommend a wine."

"Fish," Tananda said.

"Me, too," I said.

"Then a white or a green would be your best choice."

I grinned at Tananda. "I think we'd like a nice green from somewhere in the middle of your list. We've got a green theme going, and I think it'd be fun to continue."

For some reason my joke made Tananda blush again.

"As you wish, sir." The Deveel held out her palm. I dropped a tip into it, not too much or too little, I hoped. She seemed pleased by it, or as pleased as any Deveel was to get a portion of the contents of your money pouch instead of the whole amount. She snapped her fingers. In an instant, a brown glass bottle and a pair of tall, delicate wine glasses floated gently toward us. The wine steward plucked the bottle from the air, ran her talon around the foil seal, and extracted the cork, all with one hand. I almost applauded. She poured a little for each of us. I tasted it. The pale green wine was as unlike my normal tipple as could be.

"This is great," I said.

"Mmm," Tananda agreed.

After filling our glasses, the Deveel withdrew discreetly, to be replaced by a young Imp who supplied us with bread (woven basket) and water (cut crystal pitcher), the elderly Deveel who snapped open our napkins and set them on our laps, the pair of young, perky girls who replaced our table settings with a whole new set of plates, cutlery, and glasses, all of whom extended their palms to me before or after service was rendered. At last, an unctuous male Deveel appeared armed with a gleaming ivory square and a pencil. He bowed to Tanda, then to me.

"May I have your orders, sir and madame?"

After some urging from me, Tananda went down the menu with a hunter's eye. I followed her example, ordering appetizer, soup, salad, and one of the fish dishes. I had never heard the name before, but if the food was anything like the wine, I was in for a treat.

"And, sir," the waiter said, "it is green. As sir has expressed his preference, we wish to please."

That made *me* blush. He withdrew, bowing. Tananda let out a low chuckle that only I could hear. I hope. I covered my embarrassment by blurting out conversation.

"I . . . er . . . got a message from Chumley today," I said.

Tanda's eyes went wide, and she looked around. There was a discreet screen of magik between each table intended to mute sound. I realized I could scarcely hear the diners nearest to us. She turned back and whispered, "You did?"

I felt awkward. Maybe I shouldn't have mentioned it. "Uh, yeah. I, uh, *heard* he's fine. Enjoying the weather."

Tananda's mouth curved in a rueful smile. "I'm happy to hear that. I do worry about Big Brother when he's out of my sight. You know I couldn't tell you where he goes. As far as I know, it doesn't interfere with anyone else's assignment."

"I don't think so, either, but it's always good to know he's . . . around."

If I had said I had seen him in Ghordon, I might blow his cover. I had no idea if his assignment was dangerous, but I was utterly unwilling to put Chumley or any of my friends in danger.

"Well, tell him I love him the next time you send him a message," Tanda said. She smiled at me. "Big Brother and I are so glad you're back in town. I know I visited the inn once in a while, but it hasn't been the same."

"I know," I said. "I felt that way, too. It took a while before I was ready to come back. Then I almost ruined everything when I did."

"Don't beat yourself up, tiger. We'd all been thinking

about you so much that it took us a moment to realize what your return meant. I'm glad that it worked out."

"Bunny seems to be handling the presidency well. Better than I ever could."

"Family training," Tananda said, "although she told me the titles generally get passed to a male heir. Not always, of course. She's nervous about making sure the business runs smoothly."

"Gosh, you could never tell she was nervous," I said.

"Oh, she is! She wants to get everything right. I keep telling her that we trust her. She doesn't have to try so hard."

I smiled. "She's one of the most competent people I know, present company excepted."

Tananda grinned. "Thanks, but you don't have to compliment me. I like my job. When the gang broke up the first time, I did some freelance assignments, and a few with Big Brother, but I missed the camaraderie. I've really never been so close to anyone in my life who wasn't family."

"Me, neither," I said, looking deeply into her eyes.

An uneasy silence fell. I was almost grateful when a Deveelish maiden brought a bowl and towels for us to wash our hands. A chandler arrived to trim the wicks of the candles on our table. The appetizers, Deveelish dancing dumplings, arrived. By then, the awkward moment had passed.

That would have been a good time to bring up the subject of Aahz's health. Then I had a good look around the restaurant, and realized I couldn't. It wasn't just Tananda's discomfort, though that was a big part of it. Instead, I asked her about growing up on Trollia. She didn't mind talking about her childhood. I found it an eye-opening conversation. I asked a few leading questions and listened with fascination while she did most of the talking. Finally, she was relaxed enough to laugh. We started to lean closer and closer to one another. I admired the shape of her face, the charm of her features.

"Madame and sir, the soup," a Deveel server announced.

We sprang back, I very reluctantly.

The food was every bit as good as Nunzio had said. I

enjoyed all the courses. I couldn't have described what was different about the taste of the fish from all the ones I had eaten before, but it was better. The service was unbelievably smooth. Our empty plates were whisked away without a fuss, by magik. No crumb ever marred the perfection of the white tablecloth for more than a moment. Our glasses always held exactly the right amount of wine.

At last, time came for dessert. Over the years, I had learned some of Tananda's likes and dislikes, including her favorite flavors. When I had discussed her tastes with the maître d', he had laughed as if I had just told him a good dirty joke and given me a lascivious wink. I hoped the dish wasn't an obscene suggestion of some kind.

I watched her face as the dessert arrived. To me, the rounded shapes in the dish didn't seem suggestive of body parts or anything I could construe as objectionable.

"Passionfruit and angelberry sundaes!" Tananda said. She looked delighted, which made me feel great.

The wine steward appeared once more, to pour a lighter vintage than the one that had accompanied the savory courses of the meal. It went down pretty smoothly, too.

"I hope you're enjoying yourself," I said, reaching out to touch Tananda's hand. She held very still.

"I am, Skeeve. I can't tell you how much."

"That's great." I looked into her eyes. They were a lighter green than her hair, almost like tourmalines. "I've been hoping for a chance like this for a really long time. I'm really happy that you said you would come out with me."

"Skeeve . . ." Tananda looked at me searchingly. "You know, I'm a lot older than you are."

"That doesn't matter," I said. "Honest. That's never mattered between us. Has it? At least I don't think it matters."

Tananda drew her hand back. "But it matters to me. And, actually, I'm seeing someone. . . ."

"That shouldn't make any difference to us, not here and now."

Tananda tried again. "I don't know how to tell you this, Skeeve—don't get me wrong: this was a wonderful date, and you were so sweet to ask me—but, well, you have to know that nothing would ever work out between us. I know this hurts a lot of guys' egos, but I've always thought of you as the little brother I never had."

I whistled. Patrons at nearby tables turned to stare at me. "That's great!" I exclaimed. "That's perfect!"

Tananda blinked. "It is?"

"Oh, well, yeah." I couldn't believe how relieved I felt. "That's just how I hoped you would feel. I mean, I have tried going out before, like with Cassandra.[4] Things just went too fast. I never got to know her; and, well, you know what happened. *Everyone* knew. It was a big mistake. I made a fool of myself, and I didn't handle it well. None of my attempts to find a girlfriend have worked out. The problem is that I just didn't have a lot of experience dating while I was growing up on Klah. If you don't mind, I could really use your advice on how to treat a woman the way she wants to be treated. There just aren't a lot of people I can trust with this sort of thing. I mean, to everyone else I'm supposed to be the Great Skeeve. I should know everything, and I don't. I knew *you'd* tell me the truth, because you're one of my best friends. I've always prized your honesty. Give it to me straight: how'm I doing?"

Tananda threw back her head and laughed. "Oh, Skeeve, you don't know how much you worried me. How much you worried all of us."

I grinned. "I know. I can see Aahz back there in the corner trying to pretend he's a potted plant. That's Massha and General Badaxe in the front table. They might be disguised as Deveels, but look at the way the tables on either side of them are pushed out to give them enough room. Bunny brought our entrees. You couldn't conceal the way she walks with any kind of illusion. And Guido's in the kitchen, isn't he?"

---

4. For the fullest account existing of Skeeve's date, read *Sweet Myth-tery of Life*, available in plain brown wrappers at your local bookseller.

Tananda's eyebrows flew up.

"How do you know?"

I drew the miniature crossbow quarrel out of my folded napkin and held it up. "This was in my soup. I've picked birdshot out of game hens, but you don't have to shoot squash."

"I guess the jig is up," Tananda said, looking sheepish. "We were just concerned about you."

"I appreciate it," I said. "You didn't think . . . ?"

The look on her face said she had, but she said, "I hoped not, but I didn't want to refuse automatically before I knew what you wanted. I had to give you a chance. You're one of *my* best friends, too." She leaned over and kissed me. The potted plant in the corner rustled fiercely. Tananda drew back and laughed again. She beckoned to it, and Aahz emerged with all the finesse of a child who didn't want to be kissed wrestling his way out of his great-aunt's grasp. He stalked over to a nearby table and sat down at it as if he had just taken a wrong turn coming from the men's room. I shook my head.

"How'd everyone know where to come? I didn't tell you the name of the restaurant. It was meant to be a big surprise."

Tananda looked a little embarrassed. "You asked Nunzio for recommendations on good places to eat. If there's one thing the Mob knows, it's good food."

"He told you?" I asked, dismayed.

"No. He respected your confidence. He didn't want to say specifically, but we narrowed it down based on where you said it was. You noticed everyone else left this evening before we did."

I lifted my shoulders sheepishly. "I guess I did, but I didn't think about it. They came out here first to spy on us?"

"Maybe a little," Tananda admitted. "That's not the only reason. We have to look out for each other. We've got some open investigations, and the proponents might just consider it a Crom-send if one or two of us were out in plain sight alone. Not that we all can't take care of ourselves," she added.

"You must have noticed how Aahz never sits with his back to a door or a window. You've been doing it since you started hanging out with him, too. It's just smart planning."

I nodded. "See? One more thing I didn't think of but I have to take into account. We're in a high-risk business. We have enemies. We've got assets. I've got to think about my date's safety as well as whether she's enjoying herself."

"So is there a name to that 'she'?" Tananda asked, her bright green eyes narrowing into merry crinkles.

"No," I said honestly. "Nobody."

"You don't have anyone in mind right now?" Tananda wheedled. "Really? I mean, it isn't any of my business if you do."

"No, I swear. I just wanted to get some experience taking someone out and showing her a good time. If you don't mind. Now that Bunny's my boss, I thought it would be out of place to ask her. Massha's married. Pookie doesn't give the kind of advice that really works for me."

"You do tackle everything as if it was a magik lesson, don't you?"

I felt my cheeks burn. "I'm not trying to be calculating. I'm just so good at falling over my own feet. It makes me nervous enough when I meet a pretty girl. I'd like to look like I know what I'm doing. I mean, to a certain extent." I was horrified, worrying that she might think that I would push things too far. But I should have trusted her.

Tananda smiled gently and put her hand back on mine. "I understand exactly what you mean. Believe me, girls feel the same way."

"Really?"

"Really. Do you want me to fix you up with anyone? I've got a cousin about your age who's a lot of fun. You could try out your skills on a real date."

I held up my hands. "No, thanks, not yet. I'm not looking at the moment. If it happens, it happens. Besides, I had fun. Did you?"

"Yes, I did," Tananda said. "It was wonderful. Thank

you, Skeeve. I guess we both learned something this evening."

"Then would you be willing to go out with me again? As a friend and advisor?"

"Any time, tiger," she said, lowering her eyelids so she could look at me through her lashes. "You don't need any advice from me, not really. If you need a testimonial for some lucky lady, just let me know."

I floated away from the restaurant happily. That night, I had great dreams.

ELEVEN

"Would I steer you wrong?"
—E. PONZI

When Aahz and I left for Ghordon the next day, the subject of my date with Tananda was off the table by tacit agreement. I was pretty sure all of my partners had heard everything we had said to each other. On the one hand, I was a little embarrassed that my attempts to learn how to date had become a spectacle viewed by almost the whole group. On the other, having it known among my partners was not exactly public knowledge. It made me feel good to know that they cared about me enough to make certain I wasn't making a huge mistake. Not that I hadn't dreamed about finding someone like Tananda, but as I had said, and meant, she was the big sister who always told me the truth. I was lucky to have her and the others on my side. They'd all given me good advice on relationships before, but not really on how to get one started. As in so many other things, I needed to go back to square one and relearn the process from scratch. Fortunately, I had good as well as bad examples all around me.

The sun was just peeking over the eastern mountains when we popped into the building site. Ghords arrived on

Camel-back, flying carpet, or hanging on to one another in a string trailed by a flying Sphinx.

"I always hated commuting," Aahz commented, watching the fliers descend onto the long pier. But these were frequent fliers, accustomed to the discomfort of their transit. They bent their legs just before they touched down so they didn't hurt their ankles, though the odd, squarish way they held their shoulders suggested that hanging from their arms all the way from the main city of Aegis threw their backs out somewhat.

The Scarabs were already there, burrowing upward in huge numbers. They lived just below the surface of the sand where it was cool. They were already at the tiny shrines that represented their ancestors, singing high-pitched snatches of verse, lighting incense, pouring out drops of beer and sacrificing berries to placate the Ancients into blessing their workday.

"Quaint," said Aahz, dryly. "C'mon, I want to talk to Beltasar before she gets going."

It was not difficult to locate the shop steward. She was at the center of a swarm of circulating Scarabs, all buzzing with orders as well as gossip.

She noticed Aahz as we approached. "Your framework is on the agenda."

"I've got a potential client stopping in around lunchtime. Will it be ready by then?"

"By morning break, if the magician has no trouble," the Scarab assured him. "Do you question our competence? I only have four hands!"

"Don't get your wings in a wringer," Aahz said. "Just trying to drum up some business."

"Who is it?" I asked, as we headed for the office building.

"An old acquaintance from Perv," Aahz said. "Bendix owns a law firm. Thought he'd like to take a look around. I'm not going in for the hard sell. Shouldn't have to. A deal this good will sell itself."

But Bendix was not as easily persuaded as Aahz thought

he would. We stood at the top of the new invisible framework overlooking the unfinished pyramid. As Beltasar had promised, though the spells left the staff magicians panting, it was completed in time. Aahz had borrowed the illusion wand from Samwise, and pointed out all the future attractions of the site to Bendix, but the Pervish lawyer kept coming back to the same point.

"So you want me to invest in a big piece of nothing?" Bendix asked, as if astonished that he should even have to ask. He was taller and thinner than Aahz, almost as tall as me. His lower jaw thrust forward and his brow crouched over his eyes so he always looked as though he was scowling. At the moment, he *was* scowling. So was Aahz.

"Bennie, this is the chance of a lifetime," Aahz said, in his most persuasive tone. "Look over there at the finished one."

"But you're asking me to invest in something on which you haven't even broken ground. I like to see what's on the table before I write a check, Aahz. I don't like the idea of buying a siskin in a satchel."

"What's a . . . ?" I began. Aahz gave me a quick gesture to forestall the question.

"Is that one over there for sale?" Bendix asked.

"That's a rival operation," Aahz said, dismissively. "Not connected to this project."

Bendix was not so easily deterred. "Well, how do I buy a piece of that? Maybe you can introduce me."

"You couldn't afford it. It was privately funded. One owner."

"That guy has the right idea," Bendix said. "He the king or something?"

"Something like that," Aahz said, changing the subject immediately. "But he had to fork out the entire price of his pyramid. Your wife would never put up with that."

"You got that right! You should have heard her when I wanted a new crystal ball for the office."

"Well, this is just a small piece of the whole thing, and you get the benefit of everyone else's investment. All you need to finance is a millionth of the total. You can have bragging rights that you were in on this one from the start."

Bendix stroked his chin. "That's appealing. But how much are we talking for a nice spot near the top? Say, the third level?"

"Only fifty thousand gold pieces."

"What?"

I covered my ears to shut out the bellow.

Deals between Pervects were nowhere near as loud or shrill as those in the Bazaar, but they escalated a lot faster to imprecations and counter-accusations. I had more respect than ever for Aahz's vocabulary by the time he and Bendix paused for breath.

The Pervish attorney gasped in air in outrage.

"You've got to be out of your mind. You say *you* invested in this . . . this non-hole in the ground? I used to have some respect for your brain, buddy. The sun must have baked it out of you."

"I'm not nuts!" Aahz insisted. "It's a great deal! You'll never find one like it."

"No, not unless I want to help some scam artist move his late uncle's nonexistent millions out of the dimension! Fifty thousand! When I think what I went through over a crystal ball—you know Deplora. She'd tear my claws out. That's it. Forget it."

Bendix pulled a small device out of his pocket. With his eye on the small flat screen, he started moving it around. When it was in line with the wavy blue line in the sky, he reached for the red button below the screen. He was leaving. It looked like no sale. I gave Aahz a look of deepest sympathy.

Aahz's yellow eyes seemed to smolder into a blaze. He drew himself up as if calling on internal strength. Then he reached out and put out a hand to forestall Bendix. As if prying the words out of his mouth with a crowbar, he managed to eke out a single sentence.

"We . . . might be able to work out a . . . discount."

I was so taken aback at the concept that it took me a

moment to remember to breathe. Aahz? Negotiating a *discount*? On a multi-thousand coin deal? For someone else? When it took all of us to remind him not to stiff waiters?

Bendix was similarly impressed. His eyebrow ridge shifted upward. He whistled. "You must really want this bad, Aahz. What's the catch? Pervects don't give something for nothing."

Aahz waved a hand. "It's not for nothing. Your partners are gonna be envious about your new asset. You can share the wealth with them—and I'll make sure you get a discount off your own stone in return."

"How much are we talking?"

Aahz countered the question with a question. "How many senior partners in the firm?"

Bendix turned up a palm. "Ten. But my name's first on the letterhead. What consideration are you willing to offer me, as most senior partner—and an old friend?"

"Five percent," Aahz said promptly, even though the words sounded as if they hurt as much as major surgery. "Each. If they each buy a stone of equivalent value, yours is half price. Find twenty prospects, and it's free."

Bendix eyed him. "Sounds too good to be true."

"It's the deal I'm getting from the developer. I'm getting such a great bargain I'm passing the savings on to you. I still get a piece of the action, but I'm more interested in sharing an opportunity. Like I said, it's once in a lifetime."

"That's not what the sales brochure says. There are going to be twenty of these pyramids here in two hundred years."

Aahz draped an arm over his shoulders and drew a panorama with the other palm. "Yeah, but this is gonna be the showpiece. The tallest. The most well-equipped. You get to choose the parts of your life story you want carved on the sides. Think of it, pal: your most successful cases engraved the way you want them remembered. Never mind the *Pervish Law Review* that'll get backed up in some hard drive somewhere. This'll be out where anyone can read it, forever. And how about your other exploits, huh? When we were young? How many babes in that cabana fell for you over

that weekend? Wouldn't that look good in a stone frieze?"
He nudged Bendix familiarly in the ribs. "It'll all be written
in hieroglyphs—you don't have to tell Deplora what they
mean."

Bendix was starting to get that same dreamy look that
Aahz had had when Samwise talked him into buying. He
snapped out of it momentarily, and the brow ridge went
down again. He glowered.

"I'll bet every tooth in my head that you're not giving me
the same discount you're getting."

"I'm full-time on site," Aahz snarled. "You want to set
up shop here, too? I thought you had a full caseload."

"No, no . . . but you'll have to give me your word you
won't let any of my partners have the same deal as you gave
me. I want it to be exclusive, or there's no deal."

Aahz raised his hands. "What arrangements you make
with your partners is up to you. I don't care if you charge
them double. I don't care if they pay you in marshmallow
bunnies as long as Samwise gets paid in gold. I'll even give
you the contracts to sign them up yourself, so they never have
to deal with me at all. Now, let's talk about location. . . ."

By the time Bendix *bamf*ed out of Ghordon, Aahz was
strutting with pride. The Bendix Frimmis Wisten Katz and
Associates wing would almost fill the level third from the
top. In keeping with Bendix's status, he took a corner tomb
with a stunning view of the western mountains.

"Things are looking up, partner," Aahz said.

TWELVE

"I didn't know my own strength."
— SAMSON

But when our waiting Camel brought us back to Phase One, instead of looking up, we found that things had actually gone *down*.

We pushed through a frantic crowd of workers clustered around the northeast corner of the pyramid. Everyone was shouting. I looked where they were pointing.

To my horror, the house-sized corner stone had tilted downward. Part of its outer corner was buried in the sand and sinking fast. The whole structure looked threatened. The slabs above the tilted one were at risk of slipping or cracking. Ghord workers in loincloths had thrown themselves against the massive block. Others had dashed to their shrines to invoke the assistance of their ancestors.

Countless Scarabs dug away at the foundation to get at the lower edge. A rooster-tail of sand flew under their feet. As soon as it was visible, they swarmed under it, dragging ropes and harnesses.

"Heave!" the beetles shrilled in their tiny voices. "Heave!"

The block stopped tipping. I held my breath as the mass of workers surged together, pushing with all their strength.

More Scarabs swelled the ranks, but they couldn't bring it back to level.

"No!" Beltasar shrilled, audible over all the others. She hovered in mid-air, pointing her tiny hands to direct her workforce. "Reinforce the corner! Division One, down to the superstructure! Division Two, scaffolding!"

"Hup one! Hup two!" The beetles formed themselves into wedges, driving the stone upward, a fingernail's breadth at a time.

"Pray harder!" shouted the Ghords. "The Ancients will raise the stone!"

We found Samwise in the middle of a gaggle of supervisors. The Imp spread out a rolled papyrus. All the section bosses argued with one another over who or what was to blame.

"What can we do to help?" Aahz asked.

"Nothing, my friends, nothing," Samwise said, waving us away. "We have this under control."

"Doesn't look like it to me," Aahz commented.

"I know it doesn't look like it," Samwise said, "but we are handling the situation correctly. First we confer. Then we act. Now, will you kindly leave us alone? This delay is putting us hours behind!"

Fortunately, the Scarabs weren't paying attention to the Ghords, Imps, and other two-legged beings. They had enlisted other help. A flying wedge of beetles carried harnesses out to the sands where Camels waited. They threw collars around the Sheep of the Desert and fastened them.

"All hands on deck," Beltasar shrilled. "Division Three, we need to get elevators underneath it at once, before it all tumbles down on us! Ready? Heave!"

The Camels swam away from the pyramid, pulling as hard as they could. Slowly, the stone began to lift. Several Scarabs, standing on their front feet, rolled six-pointed metal spikes toward the opening gap with their hind legs. Just as they were about to insert them between the tilted stone and the foundation the big stone dropped. The building jacks went flying.

I heard a loud twang. The Camels were yanked bodily right out of the quicksands by the weight of the building and dragged along the pier. They came to a halt, lying on their sides, looking dazed. Shaking themselves, they rose on four paddle-like feet.

"Camels got legs," Aahz said, enlightened.

A couple of them heard him and exchanged shocked expressions.

"Now we'll have to kill him," the first Camel said.

"Not now," the second one whispered. "Everyone is watching."

"No, no, no!" Beltasar screeched, zipping around in frustration. "Try again! Everyone back into position."

The Ghords, Scarabs, and Camels all made their way back to their starting points. The beetles dug down.

Aahz and I hurried over to the hovering supervisor.

"You're the only one doing anything practical," Aahz said. "What can we do to help?"

"Nothing!" Beltasar shrilled at once. "Perverts are in the way. We can handle it! Is everyone ready?"

Aahz's protest of "It's Per-*vect!*" was drowned out by the voices of thousands of Scarabs.

"Ready!"

The Camels waded back into the sand, and their mysterious legs disappeared beneath the surface. They braced the harnesses on their chests and looked back over their shoulders for the word. The Scarabs rolled the jacks back into place. More beetles forced their way under the now perilously leaning slab.

"Oh, for Phoenix's sake," Aahz said, angrily. "A blind bat could tell they're making it worse!"

"What should they be doing?" I asked.

"Bracing the foundation," Aahz said. "They have the right idea, but they're doing it wrong."

Aahz's assessment was all too accurate, as the heavy stone creaked against its restraints and continued to slip.

"Pray harder!" the Ghord supervisor shouted at his staff.

"Are you idiots just going to stand there and let the whole

thing come down?" Aahz bellowed at Samwise. "You'll be paying me to consult on nothing if you don't shore up the underpinnings before you relay the slabs."

"I say we consult on whether the corner slab should be replaced entirely," the chief Ghord scribe said, frowning and stroking his chin. "Clearly it doesn't wish to be there."

"But that is where the customer paid for it to be," Samwise moaned. "Why does everything have to happen to me? What do you think we should do, Aahz?"

A loud creak made everyone look up.

"It's going to go," I said. I ran to Beltasar. "I'll do anything to help," I offered. "I'm a competent magician. I have plenty of experience. I'll follow your instructions to the letter."

The huge slabs groaned. I was afraid they would crack at any moment. I could tell that the Scarab was vacillating between breaking the rules and letting the project in which they took so much pride be damaged.

"Let me help!" I said.

"Klahds are more useless than Perverts! You will only get in the way."

Ghord workers wailed as the corner slab above the tilting stone started making grinding noises. I offered desperately, "I'll sign a waiver. You can blame it all on me. You can even fine me if you want for interfering."

That got her attention. She slewed her big turquoise eyes toward me.

"All right! Can you lift the edge of the stone up so we can get a jack underneath?

"I'll do my best," I said.

I closed my eyes and concentrated. I pictured the thin yellow line of magik twisting underneath our feet and let the force line flow into me until my hands were almost stinging with the power. I pictured my hand under the edge of the stone, lifting it gently.

It wouldn't move. I opened my eyes. The slab was just where it was. The Ghords who had expected their burden to be lifted off their shoulders looked disappointed. Beltasar was furious. She butted me in the chest.

"Ow!" I protested.

"Useless! I told you Klahds are useless!"

"Give him a chance," Aahz roared. "C'mon, kid, pick it up!"

I absorbed some more power from the yellow line. I was used to using magik to raise myself and possibly a friend or two, but this stone weighed more alone than the whole staff of M.Y.T.H., Inc., put together and then some. I felt myself sweating. Stone grated on stone. The noise set my teeth on edge.

"Go away, go away, Klahd!" Beltasar screeched. "You are not helping!"

I opened my eyes. Aahz was at my shoulder, along with the entire management staff. They were wringing their hands. "What'll I do, Aahz? I can't lift the stone."

"Don't pull," Aahz advised, calmly. "Push. Picture yourself pushing up from the bedrock under the stone. I'll let you know when you get it level. C'mon, kid. You can do it."

The yellow force line wasn't strong enough. The next nearest line was the surging black line. I felt nervous about dipping into it. Compared with the thinner ones nearby, it was a raging bull instead of a friendly dog. But I didn't have a choice. I needed power, a lot of power. I reached out to it.

Wham!

I often wondered what it felt like to be struck by lightning. Some races reveled in it, like my buddy Gus the Gargoyle, who would linger outside during the most terrifying thunderstorms hoping to be electrified by those blinding strikes of power that would fry a Klahd to a cinder. That's what I imagined as the force from the black line surged in through my fingertips and burned its way along my body. I tried turning off the flow, but it was stronger than I was.

Power roared into me, overspilling my batteries and filling every inch of my body. I felt as if I had drawn in the entire force line and become part of it. I had never used a more powerful source in all my experience. That explained why even the humblest Ghord used magik readily. It was more plentiful than food or water in this dimension. I hoped that I'd worked with enough force lines in my time to handle it. I directed the flow downward, letting it carry my consciousness with it.

My senses felt for the bedrock. It wasn't where I expected it, directly underneath the foot of the pyramid. Instead, the gigantic structure stood on a kind of aggregate, like compacted sand, over twenty feet thick. This pad of sand had broken off at the edge, crumbling more every time the stones above it shifted. I had to reach down farther than I dreamed until my mental hand touched something truly solid. The magik told me this was indeed the bedrock. Upon it I built a pillar of magik. I filled it in with more and more power from the force line, as though it was the upward surge of a fountain. It reached the bottom of the tipping stone and pressed against it. I felt it move. Yes! I heard voices around me exclaiming. And cheering. And gasping.

I felt a hand on my shoulder.

"Uh, kid, that's too much."

I opened my eyes and looked at the pyramid. Or, rather, where the pyramid had lain. There was nothing ahead of me except . . . a big square shadow.

I raised my eyes. I gawked.

The whole pyramid hung about thirty feet in the air.

"Wha—?" I choked out. "Uh, how . . . ?"

"Perhaps," Beltasar said, a lot more respectfully than she had sounded before, "you can hold it there for just a little bit."

"Careful!" Samwise shouted. He ran to my side. "Oh, careful, Skeeve the Magnificent. I had no idea that you lived up to all that hype going around the Bazaar. I thought you were merely paying for the publicity. No one ever told me! You are so much more than I expected, even more than Aahz's reputation. Be careful! Don't let the carvings get scratched!"

"Don't pester the kid when he's working," Aahz said, dragging him back. He looked disgusted.

My eyes refused to believe what I had actually accomplished, but there it was. I had to grin. All those years of

straining to pick up tiny objects, all the times that I had
nearly dropped people for lack of confidence, and I was
juggling a whole building—well, the first three tiers of one.

At my thought, the stones started to wiggle. Beltasar's
people let out a shrill wail of concern. Samwise wrung his
hands.

No, don't juggle! I told my subconscious, hastily thinking
of stillness and calm. That was better. I wiped my forehead
with my sleeve. A crowd began to gather around me, staring
up at the pyramid in the sky.

"Do you think we should leave it there?" asked one of
the Ghord supervisors, a male with the head of a snake. "It's
very impressive."

"The underside would need more decoration," said the
chief scribe, a woman like a quail with three feathers growing out of the top of her head. "We would have to get instructions from the property owners on what to put on the
bottom."

"That will change the terms of their contracts," Samwise
said. He plucked the Pyxie from his pocket and whispered
instructions to it. The Pyxie dove back in. I heard faint
rustling sounds.

It wasn't easy, holding the pyramid aloft. No one seemed
in a hurry to get anything done. Consultation went on end-
lessly, delaying Beltasar and her workers from the repairs.
Aahz kept telling them what would go wrong whatever
choices they made. My shoulders started to shake. No matter
how much power was available, it was still going through
one mortal Klahd magician—me.

"Look, guys," I began.

"Hold it, kid," Aahz said, raising a hand. "Samwise, you
gotta mix in some larger grains into the mix. The little stuff's
just eroding. It'll blow away during the next sandstorm."

"*Our* climate spells prevent sandstorms in this locale," a
female Ghord magician informed him with some asperity.
"Perhaps it has been too long since you studied advanced
weather magik?"

"Listen, sister," Aahz said, dangerously, "I've supervised bigger projects than this, in dimensions where the primary currency wasn't scorpion tails and beer. You need physical matter to supplement the magik. Any idiot who lives in a structure more complicated than a blanket flung over a stick could figure that out."

"That is enough," the chief scribe said. "My people will not work with this savage. He does not appreciate our culture."

"Of wasting time?" Aahz asked. "Pal, every office in every dimension has the same culture as yours. The heat death of the universe is gonna be due to meetings, not inertia."

Now my arms were starting to shake, too.

"Aahz!" I yelled.

Aahz snapped out of lecture mode. "That's just what I mean," he said. "You get a top-flight magician volunteering his services, and you waste his time! That's going on our billable hours, Samwise."

"No, no, that's not in our agreement!"

"Show me where Skeeve signed off on it," Aahz countered.

"Fools!" Beltasar screeched, breaking off from the group. "Division One, prepare to reinforce foundation, now! Division Two, ready to relay sealant layer! Division Three, containment spell!"

"Ready!" they shrilled.

"Go!"

Millions of Scarabs rose into the air and spread out across the huge empty square. They dropped armfuls of what looked like glowing dust. Where it touched, the ground lit up. I saw that not only had the corner nearest me collapsed under the weight of the building, but the foundation was covered with little cracks that gleamed like hot gold wire. The cracks melded and sealed up by themselves. The next swarm of Scarabs dropped black dust. That covered the glow in a layer of darkness. The third group filled the entire gap between the bottom of the pyramid and the ground with a network of tiny fibers like spiderwebs of magik. I felt the bond form. In fact, my fingers felt as if they were sticking together like glue. I had to force my eyelids open again when I blinked.

"Well done! It will never shift now, not if the whole dimension goes away." Beltasar let out one more shriek. "Division Four!"

No one responded.

"Division Four! You, Klahd! That's you!"

"Me?" I turned a blank face to her.

Beltasar pointed a tiny fist at me. "Yes, you, Skeeve the Magnificent, lower the pyramid, please. Gently. Gently!"

I lowered my trembling arms very, very slowly. The enormous square base sank with them until it was about my eye level. I caught a glimpse of Samwise's anxious face. He made me nervous. I was afraid I would drop it, ruining the work of hundreds of beings. I closed my eyes and concentrated, putting him out of my mind. If I could raise the pyramid, I could put it down safely.

My hands shook like leaves. I heard a nerve-wracking rumble and everyone moaned. I forced my wrists to go rigid. In my mind's eye, I saw the tiers of stone settle onto the enormous square of sand. I had to open my eyes to make sure. I had landed it without even a thump.

"Way to go, kid!" Aahz shouted.

I grinned.

Beltasar hurtled into my shoulder, the Scarab equivalent of Aahz chucking me with his fist.

"Well done, well done!" she trilled. "We shall vote on making you an honorary Scarab! And," she added generously, "there will be no fine against an unlicensed builder on site! However," she turned to Samwise, "I call for fines for running an unsafe construction zone."

"How about that?" I asked Aahz. I was still marveling at having moved a whole building by myself.

Aahz gave me a wry half-grin. "Remind me to call you if I ever need to change a tire."

"Into what?" I asked. I was proud not to have to ask what a tire was; I had visited Perv and seen the vehicles they drove. But Aahz still looked exasperated.

"Thank you, thank you," Samwise exclaimed, rushing up to pump my hand. I nodded. I had never felt so exhausted in my life. "No wonder they call you Skeeve the Magnificent! I had no idea!"

I felt proud. Me, the same apprentice who had been unable to light a candle for Garkin, or make a feather fly without drenching myself in sweat! I had lifted an entire building and not cracked a single brick. The Scarabs and Ghords kept glancing back at me. Glyphs flew back and forth around the site, and everyone who received one looked at me, too. I rubbed the back of my neck with both hands. Now that the power had abated, I was no longer buzzing. I felt numb.

"Sorry for not seeing what kind of fix you were in at first, kid," Aahz said, giving me a companionable slap on the back. "I don't get into good arguments like that much anymore. I love playing Deveel's advocate against office politics."

I didn't mind Aahz having fun. I hadn't dropped the ball, er, pyramid anyhow.

"What caused the break?"

"I don't know. That shouldn't have happened." Aahz scratched his head thoughtfully. "The local magik looks pretty strong. Lots of force lines. Shouldn't be this full of problems. That foundation ought to have held a dozen buildings this size until the second day of forever. I wonder if Diksen had the same trouble. Do you know if he did?" he asked Samwise.

The Imp turned from his admiring regard of me, to my relief.

"Of course not, Aahz! As far as I know he has had no troubles like mine at all."

Aahz was unimpressed. "You're not a magician. How would you know? He might have had to counterspell someone's interference, or counteract a curse."

Samwise was indignant. "I just know! He would have said something. . . . Well, *mumbled* something. Diksen doesn't like to talk a lot. . . . Well, not to me."

"I can't see why not," Aahz said dryly. "All right, Skeeve, what do you say? Shall we drop in on the neighbor and get a heads up?"

"Sure," I said. "I want to get a look inside that ball of water."

"Let's go catch a Camel." Aahz headed toward the walkway that led to the pier.

"No!" Samwise sputtered, jumping in front of us. "You don't want to do that. He hates to be bothered!"

"It's no bother," Aahz said, handing him aside firmly. "It's a courtesy call, two master magicians, new in town, stopping in to pay respects to the local head honcho. He's probably wondering why we haven't come around before this. We ought to pick up a box of oranges or a bottle of booze as a gift."

"But why?" Samwise wailed, wringing his hands as he strode to keep up with us. "Why bother Diksen?"

"It's not a bother," Aahz explained, starting to lose his patience. "It's the neighborly thing to do, since we're going to be working around here for a while. I'd like to ask him what his take is on the accidents, see if he's been having trouble he can't explain."

"Oh, no," Samwise exclaimed. "You don't want to do that!"

Aahz studied him. "The more you tell me not to visit Diksen, the more I want to do it. You're starting to make me think you never worked for him at all."

Samwise raised his hands in protest. "Yes, I did! Really, I did. He's a good guy, honest, Aahz. He just hates, I mean, *hates* interruptions. We parted on good terms. It's just that's one of the reasons I left. His studies were more important than good employee relations." He rubbed his backside, and I guessed a little of how the magician had expressed his displeasure at being bothered in the middle of his studies. That made up our minds to try and talk to him as soon as possible. "I just want to prevent you from making the same mistakes I did."

"You've warned us," Aahz said curtly. "Is there security around the pavilion? Are we going to have to fight our way through cold-seeking lasers or anti-personnel cantrips?"

"Nothing. I once suggested an array of stasis bombs, because he has some really valuable artifacts in that office suite, but he didn't want to bother. There isn't really a need for special security measures around Diksen."

"Why not?" I asked.

"He's a very powerful magician," Samwise said, as if that ought to have been obvious to me. The hero worship of a few moments ago was already relegated to the past. "He can do things to people who piss him off. Personally."

"Um, what kind of things?" I asked, glancing at Aahz. We were better off being prepared.

"Oh, you know, the usual kinds of catastrophic magik: transformations, banishments . . . death. You know." The Imp squirmed a little.

Aahz and I exchanged a look. I wondered if Samwise had ever really witnessed any of that revenge. Sometimes having the reputation for being the biggest, baddest, toughest, meanest magik-slinger in town was a whole lot better than ever having to prove it.

We left Samwise protesting and called a Camel.

THIRTEEN

"Should auld acquaintance be forgot?"

—INSPECTOR JAVERT

Now that Aahz and I had become known as people who paid for service and even left tips (Aahz's a little less generously than mine), we were customers to be sought after among the local transportation industry.

"Mister Skeeve!" cried Tritza, a Camel with rich sable hair and eyelashes three inches long. She sidled up to the pier and fluttered her eyelids at us. "Climb up, climb up. Beautiful day for a ride. Where are you going?"

"Not your turn for a fare, Tritza," snapped Mobor, a stout Camel whose fur was patchy brown and white. He cut in front of her and made it to my feet first. "It is for me to ask. Where would you like me to take you?" he demanded, turning his piebald snoot my way.

I couldn't decide between the two. They were both reliable, safe drivers, and hadn't tried to cheat me too badly on fares. Yet.

"You know you shouldn't take the first or second cab to offer itself," Aahz said dryly, as the beasts clamored for our attention.

"Why not?" I asked.

"Rules of Victorian detection," he said.

"What's a Victorian?" I asked.

"No fun, uncomfortable clothes, really awful food," he replied, and counted off among the Camels waiting for our attention. "Eeny meeny miney moe, catch a taxi by the . . . you guys have toes on those feet you don't want anyone to see? Forget it. Balu, you win." He beckoned over a young Camel. "You're reliable. You promise not to glyph while driving?"

"No, sir, no!" Balu exclaimed, then looked down guiltily at where his forepaws would be if they were visible above the sandline. "I will stop, sir. Climb aboard."

"Not fair!" complained Chibar, a tan Camel.

"He jumped the line!" Tritza protested.

"The end of the line is where he belongs," insisted Obrigadu, a jet black Camel.

Aahz and I paid no attention and clambered in between Balu's humps. The young Camel looked pleased with himself. He eased smoothly away from the jetty. The others crowded in, bumping him. He bucked as if someone pinched or kicked him underneath the surface of the sand. Aahz and I bounced.

"Hey!" I protested. The others looked shamefaced and moved a little farther away.

"Where do you wish to go?" Balu asked over his shoulder.

"Diksen's pavilion," I said.

Suddenly, the Camels stopped and stared. "You don't want to go there," Mobor said.

"Why the hell not?" Aahz asked.

"He is merciless to intruders," Tritza said, her eyes wide. "How do you think Mobor lost most of his hair?"

"I told you, it is a bad haircut," the piebald Camel protested. "She is lying, sirs. But she is right about Diksen. He is a terrible Ghord."

"What about it, Balu?" Aahz asked. "Are you going to chicken out, or will you take us?"

The young Camel swallowed hard. "If you will protect

me, I will take you. But it must cost extra, sirs. Hazard pay is required for certain destinations."

"Hazard pay—!" Aahz bellowed.

"I'll pay you double the usual fare," I cut in. "Can we go? I want to get there before business hours are over."

"Very well, sir," Balu said with a sigh. He paused. "One moment. I must glyph to my wife to tell her I love her, in case I do not come back."

"It can't be that bad," Aahz snapped. Balu said nothing, his forepaws busy beneath the sand. In a moment, he kicked out into the quicksands and set out due east across the desert. The other Camels bade him a mournful farewell.

I shrugged. "Maybe it could." We had met plenty of powerful magicians in our time, some of whom wanted to kill us, like The Ax (who became a close friend later on),[5] some of whom were actually insane, like Istvan, and some of whom just liked being the only ones in town with power.

As we cut across the expanse of desert, Samwise's low-rise project disappeared behind the sand dunes. In no time, you wouldn't have been able to tell anything was there except for the tiny shapes of glyphs flying around and the magikal framework that thrust upward from the partially finished pyramid. Ahead lay the gleaming white of Diksen's building. At sand level, it was awe-inspiring and beautiful, but from a magician's point of view, it was completely overshadowed by the much smaller shape hovering behind it, yards above the desert floor.

Yes, so a ball of water was ostentatious in an arid dimension, but it was truly impressive.

Aahz and I offered guesses on what kind of power structure he used to keep its shape, and whether he had problems with evaporation or not. I looked forward to friendly discussions with Diksen. I admired his imagination.

---

5. To discover the secret identity of the assassin magician known as The Ax, read the thrilling *Little Myth Marker*, a volume no library can be complete without.

We were able to get within a dozen yards of the pyramid's base. The afternoon sun glared at us from the tilted white wall. I had to throw up a sheet of magik to keep us from being toasted from sheer reflected heat. Balu veered around the square foundation and made his way toward the glimmering office building, which looked just like a giant crystal ball.

I took a good look around. Samwise had been right. I saw no security measures, not even lines of force laid down to prevent intruders. Diksen clearly felt he had no reason to populate his remote fortress with the army of guards that Samwise employed. I felt a twinge of envy for the kind of reputation that could keep people away without what I considered the minimum of actual protection. I said as much to Aahz.

"Don't count him out yet, kid," Aahz said, peering even more critically at the two structures than I had. I felt a little annoyed, but I had nothing on Aahz when it came to functional suspicion. He'd saved me before by assuming the worst about other people. I hated to think that I was naïve—but I had to be honest: in comparison with him I *was* naïve. Still, I hardly ever found a problem with assuming the best about other people.

Diksen was so unconcerned about intruders that our Camel managed to glide directly underneath the wavering sphere.

"How do we get in?" I asked.

"It's water," Aahz said. "We'll swim."

Making it look good for Balu, Aahz held out his arms and pretended to be dredging power up from one of the force lines underneath the desert floor. I sat watching him, but I was the one who really internalized some of the available magik and lifted us straight off the Camel's back.

"Wait for us," Aahz called down to Balu. The Camel nodded nervously at us, and the sand in front of his chest began to roil. He was glyphing to his wife again.

"Blub!" I exclaimed, as my head plunged through the water barrier. Aahz grinned at me, bubbles filtering out between his teeth. I had not been paying attention, as he had, to how high we were rising. The outer shell of the sphere was more than eight feet deep. Once I was completely surrounded by water, I kicked with both my feet, desperate to reach air.

My lungs burned. My cheeks bulged as I struggled to hold in my half-breath. A solid rim that rested on the interior surface came into view. I swam to it, grabbed the edge, and pulled myself up. There, I lay there on my back, gasping in as much air as I could.

"Good afternoon," a young Ghordess said. She sat cross-legged on the floor, which I now observed ran in a broad ring all the way around the bottom level of the bubble of water. A fold of her linen skirt was stretched across her knees to create a level platform. On it lay a papyrus sheet inscribed with a dozen symbols. The feather pen in her hand was black with ink at the end, as if I had interrupted her in her work. "May I help you?"

"Hey, baby," Aahz said, with an ingratiating grin. "We'd like to see your boss."

She regarded him primly. "Do you have an appointment?"

Once I had recovered from nearly drowning, I realized that she was a very pretty girl by Klahdish standards. She had a narrow face with large, dark eyes and high cheekbones. She wore the usual headdress, but I noted that there was a hole in the middle on top of her head to make room for three tall feathers like the one in her hand. The rest of her hair hung like long strands of black down. A couple of large, sand-colored cats sat on pedestals behind her and batted at the erect plumes. It seemed to annoy her, but she did not chase them away or even chastise them.

Even though there were no chairs, the rest of the office was modern, even more modern than Bunny's back at M.Y.T.H., Inc., headquarters. A computer, a philosophical device with which I had become familiar in Kobol, sat on a low table behind her. The three rows of keys were marked with hieroglyphs. Ornamented chests stood with their lids flung back to

expose rolls of papyri with colored labels stuck to the uppermost edge. From where I sat I tried to read the glyphs on the
labels, but I was too far away. A sharp glance from the secretary reminded me I was snooping. I gave her a grin.

"We're new in town," I explained. "Visiting magicians.
This is Aahz, and my name is Skeeve. We thought it would
be polite to drop in on Diksen and get to know him a little.
We'll probably be around for a month or so."

She beamed at us. "That is good news!" she said. "He
will welcome you with a full heart."

"See," Aahz said. "That's not what we heard."

"Oh, no, he enjoys conversation with other magikal
practitioners."

One of the cats took a swipe that bent all three feathers
over the girl's eyes. She raised a hand to straighten them,
and the cat recoiled with a protesting mew.

"Oh, I am sorry!" she exclaimed, turning to bow to the
animal. She put her hands together and closed her eyes,
intoning a phrase I couldn't understand, but which sounded
like the ancient Aegistian that some of the Ghords on site
used to offer apologies to the ancestors.

"Why don't you just shoo them out?" I asked.

She gave me a look of outrage. "They're sacred cats! I
can't do that. You can't tell them to stop. They must do
whatever they are divinely inspired to do."

"She must just like being inconvenienced," Aahz said.
"Beats working. How's your boss's schedule looking for
now, sweetheart? Has he got a couple of minutes?"

"I will ascertain. It is not my employer's custom to be
interrupted in the middle of the day, yet he would be pleased
to become acquainted with you as brothers in the arts magikal, of that I am sure." She put aside the letter she was
writing and picked up a scroll on the edge of the table near
the computer. "Hmm," she said, unwinding it. "It would
appear that he has finished his noonday meal and medita-
tion. For the next hour he will be reading from ancient texts."

"How ancient?" Aahz asked. "Like a millennium ago,
or last week?"

"Oh, very ancient," the girl assured him solemnly. "But it is a forgivable interruption under the circumstances, and the texts will become even more ancient in the waiting. It would be an honor to assist the three of you to meet. My employer will take great pleasure in your visit."

She raised her eyes to the heavens and put her hands out, palms up. "O great Diksen, he of the endless wisdom . . ." she chanted.

"Looks like Samwise was wrong," Aahz said to me. "He said Diksen wouldn't stop for visitors. The guy sounds reasonable to me."

". . . Worker of wonders, son beloved of Maul-De and Omphalos, brother to—did you say *Samwise*?" the girl asked, halting her invocation.

"Yeah," Aahz said. "We're working with him on the big project across the way." He gestured vaguely toward the west. Through the wall of water the partially finished building was a wavy blob.

The girl stood up, scattering the sacred cats and her manuscripts.

"I apologize deeply to you honored gentlemen, but I must ask you to leave."

"What about meeting Diksen?" I asked.

The girl's cheeks flushed. "He is not available. I am greatly sorry, but no one will be allowed in to see the magician."

"No one? How come?"

"No one," the girl said firmly. "No way, no how." She pointed toward the shimmering floor that we had swum through. "Please go and do not return."

Aahz and I shrugged at one another. We weren't going to insist. As far as we could tell, everything was running smoothly in Diksen's domain. Aahz wasn't going to leave as though he had been chased away.

"I can tell when a guy's too busy," Aahz said. "Tell him if he can get over the snit, we'd still like to buy him a drink sometime. See you around, babe."

Now for a smooth exit.

As Aahz stepped off the edge of the office floor, I stretched out a small magical platform underneath his feet to lower him elegantly through the building's outer shell.

Just as I did so, something large flashed by in the water. It was too fast for me to pick out more than just its streamlined shape. I was so surprised that I was distracted from my spell. Aahz plunged in feet first. With an irritated look at me, he plummeted out of sight. The girl laughed musically. I blushed, hoping that Aahz couldn't hear her.

"Excuse me," I sputtered.

The girl kept laughing as I dove in to follow my partner.

FOURTEEN

"What's good in theory doesn't necessarily work in practice."
—T. LYSENKO

"I said I was sorry," I protested once more. Aahz glared at me and stuck his nose back into the bucket-sized mug of beer.

"'Sorry' doesn't clear the water out of my ears," he said.

"C'mon, Aahz," Tananda said, scooting closer to him on the wooden bench of our new favorite bar in the Bazaar at Deva, the Over Easy. "He was a little surprised, that's all. It's happened to all of us."

While most of the others at the table with us weren't magicians, everybody nodded. Mistakes were just that: mistakes.

"I am sure the Boss didn't mean to inconvenience you," Guido said, keeping his voice neutral. Beside him, Nunzio nodded. Gus the Gargoyle, off duty that evening from the Golden Crescent Inn waved his cup of molten lava. Bunny and Tananda agreed.

"It was a bad time for an *enchantus interruptus*," Aahz said, his eyebrows down. "Here we were, trying to convince the secretary that we were master magicians to be taken seriously, in spite of our connection with a former employee who left a bad impression behind him, and we ended up acting like a couple of comedians from Vodville."

"Where's that?" I asked, before I could stop myself. Aahz turned the glare up another notch. "I'm sorry! I saw something in the water."

"It was me," Aahz growled. "There was *nothing else* there. It must have been a trick of the light. You should have kept your mind on your spell. I fell out of the sky like a rock. The only reason Balu didn't laugh when I dropped onto his back was that he was scared about being there in the first place."

By contrast, I had floated down from the giant bubble like a snowflake, and Aahz still resented it. I offered to buy his beer that evening to make up for it. He was on his third. I nursed my single glass of wine, which I really needed after a day like that.

"How's your mother?" I asked, eager to get the scrutiny of the group off me and onto something else.

"She's fine," Bunny said.

"Nothing wrong at home?" I urged, seeing her hesitate.

"Not really." She sat erect and settled her back against the wall. Something else was bothering her, but she fended off any attempts I made to get her to talk about it. Maybe she would open up on her own later. But she smiled at me. "What's going on in Aegis?"

Three pails of beer were finally mellowing Aahz.

"Just a little wonderworking to amaze the locals," Aahz said, very casually. "Today, part of the building's foundation fell apart."

Bunny's eyebrows went up. "That's bad. Does that mean delays?"

"Not with us there," Aahz said with a grin that stretched from one ear to the other. "Samwise was right to bring us in."

"What did you do?"

"It wasn't me—it was Skeeve, here." He brought a palm around and smacked me on the back so hard I almost went face down in my wine. "I've never seen a Klahd channel magik better. He picked the whole damned pyramid up all by himself!"

"Wow!" Bunny squealed. "That's amazing!" She leaned over the table and gave me a big kiss. I felt proud of myself.

"Felicitations," Guido said. "That was a mighty feat."

"Truly historic," Nunzio agreed.

Their words were more than encouraging, but their faces told a different story. They were worried.

When I thought about it, I realized that I was worried, too. It wasn't like Aahz not to add some self-aggrandizement to a story if at all possible. Instead, he launched into a detailed narration of how when the project management got bogged down in bureaucracy, I had come through with a never-before-seen exhibition of magikal expertise. I was shocked. Then I realized everybody was looking at me.

"It was nothing," I mumbled into my drink, embarrassed to look up at the admiring scrutiny of the others.

"It was good work," Aahz said. He accepted another bucketful from the barmaid and raised it. "*Slainte*, partner."

He took a deep draught, then spat it out all over everyone on the table. I jumped back, wiping noxious liquid off my face.

"What the hell is this?" Aahz bellowed. "This tastes like ammonia!" The barmaid ran back to him.

"Oh, Mr. Aahz, I am so sorry!" she exclaimed. "I picked up the wrong pail! This is the mop water."

"I know the beer here is weak, but you think I wouldn't be able to tell the difference?"

"I didn't mean to," the barmaid said, blotting all of us with the edge of her apron.

Tananda did her best to contain the smile that tried to crease her lips. She and Bunny affected innocent expressions when Aahz turned his glare on the rest of us.

"Bad luck, Aahz," Guido said. "You must admit that it is an honest mistake."

"I'm getting tired of mistakes!" Aahz growled.

The barmaid returned with the manager, Lucanzi.

"Mr. Aahz, I can't tell you how sorry we are," he said, twisting his hands together. "We prize your custom. We are very proud that M.Y.T.H., Inc., visits our establishment."

"Are you feeling sorry enough to comp the refill?" Aahz asked, sourly. "How about a round for the table?"

"Well, yours, sure, Aahz," Lucanzi said. Deveels weren't any better about compensating customers than Pervects were.

"What about the ladies here? They got all dressed up to come to this pigsty, and they end up decorated with floor squeezings! Look at the stains on their nice evening wear."

Lucanzi eyed Tananda and Bunny. I could have gotten the dirt out with a twitch of magik, and Lucanzi knew that, too, but it was the thrill of the chase for Aahz and the manager. Tananda had her knife out of her sheath and was cleaning her nails with it. Bunny somehow managed to look innocent and formidable at the same time, a combination that I could never have achieved in a million years.

"Well, all right," Lucanzi began.

"And my friends here?" Aahz waved a hand to indicate the rest of us.

"Now, just a minute! You're not going to suggest that washing those cheap suits is the equivalent of a pint of my best beer!"

Guido stood up and looked down upon the Deveel host from a height at least a foot greater than his. "Whose suit is it you are callin' cheap?" he asked.

Lucanzi smiled weakly. "No offense, good sir," he said. "All right, all right. Carnita, drinks for the table. One round on us. No more!" He gave Aahz a fierce glare. Aahz sat down again with a grin. He'd gotten what he wanted. I remembered just then it would have been his round to start with. He had managed to get it without paying for it.

"Nicely done," Nunzio observed.

Aahz accepted the accolade and a fresh, foaming bucketful from the chastised barmaid. He took a deep drink.

"It's all in how you handle the situation," he said.

"So, any luck on your other project?" Tananda asked,

looking at me lazily from underneath her eyelashes. I shook my head.

"There's really no time to meet girls on the job," I said, keeping my voice low. I didn't feel comfortable talking about my dateless state in public, but she had asked, and deserved an answer. "I mean, I've seen a few nice girls in Aegis, but we're too busy running around taking care of crises. I'm also coming along when Aahz takes a client up to sell him a stone. I don't get to spend more than a minute or two around the water cooler with anyone."

"Give yourself a chance," Tanda suggested. "You don't have to look for the one-and-only right away. Just someone to have fun with over a drink or a cup of coffee will be good to get started."

"I feel awkward just trying to ask someone out. I never know when it's the right time to offer. I think I'm pushing too hard."

"The more you practice, the less awkward you'll feel," Bunny added. "Heaven knows I have heard some rotten pickup lines, but those are from the guys who think all they have to do is beckon and girls will just drop everything for them. It's guys like you who interest us more." She looked me up and down the way she had when she first arrived at M.Y.T.H., Inc., dressed up like a dressmaker's mannequin wearing enough makeup to open her own line of cosmetics. That really made me feel awkward.

"What should I say?"

"Something that sounds natural," Bunny said. "Something sincere about what attracted you enough to approach a girl."

"Just don't take any advice from other men," a slender Deveel woman at the next table said, turning to poke me in the chest with a sharpened fingernail. "Excuse me for listening, but guys will tell you the worst possible lines so they look good in comparison."

"I think you're right," Tananda said. "I can't believe some of their lines! They couldn't possibly have come up with them up on their own, because they'd die of shame if they thought about what they were saying."

"Men have no shame, baby," said a large woman in a dress that struggled to stay fastened around her ample bosom. "They want only one thing." She shifted her shoulders, making her assets roll from side to side.

"Hey, I didn't think we was so obvious about it," said the skinny male at the two-top table with her.

"Are you kidding?" The woman laughed. He laughed with her. I guessed it was an old joke between them. I had never been able to joke with a woman in whom I was interested. Part of me longed for that kind of intimacy, but I wasn't sure how one achieved it. I opened my mouth to ask.

"What's it all about?" Gus asked, his gaze shifting bemusedly from one female to another. "Why do you ask, Skeeve?"

I clamped my mouth shut.

"He's writing a book," Nunzio said suddenly. I was undyingly grateful to him, since all I needed was for it to get around the Bazaar that I didn't think I could get a girl without help. I knew he was a true friend, because he was willing to lie for me.

"A book on dating by you? Hey, that'd be a big seller!" the Gargoyle said cheerfully. "And don't forget to put in the part about bringing the gal a present on your first date. That makes her a whole lot more receptive to a little 'who's yer daddy?'" He winked broadly at me.

I frowned. "Isn't getting to know her folks something for later on when the relationship starts to get more serious?" I asked. Gus threw back his head and laughed. Aahz poked me in the side surreptitiously with one claw tip and subtly shook his head. I felt my cheeks burn.

"Is it gonna be that funny?" Gus asked, slapping his knee. "Skeeve, you'll sell millions!"

"So, what kind of present do you recommend?" I asked.

"You gonna write it down?" Gus asked eagerly. "You don't have anything to write on."

"I can ask you again later when I've got a piece of paper," I said. "Just getting together some ideas right now."

Gus's gray forehead rippled forward, then smoothed out again. "I like to give a girl I'm interested in something small, like a can of really nice spray paint," he said. "If you know her favorite color, she'll like that. She'll think of you every time she does a little personal illuminating."

"Spray paint?" Guido asked. "That's only for girls who are possessed of stone skin."

"What do you think I dated before I found the missus?" Gus asked, puzzled. "Stone skin's the major turn-on for me. A great, cold marble complexion, that's what I really go for."

"Oh, some of us appreciate a little spray paint," Tananda said with a fetching shiver that had every man at the table watching her in fascination. "It tickles!"

"Perfume's too personal," Bunny agreed. "If you give her something from your favorite hobby, it could be a good ice breaker. Then she'll know a little about you, too."

"Never," said the Deveel girl, aiming a finger directly at my nose, "give a girl lingerie before the third date. Maybe not until the sixth. That's a present for you, not her."

"I never . . ." I protested.

"Candy's good," said the barmaid, bending her knees to rest the edge of her tray on the table.

"Something you'd actually eat," Tananda said, with a smile. "Not out of the bargain bin at World o' Stuff."

"Cheapskates," agreed the Deveel, whose name was Felina. "Sometimes they even forget to take the price tag off."

Tanda, Bunny and Felina launched into a lively and detailed discussion of gifts they had received from would-be suitors, most of which were unacceptable in one way or another. I had never really realized the depths of my ignorance when it came to the fair sex. Nor were they at all shy about discussing the shortcomings of dates they had had, in spite of the fact that there were several men listening.

"One of Uncle Bruce's men brought me an ammo belt," Bunny sighed. "Only it was the wrong caliber quarrels for my crossbow. I knew it wasn't going to work out. He wasn't paying attention. He was angling to get close to my uncle. I told him he should bring Uncle Bruce a present, if he was so interested in him. That shut him up." She put her tip-tilted nose in the air.

"Hey, Miss Bunny, men don't stand a chance if you don't cut us any slack," Nunzio protested. "The power's all on your side."

"And we mean to keep it that way," she said with a sweet smile.

"How do you strike up a conversation if you have nothing to say?" I asked.

"Ask for help or offer help," Felina said promptly. "If you're new in town, ask where the good places are to eat, then offer to take her to one of them. Pay. Don't go dutch. You'll look cheap. If she likes you, she'll treat you another time."

"Skeeve wouldn't be cheap," Bunny said. "He's a generous guy. Aren't you, Skeeve?"

"I, uh . . ."

"And how about that bum standing me up on our date, when he told everyone he was taking me out?" the barmaid asked, coming to set fresh mugs down on our table. "You would never leave a girl standing, especially in a bad neighborhood, would you?"

Before I could open my mouth, Tananda jumped in. "No, of course he wouldn't. He'd be there."

"And the last skunk that I dated," Felina said, leaning in confidentially, "started seeing another girl on the side. As if I wouldn't find out. You wouldn't do that to a girl, would you, Skeeve?"

"Uh, no . . ."

"Of course not," Tananda said. "For better or worse, he's one of the most honest guys I know."

"Honest is not always so good," said the hefty Deveel woman. "Who wants to know, really, if their hips look big in something? But you should put in that book of yours to be tactful. Tactful gets you more points than honest half the time. But if you're not fundamentally honest, you lose, guy. Do you know the difference?"

"Uh . . ."

Instead of opening my mouth, I started to look around for something to write on. Other women chimed in from around the bar.

"Open doors. Help us get a heavy package up the stairs. But if we say no, we mean it. Don't force the issue. That's insulting. Our magik's as good as yours."

"Do a little favor for her and don't expect a favor in return."

"Don't be in such a hurry! Trust takes time."

"Maybe she *is* looking for the same thing you are, but let *her* tell *you*."

"Just be nice. That means more than all the presents in the world."

Before long, I had a hundred suggestions for my imaginary book. I was going to have so much information and opinions that maybe I should have thought about writing one. It was kind of embarrassing to listen to them shooting the breeze back and forth, making unflattering statements about bad dates. The notion that I might have been one of those thoughtless men made me feel awful. I surely was guilty of at least a few of the mistakes they discussed. My biggest night out was still a blur in my head. I couldn't recall all of my date with Cassandra. At least I hadn't been cheap—in fact, I had been wildly profligate, as my bill from the credit card had shown. And while my advances had gone farther than they might have if I had been sober, they hadn't been completely unwanted, if the note she had left on my mirror in lipstick was an indication.

"Does any of this help?" Bunny asked at a lull in the conversation.

"No," I admitted. "I think I'm more confused than before."

She smiled at me. "You'll get it. Really. Relationships between men and women are as natural as the birds and the bees. Otherwise, why would there be so many people?"

I had no answer to that. I stuck my nose in my wine cup to think. Why hadn't Aahz put in his two copper pieces? He was always free with advice.

I glanced around and spotted him next to the bar counter. Aahz and the tavern owner had their heads close together in conversation. I was afraid it was something about the mishap, but it looked more like a friendly chat. Aahz was grinning widely. Out of his pocket, he whipped a contract, pointing to various clauses. While I had been listening to dating advice, he had managed to convince a Deveel to buy a stone, sight unseen.

But, no. Lucanzi took down some information on a napkin and stuffed it into the pocket of his apron. Aahz caught my eye and gave me a thumb's up. Another prospect. No question about it: Aahz was good at selling. He was motivated. Before I knew it, he would have sold all million slabs, ensuring his name at the top of Phase Two. I was impressed.

"Psst! Hey, Boss!"

FIFTEEN

"Do what I say, not what I do."
—B. FRANKLIN

I was pulled out of my reverie. Guido and Nunzio stood flanking me. At my nod, they sat down on the bench on either side of me. I took a quick look at the others. They were still debating appropriate behavior on dates.

"What's up, fellows?" I asked.

"You get any more insight into that other matter which we was discussin' the last time we met?" Guido asked, tilting his head toward Aahz.

I shook my head. "Nothing concrete. Whatever's bothering him isn't his stomach, and he doesn't show any signs of weakness. He must have hiked up and down both pyramids five or six times each today, not to mention taking a swim through a floating office building."

"He doesn't seem under the weather," Nunzio agreed. "In fact, he looks to be in robust health."

"Miss Bunny did a little checking around with Bytina," Guido whispered, keeping his lips rigid. "She inquired of Dr. Webb, but he had not had any questions from anyone resemblin' Aahz who might have been usin' an alias."

I nodded. Dr. Webb was an M.D. from Octaroo who

dispensed general medical information for free. Aahz wouldn't pay for advice if he could help it.

"Perhaps it wasn't his health he's worried about," I said. "Maybe a prophet predicted doom for him. Maybe a fatal accident or something like that? We've had a lot of mishaps on the site."

"You go on keepin' an eye on him," Guido advised. "We will keep our ears to the ground and other places. While Aahz may not be my favorite person in the world as he is to you, he is still a partner and a trusted accomplice. I will help to protect him if it is in my power to do so."

"Agreed," Nunzio said.

"Hey, what are all you lovely ladies talking about?" Aahz asked, strutting back to the table. Instead of sitting down at our table, he scooted in next to Felina.

"Oh, the differences between men and women," she said.

"So, what are the differences?" Aahz asked. "Anything special I should know about?"

"If you don't know by your age, you are never going to know!" the stout woman shouted. The others in the bar laughed.

"I'm always willing to take instruction from a smart lady like this one," Aahz said, smirking. "What are you drinking?"

"Rabbit tail," Felina said. It was a mildly intoxicating cocktail. It had a chocolate flavor, which I liked, but the kick at the end always came as a surprise.

"You know what they say about rabbits," Aahz said, after signaling the barmaid for the order.

"No," Felina said, with a smile. "What?"

Aahz leaned over and whispered into her pointed ear. She let out a peal of laughter and pushed him playfully with one hand. Aahz paid for their drinks and let his arm drift around her shoulders. She didn't seem to mind.

"I'd swear that there's nothing wrong with him," I said, watching carefully without, I hoped, making it too obvious.

"But you gotta admit," Guido said, "he's not actin' normal

for his usual Pervish self. I never heard him give credit like that without he had been pushed from behind."

"I concur, cousin," Nunzio agreed, taking a swig of beer.

"Get your hand off our little sister!"

I looked around. Before I could rise, Guido and Nunzio were out of their seats with their hands stuck into the folds of their natty jackets. Aahz was also on his feet, facing eight Deveel males. The family resemblance among them was very strong, so I guessed they were brothers. Brothers, I realized with a gulp, to the lady who had until that moment, been sitting in the shelter of Aahz's arm.

"Now, gentlemen," Aahz said, with his most ingratiating smile. "I was just keeping her company until you got here."

"Keeping her company! I saw you whispering in her ear!" said a middle-sized brother with goggly eyes.

"What was he talking to you about?" asked the meanest looking Deveel.

"Nothing. He asked me if I knew what they said about rabbits," Felina said, tossing her head.

"He asked what?" The biggest brother stepped up and grabbed Aahz by the front of his shirt.

"Now, fellows, don't make something out of nothing," I said. "Come and have a drink with us."

"You think we're going to sit down with a Pervert who is whispering dirty secrets to our sister?" demanded yet another brother.

"He don't mean nothin' by it," Guido said. "How about you gentlemen just takin' it down a couple of notches? There's other people tryin' to enjoy themselves. Youse could have a quiet evenin', too. We'll let you alone if you let us alone."

The second-biggest brother came to stick a forefinger in Guido's face. "Are you threatening us, Klahd?"

Guido took his hand and twisted it downward until the thumb was facing up at an unnatural angle. "Threats are for people who can't back it up, Deveel. I am just offerin' you some friendly advice. If youse wants a table with just your family, then take one. There's one openin' up right there near the front."

"You can't tell us what to do!"

"I want to sit with him," Felina said, tilting her head toward Aahz. "He's funny."

"He's *funny*?" the mean one echoed. "What have you done to our innocent little sister?"

"Nothing but look," Aahz said. "Any guy with normal vision would want to do that."

"You *looked* at our sister?"

"And he put his arm around me, too," Felina said, smugly.

"He *what*?" One of them grabbed for a bench and upended it, sending the Deveels who were on it tumbling to the ground. He swung it at Aahz, who ducked. The bench hit the back of another patron's head. He jumped up and took a punch at Aahz. Nunzio intercepted the blow as Guido pushed the oncoming brother backwards. The other brothers waded in to defend their sibling. The offended patron picked the pitcher up off his table and emptied it on Nunzio's head. Gus picked up the patron and hooked him on the chandelier. The Deveel threw fire spells at Gus, which just bounced off his stone exterior.

All of us piled in behind Guido, including Tananda. Bunny removed herself from the fray, taking Felina with her by the ear. While I used magik to keep the youngest brother from taking a dirty swing at Aahz from behind, I noticed Bunny giving the girl a piece of her mind. Felina's face, already a natural red, grew redder.

The biggest Deveel brother grabbed up a beer mug and crashed it down on Guido's head.

"Dat does it," the Mob enforcer snarled. He snatched the drink out of the nearest drinker's hand and smashed it directly between the Deveel brother's horns. The Deveel searched out blindly for another stein, and broke it over Guido's skull. Refusing to give ground, Guido held out his hand. Nunzio slapped another mug into it. Guido brought it crashing onto his opponent.

I was dealing with a couple of the smaller brothers. Using magik to yank curios off the wall, they pelted me with weird junk and street signs. I fended them off as best I could, while trying to keep the debris from hitting other customers. Most of them joined in the fray, some from outrage, others for the fun of a good brawl.

Suddenly, I found myself flung against the bar wall, a commemorative trophy in my arms. All of the would-be combatants were similarly pinioned. The bartender walked up and down between us, wielding a bat-shaped staff—the source, I guessed, of the spell.

"Hold it, hold it, hold it!" he bellowed. "When will you people learn? The free-for-all is tomorrow! No unscheduled fights in here tonight! Now, everyone behave or I am tossing you all out into the street!"

The goggle-eyed Deveel brother pointed a finger, which was the only body part he could move. "That Pervert started it!"

Aahz sneered at him. "That's Per-vect, and all I did was buy your sister a drink. She didn't turn me down!"

"Oh, yeah? You had to put a spell on her, because why would she talk to you for one second, let alone long enough to get your hands on her?"

The bartender kept us hanging there until we settled the argument. As the first lights of dawn began to lighten the sky, we arrived at a truce, negotiated chiefly by Guido and the largest brother, who began to recognize that, appearances aside, his baby sister might not have been totally innocent of provocation.

Once the bartender let us down, the big brother shook hands with Guido. The Deveel family removed their much-chastened sister from Bunny's custody and thence from the bar. I sat down, my ears ringing, and called for a fruit juice.

"What did you tell her?" I asked Bunny. She and Tananda had spent the last three hours of the fray sitting at a side table with the hefty woman and her slim husband.

"That men had responsibilities, but so do women," Bunny said with a sly smile. "If she wants to drive her brothers crazy, she doesn't have to involve a bunch of strangers."

"Sandbagged," Aahz groaned, accepting an ice pack for his head. The veins in his yellow eyes were ochre. "Just my luck I had to get involved with a girl who had family in the neighborhood."

I grinned. "Maybe you shouldn't have asked who her daddy was, but whether she had any brothers."

"You're learning, kid."

SIXTEEN

"Find me someone I can blame for this!"
—H. HOOVER

When we got back to the site in the morning, both of us were somewhat shopworn. Aahz was battered from getting tossed around between seven or eight large Deveel brothers. I nursed a bruise on the side of my head, but I had to admit he looked worse.

"Oh, Mr. Aahz!" Miss Tauret exclaimed as we entered the And Company office. "What happened? You look as though a building fell on you!" Her hand flew to her mouth as though trying to take back her words. In Aegis, such a thing could happen.

"I'm okay," Aahz said, rolling his yellow eyes her way. "It was pretty tough, but I got through with just a few scrapes."

She rose from her desk. "Let me get you some fresh coffee! Please, go sit down. I'll have it in your office in just a moment. What can I do to make you feel better?"

Aahz opened his mouth, then paused, looking at her warily. "You don't have a bunch of big, older brothers, do you?"

"Why, no," Miss Tauret said, her little gray ears turning

this way and that. "Just one sister. She is younger than I am."
She looked at me and flirted her eyelashes. "I glyphed her
all about you yesterday. She was so impressed that you saved
the pyramid."

"Uh, that's nice," I said.

"I taught the kid everything he knows," Aahz purred,
leaning over the desk and staring deeply into her eyes.

"You did?" She rested her elbow on the counter and her
chin on her hand.

"Yeah," Aahz said.

"Uh, excuse me," I said. I hurried into our office to look
at the previous day's paperwork. Miss Tauret had been interested in Aahz since the first day, and after last night he was
vulnerable to a little sympathetic female attention with no
possibility of reprisals from angry relatives. While I was
glad for him, I didn't have to *watch*.

Miss Tauret's attentiveness certainly cheered Aahz up.
She came in and out of our room all day whenever we were
in there, hoisting the empty beer barrel onto her meaty
shoulder as if it was weightless and, even more impressively,
bringing the fresh one in and tapping it for Aahz's conve-
nience. After I took the morning rounds of the site, I found
her rubbing his shoulders. He peered out from under the
cold compress on his eyes and gave me a wink.

The receptionist was not the only Ghord who paid us
closer attention since the day I had picked up the pyramid.
Many of the workers who had held us at arm's length got
into the habit of talking with us or glyphing when they
noticed us walking around. A lot of the girls giggled when
I went past, though they were openly friendly if I actually
stopped to talk with them. All of them were pretty impressed
by the feat I had performed. Miss Tauret let it be known to
everyone what Aahz had said about teaching me, so we were
both made much of around the site.

Beltasar was much more cooperative with me since that
day, too. She kept me apprised of the progress the Scarabs
were making. In fact, I was even present when the hardwork-
ing beetles laid the final stone on the third tier. I couldn't

take credit for it, but there were fewer accidents on site since the pyramid had been reseated. There was never a day when there wasn't *one*, but Doctor Cobra had had to make fewer pyramid calls.

The very next day the first stone of the fourth tier was laid, to great fanfare from Samwise. He made a speech and everybody was given an extra measure of beer. I was starting to like the Valley of Zyx. It wouldn't be a bad place to spend eternity.

One more milestone, so to speak, occurred during that next week. Aahz managed to sell a stone on the ground floor of Phase Two, and nagged the carvers into getting started on it so there would be something to show his potential customers. That meant laying out the foundation underneath the invisible ramps.

Swarms of the Scarabs walked backwards on their hands to roll the debris off the site. They smoothed it out in two days flat and tamped the thick foundation into place, all in less time than it would take me to paper a single wall. I was incredibly impressed. With a crowd of customers and workers on Camel-back and magik carpets sailing alongside, the slab itself, chosen by Aahz and the master scribe for its smooth sides and perfection of proportion, was transported by Beltasar's crack team over the surface of the desert. The weather, as usual, was perfect. Emissaries from the Pharaoh Suzal's court were in attendance. I wasn't happy to see Gurn there, sneering at everybody as if that was in his job description. I looked around, hoping to see Chumley, but he didn't show up. Aahz and I had not wanted to send a message to him directly, worrying that we might blow his cover in the court.

The Scarabs settled the stone at the edge of the new foundation, placing it just where Aahz and the purchaser had agreed it would go. It wasn't at a corner or in the center of any of the walls, so it must have been cheap as slabs went.

Still, it was an impressive hunk of rock. We all gathered around to watch. The Scarabs hung onto people's clothes and headdresses or hovered in mid-air to get a better view. Gurn insinuated himself just ahead of me. I had no trouble seeing over his head, but having him so close made me feel as though something slimy had wriggled into my clothes.

The master scribe, Ay-Talek, a Ghordess with the head of a fishing bird, invited us to watch from the front row as her finest stonecarver began the first line of text on the stone. Cay-Man, a Ghord with a long, reptilian face, bowed to us all and picked up his tools.

"Here we go, partner," Aahz said, his hands on his hips. The client, a used-carpet salesman from the Bazaar, stood beside us with his family clustered around him. "This is our message to the future."

Cay-Man set the chisel against the face of the smooth slab and raised his hammer. I found myself holding my breath. He brought the hammer down.

Tap!

A flake of stone leaped away, leaving a curved mark. The Ghord scribes watching broke into tremendous applause.

"What's the big deal?" I asked. "It's one little chip."

"Oh, you know," said Ay-Talek. "There's nothing more daunting than a blank slab. You can hardly think of what to write first. Once you break the gray space, it seems to go so much faster."

And Cay-Man did go faster. *Tap tap tap tap tap! Tappity tappity tap! Tap! Tap!* The first sign took shape immediately, the client's name, and was joined in swift succession by six more. I had been studying the glyphs since our arrival. I could identify a few of the signs as Cayman dug out a thin layer of rock around them and brought them up into relief. I saw the sign for the ancient Ghordess Hat-hed, followed by three eagles and a birdie.

"Golfer," Ay-Talek translated.

Cay-Man acknowledged the applause of his fellows, then went on to chisel out the figure of a man kneeling with his arms wide apart over his head. I thought back to the lexicon.

That sigil meant "this fish was that big, I swear on my life!" My guess was confirmed as an upside-down fishhook was added beside it.

"Going great guns, partner," Aahz said. "A few more hundred thousand like that and we're immortal."

Just as he said that, Cay-Man struck the head of the chisel. The carving tool seemed to spin in his hand. The next thing I knew, it was facing the wrong way. The point plunged into his palm. The carpet salesman's wife screamed.

Cay-Man knelt, clutching his hand. Tears rolled down his scaly face.

"I have an owie!" he cried.

"Don't pay any attention to him, folks!" Samwise said, holding up his hands for calm. "Someone go get Doctor Cobra."

I hurried to the carver's side and looked at the wound. To my surprise it was less than an inch long and barely bleeding.

"It's just a scratch," I said.

"It's not!" the carver wailed. "I'm going to die. Everything is starting to go black . . ." He raised the uninjured hand to his forehead. The crowd crooned sympathetically.

I rolled my eyes. He was enjoying having an audience.

Between a pair of Ghordesses barged a male with a snake for a head.

"I'm Doctor Cobra," he said. "Where'sss the patient?"

Cay-Man waved a feeble hand. The doctor homed in on him. He seized the injured limb and examined it, the snake-headed male's beady eyes scrutinizing the wound.

"It is not a serious injury," he stated, "but you will require immunization against infection."

Without further warning, he bared his fangs and jabbed them into the palm of Cay-Man's hand.

"Yow!" the carver yelled. "I hate injections!"

"Yes, yes," Cobra said, as if he'd heard it all before. "But, see? It is already healing."

To my amazement, the wound started to close up from one end to the other.

"That's remarkable," I commented.

"Nothing, really," Cobra said, modestly. "It's the second most common injury on the site."

"Let's move this slab out of the way," Beltasar ordered. "It can be completed later on! Let us place it in the Phase Two work area." She zipped over the corner of the foundation and hovered above a perfectly level floor of flagstones that had been laid down beside it.

"Let me help," Aahz said. He and the used-carpet salesman joined the horde of Scarabs and Ghords who swarmed up to move the historic stone.

"No, we do not need you!" Beltasar insisted. "Ghords and Perverts ruin everything!"

"Knock it off," Aahz growled. "This is my project!"

"On your head be it." Beltasar flitted back to the stone's destination. "Proceed!"

"Together now," bellowed Inhstep, Beltasar's assistant contractor.

Hundreds of Scarabs burrowed down and lifted the huge block. Aahz stooped and got his fingertips underneath the edge.

"Hoist!" cried Inhstep.

The huge stone rose a couple of feet. Aahz's muscles popped under his fashionable tunic as he helped move it. His strength was far greater than mine. Even with help, I couldn't have moved that slab without magik. Together, the team edged slowly over the rammed foundation, backed slowly onto the new work area, and started to lower it.

A loud rumble began. I felt the ground start to shake under my feet. I was thrown to one side. I kept from falling by grabbing onto the air with a handful of magik and hanging on.

"Yeow!"

A familiar bellow reached my ears. I flew to Aahz's side.

"What's wrong?" I asked.

"Stone. On. Foot!" he gritted out. I looked down and realized his toes were partway underneath the gigantic slab of rock. The Deveel merchant, by virtue of having hooves instead of feet, missed out on the same tragedy, but his fingers got caught. He was on his knees trying to tug them loose. Hundreds of Scarabs had been knocked flat on their faces, their six limbs spread out around them. They flexed their legs to try and heave upward.

"Gee, that's awful," I said. "Does it hurt?"

"Of course it hurts!" Aahz bellowed. "Do something!"

"No problem," I said.

Having done it once with the pyramid next door, hefting one building block posed no problem. I pressed against the unseen desert bedrock, far beneath the sands, and the block rose. Aahz staggered backwards and sat down on the paving stones. I moved the slab and set it down out of the way.

"That's the most common injury," Dr. Cobra sighed, switching his narrow head from side to side. "Give me room!" he ordered, pushing back onlookers.

"Funny thing," Beltasar said, as we stepped out of the doctor's way. "All of these people are owners."

Gurn was gone, probably back to Suzal to report on us.

SEVENTEEN

"Now we're all in this together."

—G. A. CUSTER

A crushed foot took a few days longer to heal than a cut palm, although in the case of a Pervect, not much longer. Aahz took advantage of Miss Tauret's cooing over him and kept the cast on his leg well past the time when he showed any pain at putting his foot on the floor. Even though having him out of commission meant I had to do all the rounds on site myself, I let him get away with sitting around. I felt responsible for him getting hurt. After the conference Guido, Nunzio, and I had had, I should have been watching more closely. If that stone had fallen on him, it could have killed him.

"You know, Miss Tauret's supposed to be greeting visitors, not just waiting on you," I said, as the receptionist slipped out of the room with an empty pitcher.

"You gotta enjoy the perks." Aahz stretched lazily. "Besides, I'm not going to haul my butt up and down those ramps with plaster on my leg. I don't have any clients coming by until tomorrow. It's not like I don't have any work. The paperwork never stops." He threw a document to me. "Here. Sign this."

I glanced at it. The papyrus was entirely written in glyphs, except for Aahz's signature down at the bottom. A second line had been drawn to the right of it with a symbol below. The figure of a male with the bee revolving around its head meant "skinny Klahd, hair of honey."

"What is it?" I asked.

"Progress report," Aahz grunted. I shrugged and reached for a reed pen. As soon as I signed it, Aahz took it back and stuck it in the Crocofile.

"Where's the food?" he demanded. "Hey, honey, come on with the snacks! I have to get my strength back!"

"Honey?" A face showed around the doorjamb. Instead of the gray visage we expected, it was covered in purple fur. "Sorry, what? I say, Aahz, are you up to having visitors?"

"Chumley!" I exclaimed, coming to offer him a hand. He engulfed me in one of his usual Trollish embraces.

"Good to see you, Skeeve, but mum please on the C-word, eh? The walls, as they say, have ears. I go by Wat-Is-Et here."

"Wat-Is-Et?" I asked.

"My name," Chumley said.

"I get it, but what is your name?" I asked.

"It is what it is."

"I thought you said 'what is it?'"

"No, Wat-Is-Et."

"I'm still trying to figure out what it is."

"It's very simple."

"Then what is it?"

"*Now* you have it," Chumley said, with a smile.

"What?"

"Hold it, hold it!" Aahz said, holding up his hands to stop us. "We haven't got time for 'Who's On First.' I'll explain it to the kid later." I closed my open mouth. "Take a load off! How are you doing? It's been a while. We've been expecting you to drop by."

"Oh, yes." Chumley looked a little uncomfortable. "It hasn't been too easy to get away, what with the way things have been going in the royal court. Suspicion and intrigue have been rife, what?"

Aahz eyed him. "And you're right in the middle of it?"

"Trying not to be, old thing, trying not to be! But it is difficult. The walls have ears, as they say, and even a simple gesture is enough for some of our neighbors to read. They are adept at putting volumes of meaning into a single expression."

"I've noticed," I said. "Some of those glyphs are as long as a book."

"When your means of writing is a chisel and a block, you compress as much as you can into every stroke," Chumley said. "It is a marvelous time saver, but also fraught with difficulty if you get even a syllable wrong, as I have found to my dismay."

"I won't ask what you're doing," I said. "I mean, it's none of my business. But I have to say I'm curious how you got involved in the court here."

"For once," Chumley said, "my erudition won out over my more obvious attributes."

"Huh?"

"How'd you get to be a linen-wearing bureaucrat?" Aahz asked.

Chumley sat back on the guest bench, which creaked under his weight, and threw off the curtaining headdress. "Ah, well, it started as an accident, I am afraid. The previous Pharaoh, Geezer the Ninth, had a wise man who actually went to university with me. While studying in the university library some years ago, we rekindled our friendship. Naten-Idjut was a fine fellow. We had mutual interests in the study of geology and mineral rights, but we came upon one another in the ancient lore section. Scads of old scrolls and ostraca, marvelous sources of both rumor and information.

"Naten-Idjut fell ill before he could return home. He needed to convey to his employer some important information. Leaving him in hospital, I went to Aegis as his locum and found myself as a visiting fireman, so to speak. To my surprise, I also spotted a problem that my old friend had not observed, having to do with food supply and sanitation, and was called a wise man for my pains by none less than the

Pharaoh Geezer himself. Ever since then, he and then his daughter, when he finally succumbed to old age, have called upon me when they needed outside perspective, what?"

"What?" I asked. "What perspective?"

"Whatever they require," Chumley said. "I must say, it is nice to have a job in which one can use one's own manner of speech. Big Crunch's monosyllabic verbalizations are hard on the throat."

"I think the kid wants to know, what perspective are they looking for *this* time?" Aahz asked.

"Ah," Chumley said. "Forgive me. Well, you saw part of it some days ago when you met her esteemed majesty. The Pharaoh Suzal feels that she has incurred the wrath of the ancient ones. For months now, she has suffered severe attacks of food poisoning. Even though tasters sample all her food with no signs of distress, when she eats of almost any dish, she has a bad reaction."

"Could it be some form of magikal attack?" I asked.

"I am studying all the signs," Chumley said. "More importantly, I am running chemical analyses on the foodstuffs in question to see whether we are dealing with food-borne parasites or pathogens targeted at the genetic level before I investigate magikal sources of interference. Science will reveal the truth." One of his many college degrees was in chemistry, as I recalled finding that out when a letter came from his alumni association looking for donations. Chumley had been embarrassed and ate the letter to keep anyone else from reading it. "If it does not prove to have a scientific answer, I may call in you two as consultants on the magikal side."

"I'd be honored," I said. "What do they think of her here in Aegis?"

Chumley's mouth curved in an avuncular smile. "She is a fine monarch, in the mode if not the mold of her father. She is much beloved. Her servants adore her, as do her people. I would be surprised as well as troubled if this were indeed some attempt to remove her from the throne. My spies have not indicated any usurpers threatening. Nor have any of the neighboring nations shown an interest in taking over Aegis. As you have seen, there's little arable land, and little useful mineral wealth at hand, apart from first-rate building stone. So far, I am at a loss."

"You have spies?" I asked, astonished. Chumley had always seemed to be the most straightforward person I knew.

"It's a jackal-eat-jackal world, old chap," he said. "You never know when a problem will turn up unexpectedly. Best to have all the warning one can."

"So," a voice said, from approximately my waist level, "you know our esteemed wise man."

I jumped at the sound. Gurn leered up at us. I wondered how much he had heard.

"Yeah," Aahz said, casually. "Turns out that his mama used to koochie dance at the bar my father owned. Shove off, pal. Didn't anyone ever tell you it was rude to interrupt other people's conversations? Ugly like yours is a major short-circuit."

To my surprise, Gurn looked hurt. It occurred to me that maybe he couldn't help looking like an annoying know-it-all. It might be a function of his misshapen face.

"How long have you been in Queen Suzal's employ?" I asked politely. Gurn regarded me with deep suspicion.

"My life is hers," he said.

I was touched. Gurn was a complicated guy, in everything except his devotion to his queen. I could respect that.

"We'll do everything we can to make this the best pyramid ever," I said. "Won't we, Aahz?"

Aahz regarded the interloper with distaste. "Yes. Of course."

"Do not make empty promises, Klahd," Gurn snapped, the soft moment ended.

"I don't make empty promises," I said, liking him less with every syllable. "If there's anything I can do, I'll do it."

"The word of Klahds has no weight here."

I felt my temper rising. "How about stones? If you want to step outside, I can drop one on you."

"Like you did to your so-called partner yesterday?" Gurn leered from me to Aahz. "The earthquake was a nice touch, distracting all of us from the attempt upon your friend's life. Very subtle! And will your next attempt be directly underneath her majesty's nose?"

All four of us stopped for a moment to contemplate that very pretty nose. Chumley sighed, breaking the spell. I growled down at Gurn.

"How do I know it wasn't *you* trying to mess things up?" I snapped.

"How dare you?" Gurn squealed. "I am the queen's trusted advisor!"

"I took a flight with you last week, remember? I can tell you like Diksen's pyramid better, and so does she. Maybe you want to convince the queen that she should try again to get in on it."

"You do not understand the function of a courtier at all, Klahd!" he exclaimed.

I bent down until we were nose to nose. "Yeah? So why don't you explain it to me?"

Behind him, Chumley was making the pat-down gesture again. Gurn spun around.

"Your education will be completed whether or not you like the teacher! And her majesty will be curious about the conspiracy that seems to be fomenting between her builders and one of her court officials. Is it a coincidence that you seem to be quite old friends—old fellow?" he demanded, throwing his head back to look Chumley in the eye.

"Maybe he's just easier on the eye," Aahz said. "Don't let the door hit your ass on your way out."

"Your misfortunes are not over!" Gurn snarled. He stalked off.

"Nice exit, what?" Chumley said. "Rather like an old-time movie villain. But he does bask in her majesty's favor."

"You can't put all your exits in one bask," Aahz said. "I don't care who favors him. It sure wasn't Mother Nature. The Pharaoh likes Samwise because he's doing what she wants, and by extension, she likes us. I'll settle for that, for now. By the time he comes up with a way to interfere with us, I hope to be back in Deva."

"I am afraid that he can cause us rather more trouble than we can cause him. He's an insidious little creature, and a very powerful magician. Keep your eye on him, Aahz."

Aahz made a face. "If I have to. I've got prettier things to look at."

As if on cue, in sashayed Miss Tauret with a tray full of goodies.

"I have brought you your lunch, O noble-faced Aahz," she said, twitching her ears fetchingly. "Shall I set a place for your friend and your honored guest?"

"No, thanks." Aahz turned a gaze full of meaning upon the two of us. "They were just leaving. Nice to see you, Wat-Is-Et. Come back any time."

Chumley let out a laugh. "Come, Skeeve, let us take a tour of this marvelous construction."

In his persona as the queen's wise man, Chumley attracted plenty of attention from the locals on site. Samwise shook his hand enthusiastically and invited him to check out the second and third stones just being placed on the new fourth tier. Chumley duly admired them and praised the carvers for their hard work. The Ghords bowed to him. As soon as he left one station, I heard hasty chiseling noises, then glyphs went flying toward the other Ghord emplacements. We stopped to see how the injured Scarabs were getting along. While their small limbs were wrapped in plaster like Aahz's leg, Beltasar had them sorting out different sizes of sand and gravel, some pieces so small I could barely see them. Chumley praised them on their diligence in four- and five-syllable words that were bigger than they were. Everyone was very impressed.

"You seem to have established a good working relationship with the staff," Chumley observed. He glanced backwards toward the office building. "Dare I say too good?"

"Maybe," I said. I kicked a small stone. "Say, er, Wat-Is-Et, have you noticed anything different about Aahz?"

"Not at all," Chumley said. "He is a man of strong appetites, as I have always observed, but does not usually let them interfere with his business acumen. Still, he won't miss a chance to indulge himself."

"You can say that again." There I was, trying to learn the ins and outs of good dating, and Aahz was going for girls right in front of me—and they were letting him. Perhaps Tananda was right, and I was overthinking things.

"Why do you ask?" Chumley interrupted my reverie.

"Well . . ." I was reluctant to bring up my fears. It was unfair to Chumley, who was in Aegis on an unrelated mission. He had his own worries, but he must care what happened to Aahz. Yet I had asked, and Chumley was waiting for clarification. "Does he seem sick or troubled to you?"

"Aahz? No, not at all." Chumley laughed, then cut it off when he studied my face. "You are worried. Why?"

I lowered my voice. It wouldn't keep magikal eavesdroppers from hearing me, but it would discourage those who were merely listening. "Well, you know what we're selling here."

"Elaborate tombs for the well-heeled."

"Aahz bought one. Not just one, the top of the pyramid in Phase Two."

Chumley's shaggy purple eyebrows went up. "Really, old thing? Shell out for a, well, castle in the air? Why? Does he fear that mortality is imminent?"

"That's what we're trying to figure out," I said. "I don't think that he's sick—but I don't know that much about Pervish health. He might have gotten a dire prediction from a fortuneteller, but he has never really believed in them."

"Hmm." Chumley stroked the fur on his chin. "Well, he's not above status symbols, and you must admit that the peak of a pyramid is a mighty one."

"It's not just that," I admitted. "He's paying people compliments—with absolutely no self-references attached."

"Dear me!" Chumley exclaimed. "Well, that is a different

matter. Aegis, you may well guess, is full of soothsayers, including many in the employ of the queen. I will make delicate enquiries to see if they have performed a reckoning for a visiting Pervect. Beyond that, I can do little else. I can't go abroad. My presence is required here for the near future."

"I understand," I said. I knew I was asking him a favor that could interfere with his own task based on our friendship, but we were both worried. A world without Aahz—I didn't even want to think about it.

A loud ticking sounded, startling us both. Chumley reached into the folds of his robe and came out with a black-shelled insect not unlike the Scarabs. Its little face regarded me suspiciously, then tapped its undershell with one tiny foot. Chumley nodded. "This is a Death-Watch Beetle," he said, at my curious face. "Keeps good time, and is a discreet companion as well. Silent as the grave, you might say. I must get back to her majesty. She'll be trying to eat her lunch now. Poor dear."

"Thanks for coming by," I said. "If there's anything we can do to help, let me know."

"I shall. Farewell. Give my regards . . . where necessary."

Chumley went down the pier to where a Ghord was waiting with a rolled-up carpet. As Wat-Is-Et approached, the servant spread out the carpet and laid it on the air. I could almost hear the rug groan as Chumley clambered on. His great bulk caused the fabric to sag down below. With some difficulty, the carpet lurched forwards, heading for the mountains. I felt good about having another ally here, as long as we had to deal with a powerful enemy like Gurn. I had seen him at the scene of at least three mass disasters on site, though I had no idea how he was connected, or if, to Aahz's wine cup springing a leak.

Bamf!

I turned around at the sound of air being displaced.

"Where is he?" Bendix demanded.

EIGHTEEN

> *"It's not a bug, it's a feature."*
> —W. GATES

"Where is he?" Bendix spun in a circle and ended up facing me. He jabbed a rolled up document at my chest. "Where's Aahz?"

"Can't I help you?" I asked.

"I doubt it!" the Pervish lawyer snarled. Veins stood out in his yellow eyes. I knew that meant he was furious. "Where is that son of a used-car salesman! The infomercial demonstrator! Snake oil!"

"What's wrong?" I asked.

"You were in on that, too," Bendix said, as if he had suddenly recognized me. He grabbed me by the throat. I squeaked as he picked me up and shook me. I got my wits back and used magik to put a step under my feet and pry his claws apart.

"On what?" I asked. "Aahz sold you a pyramid stone. Nothing else. What's wrong?"

"You idiots put a *curse* on me! Now it's going around my entire law firm!"

"What?" I asked. "There aren't any curses here. I admit that we've had some bad luck, but . . ."

Bendix cut me off with a gesture. "No! I checked. You don't get to my position in life without being able to tell one kind of magik from another. We have curse-checkers in our mailroom. You wouldn't believe what kind of things people send us, especially clients whose cases are unsuccessful."

Though he was shorter than I was, he strode ahead of me into the And Company offices. The reception desk lay empty. A few Ghord clerks looked at us in alarm. I held up my hands to show I was handling the situation. They looked relieved, though a couple took refuge behind their desks. Bendix marched down to the office Aahz and I shared. It was empty. The tray still lay there on our table. All the plates and bowls were empty. Bendix looked around.

"Where is Aahz? Is he hiding?"

"No, sir, of course not," I said. "Maybe he just went out for some falafel. The food's really good here."

Bendix eyed me. "Does it move?"

"Er . . . Not usually, no."

"Then it's trash! Like that lying grafter of a salesman! 'Enjoy the view of a lifetime,' he said. 'Be the first on your block,' he said. I never thought I would fall for a carnival barker's sales pitch again, but he convinced me. And now, look where it got me? My partners would be laughing if they weren't so mad. Aahz! Where are you?" Bendix bellowed. He started throwing open doors in the long corridor.

Slam! Slam! Slam!

All the rooms he tried were empty. Until we came to the supply cupboard.

Bendix jerked open the door and started to walk away automatically—until he realized it was occupied.

Aahz and Miss Tauret were there, caught in a passionate clinch. Aahz's shirt was half off, and the receptionist's usually smooth robes were askew. Piles of wax tablets and boxes of styluses were scattered around their feet.

"Oh," I said.

Aahz looked at both of us, and his brows went down in annoyance. "Do you mind? The lady is modest!"

Bendix jumped back. Aahz reached out and pulled the

door shut with a bang. We heard voices, Aahz wheedling
and Miss Tauret slightly hysterical. When he opened it
again, he slipped out into the corridor, buttoning his shirt.

"Just, uh, taking inventory," he said. "Hey, Bendix, how's
it hanging?"

Bendix gave him a disgusted look. "I can tell how yours
is. You complete moron, you stuck me with a communicable
curse!" He shook the contract at Aahz.

Aahz held out his palms. "No way! I would never put a
curse on you, Bendix. You're an old friend. I admire you.
You got in on the ground floor of a terrific deal, and I even
gave you a discount! That ought to tell you I'm serious about
this project." He tried to lead the angry Pervect toward our
office.

Bendix shook off his hand. "Tell that to my partners. The
Formican flu is going around the office like a nasty rumor,
and we lost a client that we have had for years because the
one clerk we have been keeping from ever talking to him
was the only person around when he stopped by unexpectedly at lunchtime. We had a party where the wrong gender
Pervect stripper jumped out of a cake for our oldest partner,
who's retiring. The bakery claimed that's what was on our
order. In front of six hundred guests!"

"Coincidences," Aahz said, blandly. "Why do you think
it's a curse?"

"It *is* a curse," Bendix insisted. "It's spread by contaminated pieces of paper. I brought my detector with me. Look
at this!" He took a small box out of his pocket and held it
up to the contract. The little dial on the box turned bright
red.

"It had to be in your office," Aahz said.

"I've got dispellers who come in every Friday afternoon
and go over the whole suite," Bendix said. "It had to be
something *here.*"

"Check if you want," Aahz said. "I've got nothing to hide
from you."

Bendix held the box in front of him and started going
over the office building, room by room. The dial stayed

within the green-to-yellow range. We went over most of the drawing rooms, set aside for other architects if Samwise had employed any. Nothing. Nothing registered in the front room, as the nervous Ghord clerks watched Bendix stalk around like a detective looking for clues.

"Aha!" Bendix exclaimed. He showed us the detector. It showed orange when he pointed it toward Samwise's chamber. We followed him.

Samwise wasn't there at the moment, but the plans were unrolled on one of the big, broad tables. Bendix headed toward them. I could see over his shoulder that the little square had gone to brilliant red.

"There!" Bendix said, half-triumphant, half-furious. "I told you so! The plans themselves are contaminated!"

"You're kidding." Aahz whistled. "The only thing we didn't check. Didn't even look at the plans."

Bendix was astonished. "You didn't spell-check it? What happened to you? You never used to act like an amateur."

"It was an honest mistake, Bendix."

"Honest, my foot. I want out. And all my partners do, too."

"You can't do that!" Aahz bellowed, confronting him. "We have a contract."

"Bah! Try and stop me."

"You bet I will. There's nothing in this contract that says curses invalidate the clauses."

Bendix smiled, a mean expression on his face. "You really want to take me on, Aahz? *Me?* Just back off and give me my deposit back."

"A refund! Never!"

Two Pervects arguing about money was as ugly as it ever got. Bendix reasoned, albeit at the top of his lungs, that he had thought to invest in a unique piece of real estate, but he couldn't take the liability of an extraneous curse that had the potential to embarrass him and, by extension, anyone else he chose to involve in the project. Aahz argued that the real estate was still there, would still be there, that Bendix had signed the contract, and that the clauses still held, and that curses were temporary.

"Do you know how to remove it?" Bendix asked. "Well, do you?"

Aahz fell silent.

"No. Not yet."

"Fine. Until you work out your internal problems, I want out of this project. I hope none of my partners offered a deal to any of their clients on your behalf. I'll get back to you on that. In the meantime, I'll take a check right now, for me and my partners. In full."

Aahz was humiliated beyond belief. I waited as he escorted Bendix out into the anteroom. Miss Tauret, looking everywhere except at us, made out a voucher.

"This is good through the Bank of Zoorik," she explained to Bendix. She caught my eye by accident, and her cheeks actually reddened. I gave her a sympathetic smile. Bendix snatched it up and stalked out. Miss Tauret glanced up at Aahz for support, but he was too devastated to offer anyone else an emotional lifesaver. He stalked back to our office and slammed the door.

I followed him and opened it softly.

"Can I do anything to help?" I asked.

"No! I've lost everything!" He kicked the waste-papyrus basket across the room. It bounced off the wall and fell over.

"Not everything. You still have your health. My mother always said, if you have your health . . ." I let the thought trail off. Aahz wasn't listening, and in light of my concerns, it was a bad idea to bring it up. He was so mad, he might rupture something. "You still have your friends," I finished encouragingly. That much I knew to be true.

Aahz looked up at me and snarled, "Where's Samwise?"

"I left him on top of Phase One."

Aahz stormed out of the office and up the ramps. I followed him. Samwise hurried to meet us.

"Aahz! My friend! Come and see how well we're getting on!"

"Forget that!" Aahz growled. "Diksen's plans were cursed, and you didn't figure that he had anything to protect him from light-fingered employees? Like you?"

"No, Aahz, he wasn't happy with it!"

"Did he *really* throw it out?"

"Of course he did! I mean, it was under the table, all crumpled up. I'd call that a discard. Wouldn't you?"

He was getting no concessions from Aahz. I interrupted.

"What was he designing?" I asked. "Why not use the same plans to build another pyramid? He must have had something new in mind. What was it?"

"I don't know! I told you, he didn't *talk* to me. He sort of mumbles, to tell the truth."

"Well, he's going to talk to us," Aahz said grimly. "If there's a curse going around, he's going to catch a piece of it."

NINETEEN

"A man's home is his castle."
—W. R. HEARST

We zipped straight up through the bottom of the shimmering sphere like arrows. Aahz had us land us on the rim of the lowest office floor. The secretary scrambled up from her usual sitting position, and the cats on their pedestals recoiled at the face of an angry Pervect.

"We want to see Diksen," Aahz said.

"I am sorry," the girl said. "My employer cannot be disturbed for any reason at this hour. He is meditating on the ways of the universe!"

"Taking a nap?" Aahz asked. "He can go back to sleep after I cut him a new one. Which way to his office?"

"No, sir!" the girl cried, as Aahz punched through flowing panes of water, then withdrew. "Please! Don't go that way! Or that way!"

She scuttled after us, cats at her heels, as we flew up the spiral staircase that wound around the inside of the sphere. It was much bigger on the inside than it had looked from the outside. Each level had been sliced pie-fashion into wedge-shaped rooms, tastefully furnished with artifacts and magikal impedimenta. Fountains, no doubt fed by the water in

the walls, danced and trickled in fabulous patterns. I would
have been more impressed with his skill at design had we
not been on a mission.

On the third level, Aahz threw open the first door and
barged in. A female figure, thrown in silhouette against the
translucent walls, sat up and clutched a length of fabric to
her bosom. I guessed that we had surprised her in bed. She
screamed.

"Who are you?" she shrieked. "These are my private
quarters. Go away!"

"Oops," Aahz said. "Wrong number. Sorry."

"Sorry, madam, sorry," the secretary called to her as we
stormed up to the next level.

That, too, was a private residence, but with more mascu-
line fitments. No one was in them. Aahz strode resolutely
upward. Finally, in the apex of the ball of water, under a
domed ceiling that focused the hot Aegis sun, we found
another door, this one of carved wood. It stood slightly ajar.

Aahz pushed it open. We entered a room full of floating
globes and shelves of books. I had never seen so many in
one place before.

A man sat with his back to us. He hovered in mid-air, his
fingertips tented before him.

"Diksen?"

He stirred and looked back over his shoulder, neither
alarmed nor in a hurry. He was a tall Ghord with sandy hair
and a worried expression on a jowly face that looked a little
like one of my father's hunting hounds. He unfolded and
lowered until his feet touched the floor.

"Who are you? Why do you intrude upon my privacy?" he
asked in a quiet voice. At least, that's what I think he said. As
Samwise had warned us, his manner of speaking was unclear.

"We're working with Samwise next door," Aahz said, aiming a thumb backwards over his shoulder. "He's working off
a set of plans that he said he got from you. They've been
spreading a curse around. I want to know how to take it off."

"Absurd," Diksen burbled, his jowls flapping. "Insulting,
to have you burst in like that."

"What about it?" Aahz demanded. "I warn you, I am not in the mood for hurt feelings. This just cost me a lot of money!"

Diksen's face got red. "Money? . . . More important things than money!"

"Oh, yeah? Name two!" Aahz demanded, breasting up to the Ghord magician.

"Whoa whoa whoa!" I said, getting in between them. "We started off on the wrong foot. Diksen, let us introduce ourselves. My name's Skeeve, and this is my partner, Aahz. We're part of M.Y.T.H., Inc., a group of professional problem-solvers. We work out of the Bazaar at Deva. Samwise hired us to help him out with the project next door. He said he got the plans while working for you. It looks as though they acquired a curse along the way. It's spreading and causing all kinds of havoc. I'm sure it's all preventable, but we need to find out where it came from. Can you help us figure out if it happened here in this facility, or somewhere else? Because you might have to clean one up yourself. We'd be happy to offer our services to assist you in getting rid of it, if you need it."

I put on my most winning smile.

"Won't even discuss anything so stupid as a curse," Diksen puffed. ". . . Troublesome Samwise, can't keep his paws . . . useless . . . on his own head . . . gone!" I saw what Samwise had meant about mumbling, but Diksen mumbled with menace. "Get out . . . will call for help."

"Who?" Aahz fleered. "Your secretary? Your cats? They're gonna be useful in a fight, I can tell you that!"

"Intruders . . . suffer . . . call Dorsal Warriors!" Diksen sputtered.

"Aahz!" I jumped out of the way just as something that I thought was artwork flashed and leaned out of the wall. I caught a glimpse of a pale, fishlike face as the being it was attached to threw a spear at me. He missed. Aahz grabbed the creature's scaly arm and tossed him across the room.

I had seen a lot of Ghords since we came to Aegis, but this one was different from all the rest. He did have a fish's face, with gills behind his cheeks. His legs ended in long sweeping fins instead of feet, and he had a ridge that ran up his naked back.

Aahz was scornful. "That all you got? One carp with a spear?"

He was answered by a hail of harpoons from the far wall. I dodged behind a standing bookcase. Three blades thudded into the spines of the fat, leatherbound volumes in the shelf. Aahz flattened himself on the translucent floor. He managed to avoid getting stuck by any of the weapons, but the fish-faced warriors that followed their barrage out of the water wall leaped on him. Cold and slimy hands seized me from behind.

I lashed out with a double-handful of magik heated to boiling point. The fish-men who grabbed me leaped back, yelling. I spun around to confront them. To my amazement, they all looked exactly alike.

I could see why we had not noticed them before. Their skin was pale blue, with a soft white underbelly. Their head-dresses and loincloths were green. They would have been camouflaged by the water itself. They came toward me, lowering polearms. I backed away, my hands open.

"Come on, fellows, I don't want to hurt you," I said.

They didn't feel the same way. Together, they charged me. I had nowhere to go but up. I pushed off against the floor and sprang into the air. They kept going, and splashed into the wall. I laughed.

Diksen wasn't letting his minions handle the situation alone. He pointed at a brass chain that lay coiled on a table-top. It rose up like a snake and slithered toward Aahz.

"Look out!" I shouted.

Aahz glanced briefly away from the two warriors he had just knocked against one another. The chain leaped for him. Aahz caught its ends with both hands and wrestled to keep it away from his throat. It was very strong, but he was stronger. The next warrior to appear out of the wavering wall got the brass chain wrapped around his neck. He fell back, leaving two more companions to face Aahz alone.

They lowered their spears and ran at Aahz. As they

passed under me, I used magik to pluck their weapons out of their hands.

To my horror, instead of retreating, they continued their onward rush. Without lances in their hands, they bent farther over so their heads were near their knees. The ridges on their backs sprang up into a fan of terrible spikes. Who could have guessed that the spears were the least of their armaments?

Aahz knew a lot of dirty fighting tricks. Before I could shout a warning, he dropped on his back, grabbed the first warrior by the shoulders, then kicked him backwards into the arms of his fellows. He hit them spines out. They yelled in pain as their fans got tangled.

I cheered, but my jubilation was short-lived. I had forgotten that the ceiling near which I had taken refuge was a thoroughfare for the Dorsal Warriors. Hands reached through the water and dragged me up into it.

After having been in a desert for weeks, getting dunked in cold water for the second time in a few days was a shock. I gasped, but kept my nose and mouth shut. The warriors zipped around me, prodding me with their spears. They were trying to force me down the face of the sphere. I didn't want to leave Aahz, and I didn't know how long I could hold my breath.

I made a big bubble around myself. The trouble was, I didn't have any fresh air to put in it. While I was concentrating on filling it with breathable air, the Dorsals discovered that they could kick the bubble around like a ball. I found myself tumbling head over heels. The fish-men wore expressions of glee. In a minute I would be too dizzy to know which way was up. Then they decided to change the game. They curled up with their arms around their knees, and prodded my bubble back and forth with their spines.

The air started leaking out in streams of little bubbles. I added magik to the shell to try and keep it intact, while urging it back toward Diksen's office. A group of warriors swarmed around me and kept prodding the bubble downward. I had just enough time to see Aahz in the hands of a dozen Dorsals. He wasn't going without a fight, either. As I passed, he tried to leap toward me. The warriors tackled him and sat on him.

A solid kick from one of the warriors sent my bubble flying over the top of the sphere of water and down the far side. I tried to stop my headlong descent, but I didn't have anything to use for brakes. I stuck out my legs.

"Yeow!"

The Dorsals rolled over and stabbed me with their spines. I was starting to get seasick. Enough! I let the bubble pop. The warriors uncurled and grabbed me by the arms. I didn't have very much magik left. I charged up my fingers until they had the stinging power of an Eelectric, a fantastic beast Aahz had introduced me to once. Then I touched my escorts.

They couldn't make any noise in the water, but they lit up and their bodies went rigid. I kicked loose and crawled through the water. I was at the bottom of the sphere now. If I didn't save myself, I was going to fall right out. I saw the ring-shaped floor of the reception room and grabbed for it. I swung myself up and gasped in a deep breath of air.

The secretary was back at her station. She recoiled in surprise.

"Behind you!" she cried.

I glanced back over my shoulder. Aahz, too, was surfacing, followed by the entire chorus line of a bad water ballet. The Dorsal Warriors grabbed us both and dragged us back in. I reached for the nearest force line and tried to fill my internal supply.

The next thing I knew, Aahz and I were tumbling downward, driven by Diksen's minions. I refused to let Aahz fall out of the sky again as he had the last time we tried to get in to see the reclusive magician. I made a cup of magik underneath him. Just before he dropped out of the ball of water, it caught him. He floated down toward Balu, who was waiting for us in the sand. I formed another palm-shaped pad of magik for myself.

"Come on, kid!" Aahz shouted. He reached the Camel and clambered up between its humps. He held out a hand to me.

I dropped toward my makeshift lifeboat. A phalanx of

Dorsal Warriors surrounded me. One of them struck out with the butt of his spear. It hit me in the side of the head. I saw stars. Kicking out blindly against the swimming guards, I felt for the edge of my magikal conveyance and swam over it. I realized, as the air hit me and rushed upward, that I had missed.

"Skeeve!"

Aahz's voice floated up toward me through a haze of spinning lights. I saw three or four Aahzes and six or seven Balus. Eight or nine green hands reached out for me. I stretched out for the one that was closest.

I smacked down on a soft surface. My body stung as if slapped, but nothing felt as if I had broken it.

"Reach out for me, partner," Aahz ordered. I looked up at the green and black blob moving toward me.

I put up an arm, but the effort caused the rest of me to push harder on the surface of the sand. I felt myself sinking.

"The slowsands have him, sir!" Balu cried.

"Fly, kid!" Aahz shouted. "Come on, you can do it!"

I reached for the power, but my magikal batteries were nearly exhausted. The slowsands started to creep over my legs, up my side and around my chest. I reached for a force line for a refill. The nearest was the twisting, writhing black line. The rush of magik was overpowering. I felt confused. The magik covered my face. No, that was sand! I picked my head up and spat. I didn't want to suffocate.

The sand was inexorable. It flowed up around my back and squeezed my chest so tightly I couldn't inhale.

I threw a skyhook upward to haul myself out. I hung onto the magical line. Balu had nearly reached me, when he disappeared from my view, smothered by the mass of golden brown. My vision went black. I heard Aahz yelling until my ears were filled with sand. The last thing I remember was struggling to move my arms or legs. I felt as if I was encased in concrete. I couldn't draw in a breath. I passed out.

TWENTY

"Sometimes you just have to dig a little deeper."
—THE SEVEN DWARVES

My vision cleared, but still all I could see was golden-brown sand. I gasped in air. There was plenty of it, sweet and moist. I was no longer suffocating. What a relief!

I realized that the layer of sand was a ceiling many feet over my head. I must be in a bubble or something like it. Still, I couldn't move. My arms and legs were bound together as thoroughly as they had been by the slowsands. I looked down.

I lay on a wooden table. Gilded animal heads on finials marking the corners of the table looked back at me. My entire body was wrapped in linen bandages about three inches wide, lapped in a complicated pattern from my feet to my neck. My arms were crossed on my chest. I had seen the pattern somewhere before. A memory tickled at the back of my mind. That was right! When I was a young boy, my schoolmaster had brought in a speaker, a man who had traveled to exotic lands. He had stories to amaze us, and showed us plenty of strange artifacts he had picked up along the way. One of his exhibits was a dead body in a long box. The corpse had been wrapped from head to toe in bandages just like these. Its face was dried out instead of rotten. It wore an expression of terror and woe, as if it had been buried alive. Was I about to undergo the same torture?

No. No one was going to stick me in a box! I had to get free, get back to Aahz.

I had plenty of magical power available, thanks to the force line, but I couldn't figure out how to unwind myself. Instead, I envisioned a pair of giant scissors. I ordered them to start cutting at my neck and work downward.

At the sound of the first snip, a shadowy figure that I had not noticed before turned away from the quivering golden light of a table lamp. It advanced upon me, its eyes shining orbs of black onyx, huge in a shrunken, desiccated face. Its mouth was open in an O.

"No!" it wailed at me. "Don't!"

I recoiled, but I couldn't get away from the creature until my arms and legs were free. I ordered the scissors to snip faster. The coils of linen flew away from me in a whirlwind. As soon as I could move my knees, I leaped up and off the table on which I had been lying. The skinny figure made for me. I put the table between me and it, dodging this way and that.

Then the cold hit me. I started shivering uncontrollably, so much that the figure had no trouble coming around and laying its bony hands on me.

"I told you not to," it said, in a gentle, throaty whisper. "Be calm, Overworlder. You have been almost drowned and battered by the sands. You are safe now. We wrapped you to keep you warm. You are not used to our climate. Sit down on the bier."

Unable to speak or move, I obeyed. The skinny being picked up the lengths of linen. With lightning fast movements, she, for I must call her she, wove them together. Instead of a shroud, she formed a jacket with a high neck and long sleeves, and all in less than a minute.

"Here," she said, holding it out to me. "Maybe this will be more comfortable. We didn't want you to hurt yourself while you were recovering."

I put it on and tied the tapes that fastened it. Not only was it handsome and well made, but it was warm. My shivering slowed down and eventually stopped.

"Where am I?" I asked.

"This is the land of Aegis," she said.

"But Aegis is hot and sunny," I said.

"This is Lower Aegis," she explained.

I eyed her. "Are you a Ghord?"

"No. We of Lower Aegis are Necrops. My name is Aswana. I am a healer of the royal hospital."

"I'm Skeeve," I said. "How long have I been here? Wherever here is?"

"You have been in my care for some hours," Aswana said. "But who knows how long you were falling through the sands or from what direction? The slowsands do not release their victims easily. And it is rare that they give us a visitor who is alive, I am sad to say. You must be a powerful magician."

"Why do you say that?" I asked.

"First, you were able to clip off your bandages though your hands were tied," Aswana said, her skeletal cheekbones lifting to reveal a toothy smile. "But secondly, you survived your descent. We are glad to have rescued you. We have few visits from those who live above."

"I don't know why," I said, trying not to cringe away when she laid her hand on my arm. I kept telling myself that she was not like that corpse in a box. She was a living being, and I had seen far worse. She only *looked* like the living dead.

"We are very glad that you have recovered. Would you like some refreshments? Come with me. Our king has said that he would like to meet you when you had recovered."

"I've got to get back to the Valley of Zyx," I said. "My friends. They must think —" I swallowed uncomfortably at the thought. "They might think I'm dead."

Aswana patted me again, and I tried not to recoil.

"We will ask the king to help you. He is very wise and kind."

. . .

"Welcome to Necropolis!" said the tall male on the throne. He had a narrow face with high cheekbones and straight brow ridges. His cleft chin was nearly fleshless like the rest of his people, but he was not unhandsome in spite of it. Nobles and wise men and women surrounded him. All dressed in clothing woven of the wide linen bands, many studded with amulets and charms. Such skilled tailoring impressed me. It occurred to me that Bunny might enjoy something made by them. I also realized it was a wealthy nation. The king's high-backed throne was pure gold, with inlaid precious and semiprecious stones forming pictures. The nobles' chairs weren't as large or as elaborate, but impressive as well. They also went in for magnificent jewelry, wide collars and bracelets, like those worn by the Ghords of Upper Aegis. The king held out a hand encrusted with valuable rings. "You may call me See-Ker. I am the twelfth of my name to rule the Underworld."

He beamed. I bowed low and introduced myself.

"Thanks for rescuing me," I said. "I was pretty sure I was going to die when I fell into the slowsands."

"They take people that way," See-Ker said, gravely. "Many of them give up hope long before the sands draw them under. You were most fortunate. But since you have reached us safely, we must have a celebration!"

"But, your majesty," I began. I was concerned that Aahz and the others would be worried about me. The last time they had seen me, I was drowning in slowsand. "I shouldn't . . ."

"Of course, you should!" See-Ker exclaimed. "Be seated. You are our honored guest. Let the festivities begin!"

He clapped his hands. Servants ran in. One of them brought me a gilded chair and helped me to sit down. Aswana took a dainty seat beside me. Short tables with the feet of animals, also gilded and jeweled, were set before us. Servants appeared with tall glasses in gemstone colors for us and filled them with rich red wine. They placed small plates, cut out of polished white alabaster and filled with sliced fruits and nutmeats, none of which I recognized, within easy reach. Unlike the gemstones, the food had almost no color. It looked unappetizing, but when I finally got up my nerve to try a piece, it tasted good. I realized I was hungry. It had been a whole day since I had had anything to eat. I emptied my plate, which was refilled again and again by silent-footed servants.

See-Ker clapped again, and a dozen dancing girls ran out and began to gyrate upon the wide stone floor, accompanied by robed musicians pounding on drums or plucking at C-shaped harps. The dancers wore colorful garments, made of linen so fine as to be translucent. I gulped as one of them approached me and threw a length of her filmy veil around my neck. She drew me close, gazing deeply into my eyes with her shiny black orbs, but I couldn't find anything seductive about her. To be honest, I liked girls with a little flesh on their bones. These didn't have any.

The rest of the court appreciated the entertainment, though. The nobles pounded on their chair arms or waved their wine glasses. A few got up and danced with the girls, singing and whooping along with the music. Far from the city of the dead this resembled when I first saw the Necrops, they were a happy, lively folk.

Still, I couldn't stay to enjoy it for long. I sat through the first round of entertainment. I stood up and tried to get the king's attention after the girls ran off, to loud applause and shouts from the audience, but he pointed and shouted as another group came on, these dressed in loose-fitting trousers and vests.

"See my acrobats, Overworlder! They are the finest in Upper or Lower Aegis!"

One of the rail-thin Necrops knelt almost at my feet, stuck a torch in his mouth and blew a stream of fire. I jumped backwards. The king laughed.

"Good, isn't he?" See-Ker yelled. "I would get indigestion if I did that!"

The nobles laughed.

Reluctantly, I sat down again. It wasn't that I didn't enjoy the fun or the honors. I really needed to get back to the surface. I tried to look as if I was having a good time. I pinned a smile on my face for every servant who brought me food or drink, and gave a hearty round of applause to each of the entertainers who bounded on or off the mosaic floor.

I guess I wasn't as subtle as I thought. Aswana slipped away from my side and made her way to the king's side. She leaned up and whispered in his ear. The shiny black eyes grew wider, and the dried-out face nodded once or twice. Aswana smiled, bringing out those prominent cheekbones.

As soon as the thirty-piece orchestra finished their concert, the king clapped his hands. "Come here, Visitor Skeeve."

I approached the king. The musicians made way for me.

"Are you not happy here in my kingdom?" See-Ker asked. "Have we not provided all that you need? Clothing, food, amusements, friendship?"

I bowed low. "I'm sorry, King See-Ker, but an accident brought me here. My friends are probably worried sick! I have to get back as soon as I can."

"We will bring you home as soon as may be," the king replied. "It would be our pleasure."

I brightened. "Can I go now?"

"I am afraid not," See-Ker said. "It is bright daylight above us at the moment. We cannot go into Upper Aegis in the daylight. Sunshine can kill us."

"Your majesty, my friend . . . he probably thinks I drowned. I want to get back before he gets too upset."

"I'm afraid that he will already have had much time to be upset," See-Ker said gently. "What was the hour of your departure from them?"

"Late afternoon," I said, thinking back.

"You have been with us a day and a night and a day again," See-Ker said.

I felt as if I had been struck in the chest. I had been unconscious that long?

See-Ker gestured, and the servants ran to bring my chair

around. I sat without really feeling it underneath me. The king regarded me sympathetically.

"I am sorry for the shock. It lacks a few hours yet until we may safely travel on the surface. Please accept my assurances that we will go as soon as it is possible. In the meantime, try to enjoy yourself. I offer you anything that Necropolis has to make your stay enjoyable."

With that, the king clapped his hands again.

"The entertainment will continue! I summon the players to perform the royal Chi-Kin dance!"

A group of Necrop men in woven kilts ran out on the floor and began a rhythmic performance of clapping and posturing. Everybody in the audience, noble and commoner alike, joined in. They were having fun, but I just couldn't concentrate.

I also sat through fourteen rounds of Name that Glyph. I got tired of listening to unsuccessful contestants boast, "I can name that glyph in *two* strokes" because they never could. Next up came a drinking game wherein each member of the audience was furnished with a beaker of wine and a glass. A bard took his place on the stage to tell a story of a long-ago hero. Every time he said the words, "And would you believe it?" they had to drain their glasses of wine. For such thin people, they put away food and drink in quantities a Pervect would envy. I refused to drink myself into inebriation.

"Why are you so troubled, O Skeeve?" Aswana asked.

"I'm concerned for my friend," I said. "I'm afraid he's going to try and go up against a magician named Diksen. He was responsible for me falling down here into your kingdom. Have you ever heard of him?"

Aswana looked astonished. "But of course! His mother, Maul-De, comes from our people. He loves her dearly. His Mumsy is the most important person in his life."

I remembered the shadow cast upon the curtains in Diksen's ball of water, and realized that the woman had the silhouette of a Necrop. "Does his mother live with him?"

"Oh, yes. He would not have it any other way. What a good son. Any Necrop would be proud to call him hers. He is a veritable Te-di!"

I knew the Aegistian word for soft, cuddly person. "That's not how he struck us," I said. My bruises had been healed by the Necrop magik, but I remembered vividly where they were. The Dorsals had pummeled me thoroughly.

"Oh, well, he will only be harsh upon those he feels have slighted Maul-De," Aswana said. Groups of people were leaving their seats to take papyrus sheets and reed pens from a scribe. "Look, they are beginning the scavenger hunt. O Skeeve, will you be my partner?"

"I suppose so," I said, without enthusiasm.

"It lacks yet another hour or more until we can take you home," Aswana said. "Please. It is so seldom we have visitors from the surface!" She gave me such a winsome look that I relented.

"All right," I agreed. She ran to get the list, and we set off.

We left the palace and entered the city's main street. Other teams started out ahead of us, but zipped off into side streets, leaving only a few on the main thoroughfare. I was surprised how gaudy everything was. The buildings had been painted all over with glyphs and pictographs. Except for merchandise hanging up outside the shops or in the windows, I could never have guessed from the exterior what any of them sold. The Necrops loved bright colors and brilliant white. They were the liveliest people I had ever seen who looked as if they had been dead for centuries. There was a tavern or an inn on every corner, beaming with lamps. The barmaids did a brisk trade in mugs of beer. Each establishment was full of people singing and dancing and laughing.

And drinking. A sozzled Necrop staggered out of the nearest and almost into my arms.

"Happy days, friend!" he cried. He patted me on the back

and staggered for support from lamp post to statue to planter to lamp post down the street. Aswana smiled after him. She grabbed my hand and pulled me over to one side of the road to consult the list.

"We are to find the painting of a tomb of a Ghord who serves ice cream to the Ancients," Aswana said, consulting the glyphs on the unrolled papyrus. "This way! I know where that lies!"

I followed her past many squared and triangular buildings.

"Are these tombs? I thought they were houses."

"Our houses are side by side with those who have passed," Aswana said cheerfully. "We feel less lonely knowing they are near us. We also give homes to those who fell through the sands but were not as lucky as you, O Skeeve. Like that one."

She pointed to a small building indistinguishable from the houses to either side, except that the door and windows were sealed up. Statues stood outside every building, some with their left feet forward, others with their right feet ahead. This house had the figure of a Ghord with his left foot out. I could only imagine what Deveels would have thought of wasting so much real estate. I already knew what my fellow Klahds would feel about it. I shivered as we went past.

Two blocks further down, Aswana swung to a halt at a wall that had been painted white, then decorated with figures. The Ghords tended to carve their inscriptions, while in Lower Aegis, where no sandstorms would scour them off, the Necrops painted theirs. As Aswana had said, a Ghord with the head of a hawk stood with his hands up, as if he was pushing the golden dish full of multi-colored scoops toward a host of elderly Ghords with fancy hats. Aswana offered our list to the painted figure. Its flat hands reached out of the painting like those of a paper doll and inscribed a glyph on our list.

"That's one," Aswana laughed. "Now we need to find a tribute to the Ancients that directs its energy downward. What can that be?"

I looked around, feeling that I wasn't going to be much help in this game. Then I spotted it. Attached to the high, sandy ceiling was a structure that looked exactly like the one that Diksen had built on the west side of the desert.

"Is that a pyramid?" I asked, astonished.

"Yes!" exclaimed Aswana. "That is the first of the great dynastic tombs, dating back many thousands of years. Our kings and queens abide eternally in them."

"But it's upside down," I said. How did it keep from falling? Was it growing there? "Diksen built one just like that, but right side up."

Aswana grinned at me. "Point down is the normal way they are built. Only Diksen would think of building one with the point up. He is so funny! It will get buried in the sand that way, and no one will ever find it! These can never be lost."

"There's more than one of them?" I asked, looking around.

"There is one for every dynasty. They are all over Necropolis. You will see more of them as we continue our scavenger hunt. See-Ker's is out in the countryside at the far edge of the city. Someday he will join his ancestors in it, but in the meantime they are enjoying it as a picnic spot. It has a good view of the city!"

"How big *is* this city?" I asked.

"Oh, enormous," Aswana said. "It would take many days to travel from one edge to another."

I did some mental calculations and realized that Lower Aegis must be as large as Upper Aegis. Hard to believe, but it must be true.

"Why has no one up there ever mentioned this country to us?" I asked.

Aswana looked sad. "They never come here. I think they are ashamed of us."

I was sorry to have brought her mood down. "Well, I think that has to be our second clue, don't you?" I asked, brightly. "Come on, let's go add it to our list!"

"O Skeeve, you are so kind!" Aswana hugged me in her

bony arms. She got up and started running toward the upside-down pyramid. I followed her, feeling a little cheered up myself.

The painted figures all turned to look at us as we left.

It took a couple of hours to collect glyphs from all the locations on the list. At the sound of a horn blaring through the stone-lined streets, Aswana and I returned to the royal palace. The contestants regrouped in the royal hall and turned in their tally sheets.

The king's vizier stood forward to announce the results with the help of a couple of trumpeters.

"The first place goes to Er-Rand and Ma-kna-lee." Everyone cheered as a pair of male Necrops stepped forward. The king looped gold medals around their necks. "In second place, the visitor Skeeve and Aswana."

"Oh, Skeeve!" Aswana squealed, delighted. "I never guessed we would do so well!"

"It's all you," I said, grinning in spite of myself. "I wasn't much help."

"Oh, but you were!"

"I have silver medals for you both," the king said, beckoning us forward.

"Thanks, your majesty," I said, bowing low, "but the only reward I need is to get back up to the surface."

See-Ker smiled. "Then we shall go. The time has come at last. The sun will be starting to set on the surface." He clapped his hands. "Forgive me, my friends, but let the entertainment continue without us for a while! Visitor Skeeve, please accompany me."

TWENTY-ONE

"The reports of my death have been exaggerated."
—ARTHUR, REX

A horde of servants and a few courtiers accompanied the king down a long hallway. The floor, like that in the throne room, was made of jeweled mosaic, though the ceiling, like everyplace else I had seen so far in Necropolis, looked like compressed sand. Aswana and I followed See-Ker, who pointed out interesting artifacts in niches and alcoves along the hallway.

". . . And that is a bust of my father, Thoth-Fal the Third. He was a great man, a great thinker, always seeking to enlarge our knowledge of our native wildlife. I wish you would stay longer and see his water gardens. They are the finest anywhere. Such fruit! Such flowers!"

"Maybe I can come back some day," I said. Aswana squeezed my arm.

"You would be very welcome," See-Ker said. His servants ran on ahead of us and threw open the gigantic double doors at the end of the corridor. "Now, let's get going. Behold the Lunar Boat!"

I followed him into the huge chamber and gawked.

Balanced on a pair of cradles was the largest boat I had

ever seen. It was made of a white, polished wood that looked like ivory. Round openings along the upper hull could accommodate oars, but the boat also had masts for sails. The long keel was flat for most of its length, turning up only at the prow and stern. On either side of the prow were two enormous eyes. Underneath one of them was a single glyph.

"It means 'She in the shape of the yellow tree fruit like the crescent moon that sails beneath moonlight at the command of his majesty the king of Lower Aegis under the protection of the Ancients and all magikal powers,'" whispered Aswana.

"The king's banana boat," I said. "But what does it sail on?"

"Sand," See-Ker said, laughing. "I can sail anywhere in the Underworld with this vessel."

"I mean, what propels it?"

"Moonlight. It only needs to be charged once per month, when the moon above Aegis is full. It is very economical to operate. Come aboard!"

Several servants lowered a gangplank for us. See-Ker started aboard. A dancing girl preceded him, throwing flower petals at his feet. The courtiers filed on, no doubt in order of precedence. Aswana and I came last. Everyone settled into deck chairs facing the bow, each with a flower-shaped canopy.

Servants wrapped the king and all his courtiers in linen bands until only their eyes showed. I thought again of that preserved corpse at my school. The traveling adventurer had told us it was a demon, dried out and blackened by its evil life. That "demon" must have been short for "dimensional traveler," and the body must have been that of a Necrop, probably stolen out of one of the ornate tombs the Necrops used to honor their dead. Now I felt sorry for whoever it had been. If my path ever crossed that adventurer's path again, I would bring the body home to Ghord. The servants came to me with their arms full of bandages.

"No, thanks," I said, fending them off. "I've got my jacket."

"Ah, but you will need these, O Skeeve," the king said. All I could see now were his eyes. His crown and headdress had been set on top of his wrapped head. A slit was cut in the bandages so he could speak. "It is very cold in the passage among the sands, and the dust that kicks over the bows is abrasive even to toughened skins."

"Well, all right." Reluctantly, I allowed the servants to wind linen around my legs, neck, and face. I was nervous as a servant with a huge knife bore down on me, but the dramatic slash only opened the space over my mouth. I patted the place gingerly with my fingers and looked at them, but there was no blood. They carefully threaded tiny bandages around my fingers so it looked as if I were wearing gloves.

"There! You look just like one of us, O Skeeve. Most handsome. Are you married?" See-Ker asked.

"Uh, no," I said, nervously. "Why?"

"The ladies of my court found you most attractive," See-Ker said. I glanced at Aswana, who lowered her bony chin into her wrappings and giggled. "If you wished, you could have many of them at your beck."

I fingered my collar nervously. "To tell you the truth, your majesty, I'm looking for a girl who likes sunlight."

"Ah, well," See-Ker said. "But come back again to visit us any time."

The navigator came to ask me a few specific questions about our destination. I did my best to tell him where on the surface I wanted him to go, though I had never measured the actual distance from, say, Waycross's Tomb to the And Company site. He nodded and unrolled charts, which he showed to the captain, an older Necrop with bowed legs. The captain shouted orders. A few of the servants ran to pick up huge palm fronds and stand by us, ready to fan at See-Ker's command. Oarsmen took their places on benches that faced the rear of the boat and threaded oars through the holes in the sides of the boat.

"One, two! One, two!" the coxswain at the prow shouted through a megaphone. "Put some life into it!"

The rowers dipped the oars and began to pull. It felt as if nothing was happening at first. Then I felt the boat lift. The rowers hauled faster and faster. The boat made for the sand ceiling. I thought we would plow right into it, but a space opened up ahead of us about six or seven feet deep, like a bow wave. As See-Ker had predicted, sand blew over the rails and showered all of us. The servants with the fans batted most of it away, but I got a mouthful of moist, fine grains. I spat them out, to the merriment of the court.

The King's Banana Boat plowed upward at an angle, giving me the privilege of watching my descent to Lower Aegis in reverse, conscious and in comfort, in contrast to my arrival. I thought that the inside of a desert would be featureless, but to my surprise, we passed small huts, occupied by a Necrop or two and a couple of animals. Other ruins, both right side up and upside down, appeared, giving me time for a quick, curious glance before they vanished again. The tillerman never struck any of them. He must have known his route well. I had been lucky not to get caught in any of the ancient buildings myself. I never would have been found. I tried not to think about how close that fall had come to killing me and tried to enjoy the trip upward instead.

The surrounding sand started to get drier and hotter. I didn't need the increased activity of the boat's crew to know that we were close to our destination. The King's Banana Boat tipped upward more acutely. Light broke around us for the first time.

Like everyone else aboard, I shielded my eyes against the blinding brightness of the sky. My eyes got used to the orange light in moments, and I realized sheepishly that the sun had just set. It was almost twilight. I had become accustomed to a land of near darkness.

Pop!

The bubble protecting us from the sand burst as The King's Banana Boat thudded onto the surface and skimmed along the desert sands beside a gleaming, broad ribbon of a river. I stood up to scan the horizon.

I was relieved to see that the captain and the navigator

had worked out from my scanty directions the best way back
to the Valley of Zyx. We were within a couple of miles of
Samwise's pyramid. The flat top, with a few new stones
sticking up like baby teeth, beckoned to me. I felt like taking
off and flying there, but I might not have been as fast as the
lunar boat. Free now from having to tunnel, it whizzed along
like a dragon.

"How strange to see a pyramid being constructed the
wrong way up," See-Ker said, eyeing Diksen's pyramid to
our left. "It is a funny idea."

I glanced at the people moving around on the flagstone
paths that lay around the work area. It seemed as if the usual
population of the site had doubled or tripled in the last couple of days.

"Who are all those people?" I asked.

"They do not look happy," See-Ker said.

You couldn't have sailed a boat like The King's Banana
Boat anywhere without attracting a lot of attention, so I
wasn't surprised when Ghords on the site started shouting
and pointing in our direction. They began to gather in large
crowds, each Ghord with a torch in one hand and a tool or
implement in the other. I was puzzled. When we got a little
closer, I could hear what they were saying.

"Go home, Necrops! Go home, Necrops!"

See-Ker shook his head. "Why can't we all just get
along?" he asked.

A flying wedge of black specks came hurtling toward us.

"King See-Ker?" called the lead Scarab.

"Yes, it is I," the head Necrop said. "Is that you, Beltasar?"

"It is, sir. Perhaps you should not come here today. There
has been some trouble, and the Ghords are restless."

As soon as I recognized the site manager, I started to
unwind the wrappings around my face.

"It's okay," I said, pushing the bandages off my head. I
combed my hair out with my fingers. "They're just bringing
me back here."

"Skeeve!" the Scarab sang. The rest of the workers surrounded me. "Everyone is upset over you, especially Aahz."

"I know," I said, grimly. "Just make sure we can dock, okay?"

"Leave it to me!"

Shrilling out orders, Beltasar led her winged beetles back across the narrowing expanse of desert. They buzzed the Ghords until the line of carvers and illuminators broke up into small groups and put down their tools. Beltasar buzzed back to us.

"All set! I told them you are on board. It is good news, even if the Necrops scare them."

"You've met the king?" I asked. "I didn't see any Scarabs in Lower Aegis."

"Oh, yes," Beltasar said, proudly. "I learned stonemasonry from Necrop masters sent to Scarab Polytechnic University by his majesty. Class of 7492! He came to our graduation," the beetle added proudly. "He gave me my diploma with his own hands! I shall never forget that day, and neither will my nine thousand, eight hundred and six children."

By the time the lunar boat pulled up against the long stone pier, the way had been cleared.

The Ghords cowered back from the Necrop sailors who jumped out and made the boat fast, but as soon as I came off, they crowded around me, pounding my back and singing.

"We must give praise to the Ancients for your safe return!" exclaimed Ay-Talek, the chief scribe. She ran toward the nearest shrine and began to fling flower petals over the figure of the Ancient.

"Hapi-Ar will be glad that you are back!" Lol-Kit agreed. "I must go and thank him for your safe delivery!"

"That's great," I said. She smiled and scooted away through the crowd. I turned to Pe-Kid, the green-faced Ghord. "Where's . . . ?"

"And so will Oris, She of the Dual Personalities," he said. "I shall just go and offer two kinds of thanks . . ."

I grabbed him before he could run off. "Aahz. Where's Aahz?"

"We have not seen him for hours," Pe-Kid said, regarding

me with surprise. "He has been in conference. Yesterday he mustered all of the Camels in the area to search the sands below Diksen's domicile. When they were not successful, he went over the hills to the Pharaoh's palace and returned with one of the royal Sphinxes. The next morning, all these people came."

I glanced over at the crowd of strangers. To my surprise, I saw they were Klahds, like me. They weren't wearing uniforms, but they were all large, fit, and armed, like military men. I thought I recognized a few of the faces.

I went up to a big man with gray temples who looked the most familiar.

"Excuse me," I said, "but aren't you from Possiltum?"

The man's face broke into a wide smile. "Lord Skeeve?" he asked. "Good to see you again! I bet you don't remember me: Corporal Sangmeister? Lord Aahz said you were gone forever!"

I groaned. Aahz had called in not only the cavalry, but the former infantry. "Who's commanding you?"

Sangmeister aimed a thumb over his shoulder. "We're all retired now, sir, but General Badaxe is in there with Aahz. They're planning some kind of invasion. . . ."

"General Badaxe . . . ? I'd better get in there!"

I strode toward the And Company office building, getting more worried as I went. He had already enlisted Tweety and, I bet, Chumley, to assist in searching for me. Now he had called in a wall of muscle.

"I shall come with you, O Skeeve," King See-Ker said. His long legs easily kept up with my hasty stride. The shorter attendants hurried in our wake, a couple of them still trying to fan their master as they ran.

My appearance surprised the office staff. I fended off their good wishes and anxious expressions of concern.

"Where's Aahz?" I asked.

"He is in conference," said Miss Tauret, pointing the way toward our office. I glanced down the hallway. Tweety the Sphinx didn't fit all the way. His leonine backside and broad wings were halfway out of the room, which meant there was a big crowd in our spacious atelier. "He doesn't want to be disturbed. He is planning something dire, I fear." Her usually cheerful face was woeful.

Revenge against Diksen, I guessed.

"It'll be okay now that I'm back," I assured her.

I peeked over the Sphinx's rump into the room. I knew most of the faces. Aahz had called in some pretty big guns. Perched on an architect's stool much too small for his sizeable backside was Hugh Badaxe, general of the queen's troops, of Possiltum. Beside him, still clutching a bright orange handkerchief in her large hand, was Massha, my former apprentice and present Royal Magician. Mascara ran down her large face in black rivulets. She didn't seem to care. Chumley, in headcloth and kilt, offered suggestions from a corner where he would not overpower smaller members of Aahz's cabal. His purple fur drooped.

The small figure sitting on top of the drawing table with one knee over the other was Markie. She looked like a very small Klahdish child, but she was actually an adult from a dimension called Cupid, where the people were small and soft-fleshed. I knew from experience that she was capable of wreaking intense havoc wherever she went. She was there as Aahz's magikal firepower.

Markie felt she owed M.Y.T.H., Inc., several favors: first, for not outing her as a psychological hit woman, and second, for offering friendship after all she had done to us. I had even made use of her particular talents in helping to train my magik students.[6] She and I got along very well . . . now.

Aahz paraded up and back before his cobbled-together fighting force.

". . . The idea," Aahz was saying, "is to take the place to

---

6. Markie's proficiency was demonstrated in *Class Dis-Mythed*, a book you would be proud to own.

pieces and deal with his defenses from too many angles for him to react coherently to any one of them. Diksen gets no quarter from me. Markie, you've seen the bubble. Can you break it down?"

"You bet I can," the Cupy said, her small face grim. "That magician did in one of the most decent people who ever lived. I have to admit, air magik is really my strongest suit, but I can handle water, no problem."

"Good," Aahz said. "Land those fighting fish on the ground. Badaxe's people on Camel-back can handle them once they hit the sand. Unless they sink. Which wouldn't make me cry at all."

"Look, Aahz," Guido said, "fightin's not the first solution."

"What? Diplomacy? And listen to him lie to us again?" Aahz snarled. Guido subsided, shaking his head. Aahz in full flame was more terrifying than a dragon.

"I must concur," Chumley said, holding up a purple forefinger. "Did he actually lie to you? And who caused him to call for his guards? Anyone would react to a forceful approach."

"Chumley! I thought you were on my side!" Aahz said.

"I am, old chap. I am on the side of the truth, which could be a more potent weapon against Diksen's resistance than any of muscle, steel, or magik."

"The truth?" Aahz echoed. "The truth is that I am going to get even with Diksen. His secretary said he couldn't help, even after I went back and told her what happened. What he did . . ." His voice trailed off. "I don't care what happens. I want that guy's ball crushed!"

I had to get in there. I tried pushing past the Sphinx, but he might as well have been made of stone. I clambered up on his flanks.

"Sorry," I said, as Tweety turned to give me a look of outrage that swiftly turned to one of astonishment and delight.

"Skeeve!" he said. He let me slide down his forepaw.

Massha spotted me. She gawked and poked General Badaxe. He was intent on Aahz and didn't notice.

Samwise was jammed into a spot between Tweety and a bench on which Guido and Nunzio sat with their arms folded. I slid into him when I clambered down the Sphinx's shoulder to the floor.

"Skeeve!" he exclaimed, grabbing my hand and pumping it.

"Skeeve," Aahz said, rounding on Samwise. "Who did you think we were talking about all this time? I want revenge! That guy's gonna pay."

"Aahz," I said, waving a hand for his attention. "Aahz!"

"What?"

He turned to confront me, and his yellow-veined eyes widened.

"I'm okay," I said.

TWENTY-TWO

> *"Diplomacy is the practice of saying 'nice doggie'*
> *until you can find a rock."*
> —W. ROGERS[7]

In short order, I suffered a big hug from Chumley and sti-
fling embraces from the general, from all the office girls,
and some of the construction staff. Massha and Markie
enveloped me in a solid group hug, Massha like an all-over
massage with a fluffy pillow, and Markie a tourniquet
around the knees.

"Are you okay?" Massha asked.

"I'm fine," I assured her. "I just took a little trip I wasn't
expecting."

Massha threw her big arms around me again. "Don't ever
scare me like that! I think I lost eighty pounds!"

Guido and Nunzio pumped my hand until I thought it
was going to fall off in spite of the bandages. Everybody in
the whole And Company building came to slap my back,
embrace me, or shake hands. Everyone, that is, except Aahz.
When everybody else finished welcoming me home, I
looked at Aahz and spread out my hands sheepishly.

---

7. This is a *real* quote.

Aahz looked me up and down and glared. "How badly hurt are you?" he asked.

"I'm not hurt," I said. "I got a little bruised falling down through the sand, but I think that was from hitting some of the rocks hidden in the slowsands. The currents are really strong. But Lower Aegis is great. You'd like it down there."

Aahz pursed his lips. "If you're not hurt, then what are all those bandages for?"

"Oh!" I said, looking down at my attire. "These are for warmth. It's cold in Necropolis. Pretty nice, huh?"

"Dandy," Aahz said, in a peevish voice. "You couldn't have gotten a message to me? Not one crummy note to let me know that you were alive? So I didn't worry myself into a complete frenzy and make a fool of myself in front of everyone I knew?"

"That is my fault," said the king, raising his hand from his spot in the hallway. He was so tall he could be seen over the head of the Sphinx. Tweety backed out so that the king could make his way into the crowded conference room. The servants with fans scrambled in behind him and started to flap their palm fronds over their master's head.

"Who are you?" Aahz demanded. His head reached the middle of the king's prominent breastbone. The king looked down at him with his shiny black eyes.

"I am See-Ker, lord of Lower Aegis. I confess that I had everybody who could have taken a message to you engaged upon festivities to celebrate our recovery of your friend. He is a fine fellow. We of Lower Aegis are proud to know him." He nodded to Chumley, who bowed back. "I am glad to see you, wise Lord Wat-Is-Et."

"As I you, O See-Ker, sailor of the Lunar Boat. I am sorry to have missed you in your lovely realm."

"Fine," Aahz said, waving his hand in dismissal. "Now, if the mutual admiration society is done with its meeting, I've got an invasion to plan!"

"But I'm safe!" I protested. "You don't have to go attack Diksen now!"

"Sure I do," Aahz said, scowling. "The bum put a curse

on *my* construction project. He is costing me a fortune every single day it's in force!"

"Turns on a silver coin," Badaxe said, shaking his head. "Aahz, it's not necessary."

"No, indeed," See-Ker said. "I will intervene with Diksen for you."

"You?" Aahz asked, looking the king up and down. "Thanks a heap for giving my partner a lift home, and good-bye. No offense, skinny, but you're butting into a situation that's none of your business."

See-Ker was more amused than insulted by Aahz's attitude.

"You are wrong when you say it is none of my business," he said. "First, your partner is now a friend of my nation. Second, it is the concern of all intelligent beings to avoid unnecessary harm to one another. Third, Diksen's family comes from Lower Aegis, so it may be said that he is as much my subject as that of her majesty, the Pharaoh Suzal. I can tell you what I know of his plans and aspirations."

The third reason made Aahz perk up his ears.

"Okay," he said grudgingly. "Have a seat, majesty. Tell me what you know."

Guido and Nunzio hastily vacated their bench for See-Ker. The slender king took up less than a third of it width-wise than they had.

"What could he possibly tell you that I couldn't tell you, Aahz?" Samwise wheedled, as the king's minions took their place behind him with fans and at his feet with a tray holding a pitcher and golden goblet. He blocked Aahz's path. "Don't listen to this guy. I'm the one who used to work for him."

"And you said, you don't know anything." Aahz moved him to one side. "I want to hear it from a different source."

"But Aahz!" Samwise interposed himself again.

Aahz looked him in the eye. "Are you telling me there's something you don't want him to tell me? Are you keeping secrets?"

"What, like you don't have any *magikal powers* any-more?" Samwise sneered.

A low gasp echoed around the room. I started forward to prevent Aahz from ripping Samwise's head off for the insult. Instead Aahz folded his arms. I stood back, impressed. Aahz didn't even raise his voice.

"I brought you a competent magician, didn't I? Did you lose a single coin from me? No! I brought you more business. You've had my expertise and my advice, which is what you asked for. Do you want more than *that?*"

Samwise sighed. "No, I guess not." He sat down on a chair and put his head in his hands.

"Okay, your Majesty," Aahz said. "Give. What's eating Diksen?"

"He has an artist's soul," See-Ker said. "He is sensitive by nature."

"Yeah, I could just tell that by the way he threw us out of his office," Aahz said. "I'm beginning to figure out what went wrong here. What evidence can you add?"

"I do not deny that Diksen has a competitive nature. The pointed structures in my realm inspired Diksen. He wanted to bring them here first."

"I doubt he'd have had a lot of competition. There's not much attic room," Aahz commented.

"But we have few possessions," See-Ker pointed out. "Our treasure is in our families."

"Thanks for the load of sentimental claptrap," Aahz said, "but let's not get off the subject. What about Diksen? Where'd he get off setting a curse?"

"I wouldn't claim to read his mind, but I have known him since he was a boy," See-Ker said, taking a sip from the goblet poured for him by Aswana. "There was supposed to be another building begun, on behalf of his mother, who is also a Necrop. He intended to finish it while she was alive, so she could enjoy it. The carved stones under the clear surface would be her favorite stories and legends. He has worked on them for years, but he has not yet come up with plans that satisfied him. They must be just right. We Necrops live long; he had the leisure to perfect them as he chose. But before he knew it, another pyramid was under construction.

It looks exactly like the plans that Maul-De brought to show us on her visit home some years ago. She was so proud of her son. He does love his Mumsy. He is a good boy."

"You can't be sure they're the same," Samwise protested.

See-Ker regarded him with his calm black eyes. The Imp squirmed. "But I am. I saw the plans myself, and I have seen the three levels of stone you have already laid."

"Four!" Samwise protested. "Almost four!"

"Almost four, then," See-Ker conceded. "They are exactly like the tombs that we create in Necropolis. An uncanny resemblance. Have you ever been to my city?"

"Uh, no. Look, I never denied that I got the plans from Diksen. But it was okay! He wasn't going to use those anymore! They weren't what he wanted! I figured he wouldn't mind."

"You stole the plans," Aahz gritted.

"He threw them *away*," the Imp protested. "They were crumpled up on the floor. He was never going to unfold them and use them again!"

"But you did take them without his express permission," See-Ker said, his large eyes bright in the hollow, shrunken sockets. "He would see it as an insult to his Mumsy."

Samwise quivered.

"Uh . . . well, yeah, when you say it like that, I guess that's kind of what happened."

Aahz groaned. I stepped in.

"What about Diksen's character?" I asked See-Ker. "Is he likely to be responsible for the trouble that we've been having? Attacks, accidents, uh, catastrophic misunderstandings?" I glanced at Aahz.

See-Ker shook his head. "Not directly. It is against our culture to work toward the destruction of another unless he offers direct harm to us. We believe that a dishonest man will bring harm upon himself. It is a shame that he passed it along to so many other innocent people, if it is indeed his curse that is responsible for all these misfortunes. These clients of yours did no harm to Diksen."

"You can say that again," Aahz said.

"Perhaps we can appeal in that fashion," Chumley said. "A decent man would not want harm visited upon others who did not wrong him."

Aahz lifted his lip derisively. "If it was me, I'd let others suffer and make sure they knew who was responsible for it." He looked pointedly at Samwise. "Let them impose justice on him."

"All I want to do is make people happy!" the Imp protested.

"And make a bundle of money," Aahz said. "You were so greedy that you didn't check."

"Well, you jumped on the bandwagon pretty quickly yourself, Aahz," Samwise complained. "We wouldn't have started Phase Two for ages if you hadn't insisted."

"He is still not responsible for your action," See-Ker said gently. "So if you apologize to Diksen, perhaps he will forgive you and remove the curse. There is no other way. It is difficult for a curse to be dispelled by anyone but the caster."

Chumley slapped his hands on his thighs. "So, a diplomatic mission of sorts is called for. I volunteer my services."

"As do I," Tweety said, raising a massive paw.

Others around the room offered their assistance. Aahz counted up dozens of volunteers.

"Okay," Aahz said. "What harm can it do? In that case, Badaxe, we'll have to stand down the invasion. At least for the time being."

Badaxe waved a hand. "Don't worry. I didn't prepare for one. My guys are mostly out there to make sure you didn't try and charge off to do something stupid. I'll bring a few of 'em with me, just for backup."

"I hope they will not be needed," See-Ker said. "The Dorsals have no magik of their own. They are merely fierce, brave and intelligent."

"So are my boys," said Badaxe proudly. "If they're so smart, they won't fight if we come in a under truce. Evening the odds'll just make sure everything *stays* peaceful."

"Uh, Aahz?" Samwise asked with a meaningful look at me, "Do you want the *other* preparations to be suspended?"

"Yes!" Aahz said, as if suddenly reminded of an unpleasant topic.

"What preparations?" I asked, curiously.

"Never mind!" Aahz shouted. "Let's get this show on the road."

"Everything?" Samwise pressed.

"No! Not *everything*. We'll talk about it later," Aahz said, clearly not wanting to discuss it in front of me. "But get rid of the mourners, anyhow."

Samwise nodded and leaned out the door. "Cancel the mourners!" he shouted.

A cry of "Aawwwww!" echoed back to us.

It didn't take a genius to guess what kind of preparations Aahz had set in motion. I was touched. A glare from Aahz told me I shouldn't say so.

TWENTY-THREE

> *"I did it all for Mother."*
> —O. REX

The diplomatic contingent intending to pay a visit to Diksen's pavilion was a lot larger than I had anticipated, but there was plenty of room on the Lunar Boat for all of us. Lord Wat-Is-Et joined See-Ker's royal party in the stern of the boat. Aahz huddled with Markie and Massha off on one side. Guido and Nunzio insisted on staying close to me wherever I went.

"There is no way we would let you visit this guy unprotected," Guido said. "Miss Bunny was displeased when you didn't come back to Deva the other night. She has been most upset. If we let you go unaccompanied, she would be most upset with us, and that we do not need to experience."

"Granted," I said. I wouldn't want to be on the wrong end of Bunny's temper, either. "Sure. I'll be glad to have you with me."

Guido cleared his throat a trifle uncomfortably. "Uh, Miss Bunny wants to see you when you get back this evenin'. Also Miss Tananda. They were both kinda insistent. And Gleep and Buttercup were pretty broke down when Aahz brought the news back."

"I'll come back with you fellows," I promised. I felt a

pang of guilt. Poor Gleep! All this time I had been worrying about Aahz, and I had forgotten about my dragon. That was irresponsible pet ownership. I was ashamed of myself.

A few of Badaxe's men on Camel-back trailed the Lunar Boat as we plied our way over the moonlit sands toward the bubble, gleaming under that cool yellow light. Tweety sailed above us, afraid he would upset the boat, but when we arrived underneath the bubble, he came to hover at our side.

"All right, kid," Aahz said. "You know where Diksen's office is. Let's fly up there before he can split."

See-Ker held up a long hand. "I believe that we will get a more positive response if we approach him as supplicants," he said.

I elevated everybody into the anteroom. We were a huge crowd balancing on the ring-shaped floor around the pool that represented the bottom of the sphere, but no one fell in. I mean, out. Even the servants with the fans found a place to perch.

"Smoothly done," said the king.

Aahz was impatient. "Never mind the compliments. Hey! Anyone home?"

The dark-feathered secretary came hurrying out of a small door in between two works of art on the walls. She had a purse over her shoulder.

"Office hours are at an end, dear visitors," she said. "I was about to go home!"

Aahz glared at her. "We want to see the boss. Now."

"Tact, Aahz, tact," Chumley advised. He inclined his head, not daring to bow for fear of precipitating either Badaxe or Massha into the drink. "My dear young lady, I realize it is late, but may we see Diksen? As you see, we have rather a distinguished visitor who would like to speak with him." He held out a hand toward See-Ker.

The girl went wide eyed and bowed deeply to the king.

"Greetings, Matt, O feather of efficiency," he said.

"Greetings, O See-Ker, great king of Necropolis," she said. "What are you doing with all these outlanders?"

"In search of an answer which only your employer can provide. Will you summon him?"

"For you, great master, anything!" Her eyes shone adoringly. She placed her palms together and intoned at the ceiling, "O great Diksen, he of the endless wisdom, writer of spellbinding texts, worker of wonders, son beloved of Maul-De and Omphalos, brother to Zimov and Clar-Ek! Be with us here and now, I do most urgently entreat!"

"She has to do this every time she wants to see her boss?" Massha asked. "Pretty cumbersome, if you ask me."

"She is painstaking," See-Ker said. "Diksen is fortunate to have her. Good secretaries are very hard to find."

Matt brought her hands together, and the clap sounded like thunder. The hound-faced Ghord appeared before her, still clasping a book.

"What is it?" he demanded, glancing up and staring at the massive crowd in his anteroom. "Late . . . not expecting visitors . . . oh. Majesty. Would have made arrangements . . . feast."

See-Ker smiled at him. "My esteemed friend, Diksen, this is just a visit of courtesy. I bring friends."

On cue, Aahz dragged Samwise forward. The Imp's knees were knocking.

"Not him," Diksen mumbled furiously, gesturing threateningly with his book. "He is a . . . thief. Dorsals!"

I saw shapes swimming around the shell of the building. Light from the room's many lamps flashed off weapons.

"No one else, thanks," Markie said. "There's enough of a crowd in here already." She waved a hand, and the inside wall of the bubble froze solid. Thwarted, the Dorsals pounded on the ice with the butts of their spears. "Go on, your majesty!" Markie suggested, in her most adorable voice. "We won't be interrupted again."

See-Ker nodded. "Perhaps Samwise is a thief, but he is a thief willing to make amends. Will you hear him? He grovels most satisfyingly."

Diksen blew out a deep breath, making his jowls flap.

"For you, majesty . . . of course." He glared at his former employee. "Talk."

Samwise twitched. "Uh, right, well, Diksen, I know you weren't too happy with my work, but I always respected what you did! You knew I dreamed of being an architect like you. I studied the masters, but what you were doing— you thought big! Really big! I would have been satisfied to do a fraction of what you did. I would have been proud to make use of your leavings . . . and, uh, that's what I did."

"That pyramid . . . for Mumsy!" Diksen exclaimed, waving his hands. He prodded Samwise with the book. "Insult . . . dire . . . death!"

"I can tell you're pretty mad," I said, "but all Samwise wants to do is apologize. Don't you, Samwise?"

"Uh, yeah!" the Imp said. "I apologize. It was wrong of me. I'll apologize to your mother, too, if you want. It's the least that I can do."

"Summon Maul-De," See-Ker told Matt.

The secretary had a separate invocation for Diksen's mother. When the smoke cleared and Maul-De stepped forward, I was one of the few who didn't recoil. Her face was shrunken, even by Necrop standards, and her back was bent, but Diksen put his arm around her as if she was a piece of priceless porcelain. Aswana went to her other side. The old lady greeted her with pleasure.

"What is this?" she asked in her querulous voice.

"Miserable . . . thieving clerk . . . apologize," Diksen said.

She turned toward Samwise, and her wasted frame seemed to expand. She straightened up until she seemed almost as tall as See-Ker.

"Well?"

Samwise flinched and tried to flee. Badaxe picked him up by his collar and held him, legs windmilling, over the open pool.

"Haven't you got something to say to the lady?" he asked.

"Uh, yeah, of course. Maul-De, I'm sorry. I . . . uh . . . didn't think about those plans being a tribute your son wanted to build for you. I, uh, well, what can I say? I abjectly apologize. I never wanted to offend you in any way in my entire life! I have great respect for you. You're an amazing person, and, uh, I admire you and your son."

"And . . . ?" Maul-De pressed.

"And, what?" Samwise asked, puzzled.

"And you are going to take down that abomination out there?" she asked, pointing a bony finger in the direction of Phase One.

"Take it down?" Samwise asked. "I can't do that! I've got thousands invested in it! Thousands of people on the job, thousands more who have bought into it! I can't just destroy it."

Maul-De turned away with a wave of her hand. "Kill him."

Diksen pushed back his sleeves, a grim smile on his face as if he had been waiting for an opportunity like that for years. Markie and Massha revved up their respective talents and stood ready to counterattack. The Imp fell to his knees and threw his arms over his head.

"Wait, wait, wait!" I said, getting in between them. "Killing Samwise won't solve the problem. Can't we come to some other agreement?"

". . . What?" Diksen asked.

"Make it worth his while," Aahz said, nudging Samwise with his toe. The Imp was surrounded by a ring of faces, all on our side, with the exception of Diksen, of course. "We all have a stake in this. Fix it!"

Samwise cleared his throat. "Uh, listen, Maul-De, I'll make a donation to any charity of your choice of, say, ten percent of my profits."

"Twenty," Aahz said.

"Aahz!"

Samwise sighed. "Twenty."

"Not good enough," Diksen growled.

"Thirty, and I'll throw in ten percent of my commission if you take the curse off, too," Aahz said, with a warning finger held up to stop Samwise from bursting out with a protest.

"The curse is no more than you deserved," Maul-De said, narrowing her large black eyes at him. "You got caught in a trap set by my son to catch miserable thieves like you."

"But the rest of us get it, too," Aahz pointed out. "Bad luck's been following anybody who got involved with this, and that's not fair. You nearly killed Skeeve when your goons threw him out of your sphere. For that I ought to kill *you*, but I'm giving you a chance to make it right."

"He fell through the sands into our realm," Aswana added. "It was a wonder that he made it alive!"

For the first time Diksen looked abashed. He mumbled into his jowls. "Shouldn't have killed anyone . . . minor matter . . . pull out of the sand . . . buildup of bad luck. Sorry . . . both of you. You bought into . . . that . . . thing!" His hand shook as he pointed toward Samwise's construction project.

"Are you trying to say that the accumulation of misfortune is the reason that Aahz couldn't rescue me?" I asked. "But I never signed a contract."

"Don't use many curses," Diksen admitted. ". . . Threat was a deterrent enough . . . I thought."

"Turns out you were wrong," Aahz said. "It's stronger than you thought it was. How about lifting it? You can leave it on Samwise, for all I care."

"Aahz!"

Diksen waved a hand. "Not interested . . . should have been unique . . . twenty more to come . . . ruined my plans!"

"And you will not lift this curse under any circumstances?" asked See-Ker.

"Will not!"

"Is that your final word?"

Diksen crossed his arms on his chest and nodded. See-Ker sighed.

"It will hold."

"We are all reasonable people, I hope," Chumley said. "How can we cut through this Ghordian 'not'?"

"You don't, alas," See-Ker said. "It is a serious thing. The pyramid is still a fact. Come, friends, we must withdraw."

"Wait a minute," Aahz said. "Is that it? You won't even consider it? What about the rest of us? I can't sell something that I know has a curse on it!"

For answer, Diksen put his arm around his mother's shoulders. The two of them popped out of existence.

"I am afraid, gentlefolk, that I must bid you good night," Matt said. She glanced outside. Night had fallen. "I believe I have even missed the last carpet going into town."

"We can offer you a Camel," I said. "We have a bunch of them waiting down below for us. I'll pay for it."

"That is most kind of you," Matt said in surprise.

"None of this is your fault," I said. "Come on, fellows."

We returned to the half-finished pyramid feeling low.

"All is not lost," Chumley said. "We can try to undo the curse on our own. I will examine the royal library. The librarian, Alexandria, is a good friend. If there is anything in a historical text, I shall find it."

"Me, too," said Massha. "I'll research it from my end. I'll send a note to my friends in Jahk. A sports-oriented dimension like mine uses lots of curses. Some of them last over a century!"

I thanked them for their help. "Aahz and I will make the rounds in the Bazaar. If there's anything effective for sale, they'll have it."

"For a price," Aahz scowled, not looking enthusiastic.

"We'll figure this out." Hugh Badaxe gave Aahz a slap on the back. "You don't need us anymore. I've got to get my guys back. We've got to attack the spring harvest. Hay and early peas, you know."

Aahz waved a hand. "Go ahead. Thanks for the help. I owe you."

"Happy to do it, for you or Skeeve. I can leave a few men for a short time if you want. They don't get to travel much, and they want to see Ghordon. They're already making friends with some of those critter-faces out there."

"I'd appreciate it," Aahz said.

"Glad to see you among the living," Badaxe said to me, then glanced at See-Ker, "so to speak. We should go."

"Hey, big spender, can you give a girl a hand?" Massha asked, quietly in my ear. "I could use a boost to get all the men back to Possiltum. I'm afraid of burning out my transport lamp. I'm low on fuel, and it's so darned hard to get the formula." Massha's magik relied mostly on gadgets, most of them unique.

"Sure," I said. "What's it run on?

"The usual stuff—dinosaur dung, unicorn hair, dragon toenails, Cyclops sweat."

I cringed at the idea of getting dragon toenails for her. Gleep hated it when I clipped his claws; he would whimper and try to hide his paws from me. "How about I just take you all back so you don't have to burn out the light?"

"That'd be great." Massha gave me a kiss on the cheek. "Glad to see you the way you always are," she said. "It was tough, thinking what it would be like without you." Then she leaned close and whispered in my ear, "Honey, don't let Aahz pretend to be all tough with you. He cried like a baby. But don't tell him I told you so."

"Never," I promised.

Markie brushed off her tiny dress. "I'm off, too. I've got a family gathering on Cupid. I joined a singing group, the Cupy Pies. We'll be performing at the reunion. Close harmony ballads." She gave me a sideways glance which I realized to my surprise was shyness. "Come to one of our concerts some time."

"Thanks," I said. "I will. Tell Melvine I said hi."

"With pleasure," she said. "He's a changed Cupy since he was in your class. He's normally not much on showing admiration, but you earned it."

Before I could sputter out my embarrassment, she blinked out.

"Do not view this as a failure," See-Ker said to Aahz. "You may still persuade Diksen. He is a sensible man. Now that you have approached him, he will consider his feelings and come to a reasonable conclusion. It may take time. I suggest that, since you have made commitments to others, that you go on with your project. Now, we must leave before the sun creeps above the horizon."

"Prepare the royal vessel!" the servants cried.

I said my farewells to my new friends.

"Come back and see me some time," Aswana said, clasping my hands in hers. "I have so much more of my country to show you."

"Maybe," I said. She was very nice, but I found it hard to get past the sunken cheeks and dry skin over bone-thin hands. Still, the Necrops had been more help than I could have asked for.

Aahz and I went out to see them depart. They boarded their ship and took their seats. The rowers took up their oars.

The full moon had shifted, but it still lit up the sails of the Lunar Boat. The long, flat-hulled vessel sailed out into the midst of the desert and descended out of sight.

"That's the way I feel," Aahz said, standing beside me. "Sunk."

TWENTY-FOUR

"No one will ever find out about us."
—M. HARI

My return to the site in the morning was somewhat subdued. I never got to sleep. Bunny and Tananda pounced on me as soon as we arrived in the M.Y.T.H., Inc., office. Both of them had been so upset, they didn't want to let me out of their sight. They cried on my shoulder, shook me, hugged me, offered me food and drink, and made me sit between them on one of the couches, demanding to hear every single thing that had happened since I had left them the morning before.

Both of them held one of my hands. I hated to make them let go to reach for any of the snacks or drinks on the table beside us, so I concentrated on giving them every detail of my fall through the sands and ride back to the pyramid. They demanded that I repeat it all over and over until I was sure there was nothing left to tell. Then they cried once more.

"Never do that again!" Bunny wailed, clinging to me in an uncharacteristic display of woe.

What could I say?

"I promise I will try never to get sucked down through a desert into an underground kingdom," I said. She and

Tananda had to be satisfied with that. They hugged me again
and again. I'd be lying if I said I didn't enjoy the attention.

Guido and Nunzio left us sometime after midnight. Aahz
sat up with me and the ladies for a while, but he brooded in
a corner with a jug of wine, snapping whenever anybody
spoke to him. I could tell he felt left out. I did my best to
cheer him up and bring him into the conversation, but I got
tired of being snarled at. I understood that he felt responsible
for my fall, but it wasn't his fault. It had been mine. I got
distracted and hit in the head by that Dorsal Warrior when
I wasn't paying attention. Aahz would have called it a rookie
mistake, a colloquialism I had learned long ago. I pointed
that out to him, but it didn't help.

He still wasn't really talking to me in the morning. I left
him hunched over the paperwork in the office and got out.
There wasn't room enough in our atelier for both of us and
his mood.

Instead, I took a break and decided to fulfill a long-made
promise to myself to look around the rest of the Valley of
Zyx. I hired a Camel to take me on a tour. We skimmed
around the emptiness so I could get an unobstructed view
of the mountain ranges that formed the valley, then took a
long ride by the banks of the river Zyx itself. It was a magnificent, wide ribbon of dark blue silk. Despite Ghordon's
resemblance to Deva in terms of geology and climate, Deva
didn't have a river like that. If it did, it would be fronted by
luxury mansions or filled with garbage—or both. Deveels
tended to exploit natural resources to the maximum.

I finished my tour at the Kazbah, the cluster of colorful
tents at the eastern edge of the valley. My Camel dropped
me off at one end and promised to come back for me a
couple of hours hence at the other.

The Kazbah was remarkably similar to the Bazaar. I had
to check once in a while to make sure the merchants shrieking out their sales pitch were Ghords, not Deveels. Tents,

often no more than a flapping cloth canopy to keep off the aggressive noontime sun, did nothing to keep down the dust-fine sand that blew everywhere. I found myself wiping my eyes every few minutes, until I created a small spell that protected my face. The merchants offered everything from food to fine tailoring, delicate pottery to mill wheels. Local magicians, herbalists, fortune-tellers, and other seers offered their services by means of signs on which living glyphs beckoned to passersby.

I thought I would look around for little gifts for Bunny and Tananda. I was shocked but gratified how upset they had been over the prospect of losing me. When I thought about it, I was grateful for one more chance. We had just started to rebuild the camaraderie that I had left behind when I resigned from M.Y.T.H., Inc. The least I could do was bring them both a souvenir of the Zyx Valley. Maybe I could also find something to cheer Aahz up.

I threaded my way among the flapping tents. The most ancient stalls, the jewelers included, were carved right into the mountain sides. Lion-headed women with toothless jaws roared at me to come and inspect the spices or cloth or painted leatherwork or cast metal they had for sale. Everyone offered sour beer or mint tea if I would just sit down and let them show me their merchandise. Traders screamed at each other and their prospective clients, addressing them in every language until they came up with one that the prospect spoke. They were as allergic to giving change as Aahz was to letting loose a coin.

I got a lot more respect from the locals since the day I had boosted the pyramid. If I stopped to look at a display, tiny glyphs went zipping out of the shop past me into other booths along the streets. If I didn't ask about prices, the owners would snatch up a few examples of their goods and follow me, bleating about quality and pleading with me to come back.

"I will have so much more status if I can say that the visiting Klahd magician Skeeve the Magnificent shops here!"

"You will tell people who see you wear this, and everyone will come to me to buy one and I shall be rich! It would so benefit us both. Come back, come back!"

Most of the time I just smiled and kept walking, promising to go back some time, but I bought a few knickknacks just to enjoy the bargaining. I felt at home. Yes, the Kazbah was a lot like the Bazaar, traders, pickpockets, prostitutes, gullible travelers, and all.

My mind was on Aahz. He had dozens of clients lined up to see sites in Phase Two over the coming weeks, but I could tell his heart wasn't in it any longer. He was worried about the rumors that would start when it came out that a curse came with the location. What could we do about that? Treat it as some kind of premium? He had already had to give a refund to Bendix. That meant his commission was gone, too. A rug merchant from the Bazaar had wanted to sell sublets on his own. We were afraid if he did, an exponential accumulation of bad luck would devolve upon Aahz and Samwise. The more shares that were sold, the more risk they took. I couldn't think what would be worse than what had already happened, and I didn't want to find out. Diksen had apologized to us, but he had been firm. The curse stayed as long as the pyramids did. Yet we were all too committed to back out. Samwise had bills for materials, workers' salaries, advertising, magicians' fees, and union dues. He had to go on.

So did Aahz. He really, really wanted that top spot on Phase Two. He had already commissioned Ay-Talek to start on his stone herself. He had furnished the scribe with dozens of scrolls containing his exploits. She had exhibited the first glyphs she had carved on the side. They were beautifully rendered, though spelling out 'Pervect' had taken some tactful images.

Samwise avoided both of us whenever possible. He had put us in a terrible position. I would have left Ghordon in a minute and never returned, but we had to find a way to take the curse off Aahz. At the moment, Diksen's little booby-trap was still a secret, known only to the three of us, See-Ker's folks, and the friends whom Aahz had brought in as a strike force. None of those would tell, but who else had overheard our discussions? Ghords seemed to live to gossip. Glyphs seemed to shoot around the construction zone more often than before—or perhaps I was just more aware of it than I had been. We had to behave as if news of the curse could slip out at any time. Aahz spoke of damage control, but that went right back to not knowing just how to spin that piece of news. I didn't know what Samwise and Aahz would do if word got back to the Pharaoh. Considering how often he turned up underfoot, I was surprised Gurn hadn't managed to insinuate himself into our conference the other night.

I wandered into a narrow little street of cracked paving stones lined with open-topped wagons filled to the brim with odd merchandise, almost all of it worthless. I used my inner eye to look for magik items, but there was little to be had. Anything there with a touch of magik tended to have been doctored with a pinch of Pyxie dust (citrus flavored) and a wink for the gullible. My hand lit upon one item that had a little glamour upon it. I realized I was holding a model of Diksen's pyramid. It was hollow underneath.

"Ah, sir," exclaimed the lizard-faced Ghord behind the wagon. "That is one of my most popular wares."

"What's it for?" I asked.

"It is used to store cheese," he said. "The power of the pyramid prevents it from aging. Here! See the one I use for myself." He took an identical curio from the counter behind him and held it out to me. A chunk of grayish cheese lay on a square dish beneath. I thought it smelled pretty terrible anyhow.

"I'm looking for a present for a friend, but he doesn't eat much cheese."

"It will also preserve beer," the merchant said hopefully.

"He never lets his beer get old."

The reptilian Ghord whisked it away. "Well, then, sir, this is not for you. Is there anything else I can help with?"

A thought struck me, and I made my way back toward the Avenue of the Magicians. Like the items in the barrows, most of their wares were fakes, too, but I found a couple of rival vendors selling scrolls and books of magik.

"You want what?" asked the first grimoire salesman I asked.

"Cures for magikal ailments," I said. "What to do if you accidentally pick up a bad amulet, or annoy one of the Ancients."

"For that, you wish *1,001 Forms of Propitiation*," he suggested, handing me a hefty volume with a thick layer of dust on the cover. "The best way to get around the Ancients is to smother them with kindness. Here are all the known rituals and offerings for each of the old Ghords."

I fended off that book, as well as half a dozen others he suggested. None had anything to do with curses. I rephrased my query for the second sales-Ghord, a female with a near-sighted rodent's head. She frowned, her long teeth chewing at her lower lip.

"Sounds like a specialist job to me, young friend. How about a gazetteer to the dimension instead?"

"Say," I said, as if an idea struck me. "Do you ever sell anything to a magician named Diksen?"

The question caused both merchants to roll up like their own goods. I retreated. It wasn't going to be that easy to undo a spell without the caster coöperating.

Perhaps it would be better to concentrate on gift-buying. I made for the Avenue of the Jewelers. On one of her visits, the Pharaoh had worn a headband and a broad necklace made of jewels, either of which would have looked terrific on M.Y.T.H., Inc.'s new president for dress occasions. I wondered if I could find the jeweler who had made them. Since she had started choosing her own clothes, Bunny dressed fairly conservatively, but somehow her outfits managed to make her look even more sexy and appealing than the scanty garments had. When she dressed up to go out, she looked like a million gold pieces. For sticking with me during the months I spent finding myself I owed her my respect and loyalty, but a couple of little presents now and again were welcome, too. For Tananda, I thought a pretty bracelet would please her. The jewelers were delighted to talk design with me, and at least ten of them produced drawings of pieces they could produce in short order with as many gemstones as I liked, providing price was no object. I promised to consider and get back to them.

A weird aroma caught my nose and drew me halfway down a narrow passage. I found myself at a cookshop where the long-nosed birdman behind the counter was flipping a mass of something in a frying pan.

"Fresh food!" he informed me.

I peered at the mixture. It looked like gravel mixed with green sand. "Is it animal, vegetable, or mineral?"

"Better not to ask, young sir," the birdman said. "But it is delicious! Try some! Take a chance! Your stomach will thank you. Only a copper coin."

I reached for my belt pouch.

"Don't pay more than half a copper," a soft voice at my shoulder said.

I spun around. Matt stood beside me. Her cats wound around our feet.

"Hi, there," I said, smiling.

Her warm, tanned cheeks turned rosy.

"Good afternoon. My-Nah is a good cook, but he tends to overcharge tourists. Don't you?" she asked the birdman.

He bowed. "Pretty ladies like you make me forget all about profit," he said.

"Were you going to have lunch here?" I asked, glancing around. "Why don't you join me?"

"Well, I . . ." She hesitated. "Yes, thank you."

"Two bowls," I said. "And wine?"

"Fruit juice, thank you, sir. I must go back to work this afternoon."

I handed the birdman a copper coin and visited the booth next to his for freshly squeezed juices. By the time I returned, Matt was sitting bolt upright upon one of the shabby wooden stools at one of the communal tables sheltered by a pink fabric canopy in the passage. She had placed a portion of her food on a solid gold plate under her chair for the cats.

I took a couple of gingerly spoonfuls of My-Nah's food while Matt watched.

"How is it?" she asked.

"I've had worse," I said, trying to sound cheerful. It tasted like some of the nondescript bowls of food I'd bought from street vendors in the Bazaar. Nothing special, but not fatal to the diner, either.

She laughed. "It is nourishing. Beyond that I do not ask. It is either that or bring my own lunch. I am too busy when I leave for work in the morning."

An awkward silence fell. I thought back hastily to the dating lessons that Bunny, Tananda, and the others tried to hammer into me. Not that this was a date, per se, but she was a pretty girl, and I found myself unexpectedly tongue-tied trying to make conversation. "Ask her about herself," Bunny had suggested. "Show an interest."

"Do you like working for Diksen?" I stammered out. It was the first thing I could think of.

Matt didn't seem to find the question offensive. "He is not a bad boss. He pays well and he is not unreasonable in his requirements." She took a bite of her own food, then looked up at me shyly. "I am sorry that he treated you so poorly. He likes his privacy. He was not happy about having his former employee set up business so close to his, in every way!"

"Yeah, we were a little surprised to find out just how close," I said, with a grim thought for Samwise.

"It is not your fault," Matt assured me. "Are you recovered from your misadventure? You are not harmed in any way?" She studied me solicitously. "You have a bruise on your temple!"

"I'm fine," I said. I basked in her sympathy. It felt nice to have a pretty girl paying attention to me. "I just wish we could have solved the problem. Aahz is my best friend. I'm really worried about him. He's got a lot at stake, and your boss's curse is making it impossible for him to do the job he was hired to do."

Matt didn't reply. She hastily picked up her juice and took a sip.

I realized once again that I'd been the one to kill the conversation. My problems were not her concern. I ate some of my food and tried to think of a pleasant subject.

"So, what do you like . . . ?" I began.

"And how do you find Aegis . . . ?" she said at the same time.

We both laughed.

At the next table, a couple of girls were talking over a bowl of My-Nah's who-knew-what? One of them had a long narrow head with oval ears and long, flexible lips. Her golden-furred face rose on a long neck spotted with huge brown oval blotches. The other had a bird face with a short hooked beak. They were talking excitedly in low tones, but perfectly audible to us. I smiled to myself. Ghords seemed to live to gossip—or glyph, which amounted to the same thing.

". . . But do you believe it?" the first one asked the other, her voice suddenly audible over the racket in the street. "In the supply closet! That is just asking to be found, isn't it?"

"Well, you know what they say about *them*. She said he was absolutely wild . . . !"

"How fabulous!" the first one giggled.

"I *know.*"

They dropped off again into inaudibility, but it had been enough. My cheeks burned. I wanted to climb under the table. I knew who they were talking about and, to my horror, so did Matt. She smiled and shook her head.

"That is typical gossip, I am afraid," Matt said, not without sympathy. "Even I have been getting messages from friends about what is happening on the construction site."

I cringed. "And do you pass them along to your boss?" I asked.

She looked shocked. "No! Why would you ask such a thing? Messages are private. Oh, it is only your friend's bad luck that he chose her. Tauret is such a big mouth. Almost any other woman in that office would have been more discreet."

I didn't intend to tell Aahz how far word of his close encounter had gone. It could have been a function of the curse that caused him to choose the one girl who kissed and told. Or simple bad luck. There was no way to know for sure. It would be cruel to rub it in.

"Mer-ow!" one of the cats said, coming out from beneath Matt's stool.

She stood up and smiled at me. I scrambled to my feet. "I am sorry," she said. "I must go back. Thank you for our lunch. And thank you so much for arranging my ride home the other night."

"My pleasure," I said honestly. "It's our fault you were late getting away."

"You are kind. I wish you good fortune. If there is ever anything I can do for you, please ask me."

"Unless you know how to unlock the curse," I said, wryly, "I don't know what there is."

"I cannot go against my employer," Matt said, immediately tense.

"I wouldn't ask you to," I assured her. "Thanks for the offer, though. It was really nice having lunch with you."

Matt looked surprised, as if it had not occurred to her. "Yes, it was. Goodbye now." She and the cats disappeared into the crowd.

Whistling, I made my way to my rendezvous point with my Camel.

TWENTY-FIVE

"What am I? A mind-reader?"
—THE ROWAN

Beltasar met me at the pier. The Scarab held out a sheaf of miniature documents.

"Sign these."

"What are they?" I asked.

"Work orders," she said, buzzing in a circle around my head. "There are eight blocks to be moved, and no paperwork has been filed. I cannot locate Samwise. I cannot find your friend, who ordered that nothing be signed except by him or by Samwise in his presence. But you are his partner, so will you initial them so we can get going? We are burning daylight!"

I looked them over quickly. Glyphs were still difficult for me to make out, but each of these was almost alike, except for the name of the owner of each stone, and the coördinates of the location to which it was going. I took the pencil from the hovering Scarab and dashed off my name on each one.

"Thank you," she said, and shot away.

Where was Aahz?

I went back to the And Company office. He wasn't in our studio. I checked all the offices. No Aahz.

"He has not been in here in hours," said Miss Tauret. She looked a trifle miffed. I thanked her and went out to ask around the site.

"Aahz?" asked Lol-Kit, the female scribe. "The male with the face of Sober?"

"That's right," I said. I had been walking around for an hour without luck.

"Oh, he went over there some time ago," she said.

"Where?"

"Up there." She pointed a delicate claw toward the sky. I squinted into the sun, and made out a small black object hovering in the sky. "Yes, he is still there. He has been lying there for hours."

I panted my way up the steps to the top of Phase Two's invisible framework.

"Aahz!" I shouted again. "Are you all right? Answer me!"

My heart battered against the inside of my chest. Had the worst happened? Had he gone up to wait for a client and collapsed without anyone noticing?

He lay on his back at the apex of the four ramps, one arm outstretched, his hand curled around a circular object. He was lying too still. I took to the air and flew the rest of the way.

"Aahz!"

I zipped through the top of the framework and into the air until I was hovering over his face. His eyes were open.

"Aahz!"

The eyes rolled in my direction and focused on me.

"What? Can't a guy get any peace around here?"

My heart slowed a little, and I lit on the next step down from his. He had a clear pitcher beside him the size of a barrel half-filled with a pale golden liquid. I wasn't naïve enough to think it was lemonade. A chased goblet that would have made a good bucket sat empty beside it. That had been the object in his hand.

"Are you okay?" I asked. "Everybody's been wondering where you are."

Aahz sat up and sighed.

"I just needed to get away by myself for a while," he said. "These last few days have been kind of tough on the ego."

"I can understand that," I said.

Aahz poured himself a drink. He offered me the goblet. I shook my head, and he took a hefty gulp.

"You sounded like you were in a panic when you came flitting up here," he said. "Something the matter?" He aimed a talon at my nose. "Don't try to hedge. I've been watching you and the others tiptoe around me for weeks. What's on your mind?"

"Nothing!"

"Skeeve, you're a lousy liar. What's going on?"

No use in hedging, as he said, though there wasn't a shrub in sight. "We've been worried about you."

"What *about* me? I'm not the one who got lost in the sand for three days and hitched a ride home with Shrouds-R-Us."

I shrugged. "We've been kind of worried about your health."

"Why? I'm eating and drinking. Everything else is functioning just fine, thanks. What makes you think I'm not well?"

"Well . . . it's just . . . you've been nice to people lately."

"I'm always nice to people!" he roared. "What are you talking about?"

I smiled. That sounded like the old Aahz.

"It's not just that," I acknowledged. "We were concerned as to why you wanted to be involved in Samwise's project so badly. I saw your face when he started describing the pyramid stones, the carving, the mourners and everything. We've turned down working on jobs like this in the past. It's nothing special. It's construction. But you've taken this very personally. After finding out Samwise is responsible for bringing the curse on himself and everybody involved, we would have walked away from a situation like this in the past, but you've hung on. Why?"

Aahz threw himself on his back again and looked up at the sky.

"Legacy."

"Legacy?" I echoed, feeling panic rising again. "Then, there is something wrong with you? I'm your best friend. Will you tell me what it is?"

"There's nothing wrong with me!" he shouted. "I don't have to be at death's door to wonder what people are going to think about me when I'm gone. By then, it's too late. I'm not as young as I used to be. When Samwise sat down in our office and let loose with his sales spiel is when I really started thinking about it.

"I tend to live with an eye on the future, but it's not my primary focus. But, you know, as time goes by, you start to think about things. What have I ever done that anyone will remember me for? My kids don't talk to me. I've spent a lot of time kicking around, but what have I really accomplished? What's my mark on the future? Where is it? What did Aahzmandius ever do to earn a footnote in history?"

"There's M.Y.T.H., Inc.," I pointed out.

He opened one yellow eye and aimed it at me. "That's not my legacy, kid. That's yours. Bunny may be in charge now, but if you really wanted to run it again, no one would say no, not even me. Everyone in the Bazaar knows you established it. It runs on your principles. Not that that's all bad," he added.

"You were Garkin's friend," I said.

"So what? He had a lot of friends. He was a swell guy."

"I was with him for months, and no one ever dropped in on him except you," I said.

"That means either I'm too dense to know that he wanted to be alone, or he never passed the threshold of pissing me off so I left him alone, too."

"Well, if you hadn't been his friend, you wouldn't have been there that day when Isstvan's assassins killed him," I said reasonably. "They'd probably have taken me out, too. I could hardly muster enough magik to light a candle. I wasn't in any shape to fight a couple of armed Imps."

.

Aahz grunted. "So I saved your life. Maybe. You've returned the favor a dozen times. We're even."

"But you taught me everything I know," I said. "I mean, what would have happened, say, if I'd wandered into the Bazaar on my own . . ."

I let my thoughts peter out. Aahz *had* more or less let me wander around on my own, which is how I got to meet Tananda, who was now one of my best friends; and how I acquired a dragon that Aahz had only in later years admitted was not such a big pest as he had been at first. "Anyhow, you've been my mentor and my partner. I guess it may not seem like a lot to accomplish, but you changed my life. All that I have, I owe to you. And that includes M.Y.T.H., Inc."

Aahz made a sour face. "Kid, that's the kind of hogwash I expect to hear on a soap opera." He held up a hand to forestall the question that was on the way out of my open mouth. "It's a drama series in which commercial messages are interrupted by actors spouting angst at each other. And hogwash is what comes off a hog after a bath, not what you use to clean it. But thanks for trying to cheer me up. I was more looking for the kind of deed that would mean something to future generations. Changing the world, somehow."

"Maybe that's still ahead of you," I said hopefully. I cudgeled my brains to come up with a deed that would fulfill his wishes, but I wasn't used to thinking in that broad a scope. I put the notion away to confer with our friends later on.

"Yeah, well, maybe. I know a hollow rock isn't what I'm thinking of, but it got me thinking. I didn't think my day was done, but it hurts not to be able to make a splash even when I want to. I had a great rep as a master magician, and I earned it, kid. People were impressed by me. My name meant something. I had promise. Now I have to listen to small time shysters like Samwise call me a has-been. I thought waiting a century was no big deal for the joke powder to wear off, but a guy can only take so many hits to his ego."

"Everyone respects you," I said.

"Seeing is believing," Aahz said. "I couldn't do anything

to save that broken corner of Phase One. *You* saved the day. It was damned impressive. You ought to be proud of that."

"I wouldn't have been able to do that without your help," I said. It was the truth.

But I knew what he meant. The crowd that had looked for his expertise had suddenly turned away from him. It had felt good to get credit, but not at Aahz's expense. I just sat there, unable to think of anything to say that didn't sound like . . . hogwash.

Sighing, I looked out over the construction site. From our vantage point way above the desert floor, we had a great view of Phase One. The fourth tier was coming along nicely. I wondered about the well-being of all the investors and whether they were getting hit as hard by the bad-luck stick as we had been. I couldn't see Beltasar and her individual workers at this distance, but I saw the tide of iridescent shells surging and receding under each stone as it moved. Their strength still impressed me.

"You could have taken credit for saving the pyramid," I said at last. "I expected you to. That's one of the reasons that Guido and I were worried about you. You usually go for part of the glory."

"Yeah, well . . . I missed you, too, over all those months. I resolved that I wouldn't be so stingy about credit in the future. You've never been selfish about giving others their due. I could learn a little from you, too."

That made me feel prouder than any other commendation I could have received from kings or industrial leaders.

"Thanks," I said.

"Don't let it go to your head. I'm still going to call you on it if you screw up. If nothing's going wrong right now, I'm just going to lie here and soak up some rays." He patted the sweating pitcher beside him. "Want a drink? The local hooch packs a pretty good wallop."

"No, thanks," I said. I was so relieved that he wasn't going to die that I felt a surge of energy. "I'm going to go into town and check in with Chumley. He said he was going to investigate the Mumsy's curse. I'll see if he found any-thing."

"Fine," Aahz said, not looking down at me. "Don't hurry back. I'm enjoying myself."

I turned to go.

Gurn leered up at me from the next step down.

"Quite a view you have from up here," he said.

TWENTY-SIX

> *"Who let the sacred cat out of the bag?"*
> —PHARAOH SHESHONK I

I was so startled I took a step back into nothingness. My arms wheeled in wild circles as I tried to save myself. A strong hand clasped around my wrist and dragged me back onto the invisible framework.

"Watch it, kid," Aahz said, releasing me. He glared at the small courtier. "What in hell are you doing here?"

"Just as I was about to congratulate you on being saved from a sandy grave," Gurn said, with a wicked grin that did nothing for his distorted looks. "You nearly achieve it a second time."

"Get lost," Aahz said. "This is private property."

"All property in Aegis belongs to her majesty," Gurn said. "But by all means, send me away! I can go back to her majesty with the news that her precious pyramid is infested with a curse!"

Aahz and I looked at each other. It would be the end of Phase One, let alone Phase Two, if the Pharaoh withdrew her permission to build. We'd be sunk.

"How do you know that? I've been keeping an ear on the gossip, and no one's talking about it," Aahz said.

"No one but her majesty's esteemed wise man, he who travels in the outer lands until he is needed—or so he says."

"Ch— Lord Wat-Is-Et would never tell you anything like that."

"Oh, it was not me he told, but the words came from his mouth," Gurn said. "You should pay closer attention to the discretion of your friends."

"One of which you aren't," Aahz said lazily. "You keep turning up like a bad coin."

"I go where I want to, in her majesty's name!" Gurn said. "Observing, for example, all of the accidents that have occurred on the site of what should be her most glorious monument."

"*Causing* all those accidents, I wouldn't be surprised," said Aahz.

"You fool! I have been *preventing* accidents!" Gurn shrieked.

He aimed his little finger at Phase One. I reached out to stop him, and found my hands encased in a crackling sphere of magik.

"Hold your fire until you know what I am doing, Klahd," he said. "Foolish heroics . . . idiotic waste of time. Use your mind's eye, if you call yourself a magician."

I peered down. Beltasar's people were moving a stone up a ramp. It had stopped dead, Gurn's doing. I watched the turquoise dot that was the chief Scarab fly around and around them, haranguing her USHEBTIs into getting it going again. I couldn't tell what she was saying at that distance, but the shrill tone was unmistakable.

Then, a red-shelled Scarab, whom I knew as Rayd, came flitting toward her from upslope. The two of them flew in a circle, shrieking to one another, then zipped toward a portion of the invisible ramp.

It was not only invisible, but nonexistent. Gurn sneered at me.

"Before you ask, Klahd, no. I didn't do that. The curse did it."

We watched as the Scarabs called for a site magician. A female in pleated robes came hustling up the slope, obviously called away from lunch, food still in her hand, to perform an emergency repair. She put down her meal and started drawing down power from the force lines in the sky. Once the foundation was filled in, Gurn waved his hand again. The Scarabs tugged the stone into motion. They got it safely up onto the fourth tier and settled it in place.

"That's a really good spell," I said admiringly.

Our little moment of camaraderie was at an end. Gurn glared. "Don't patronize me, Klahd!"

"I'm not," I said. "I am impressed. But why not tell people what you've been doing here to help?"

"Instead of turning up like a bad coin?" Gurn threw our words back at us. "Why? It's none of their business. Just as I do not tell her majesty all the things that go on here, such as playing around with the help . . ."

Aahz scowled. "That's nobody's business, either."

"It has become everyone's business, thanks to your partner in mischief. You had to pick the one lady who talks," Gurn said, amused. "Or that one of her trusted ministers has another name? Cholmondley, is it?"

"Just Chumley," I said. "So what? Does it change what he is? His intelligence isn't fake. He's one of the smartest and wisest people I know."

"He is fortunate in his friends, but her majesty should be served with all truth. I could have you thrown in the deepest dungeons in the coldest and darkest part of Aegis!"

"Been there, done that," I said, with a yawn.

"*This* time you will not have Necrops to weave you warm underwear. To lie to her majesty is to insult the Ghords!"

"Gotcha there, pal," Aahz said, turning up on one elbow and grinning. "You're not telling her everything, either. You say she still doesn't know about the curse. That's withholding information. Or, as you insist on calling it, lying."

Gurn looked furious, as if he was about to throw his amazing stopping spell on Aahz.

"But why keep our secrets at all?" I asked, trying to defuse the situation. "You know the pyramid's cursed."

"Because her majesty sincerely wants this," Gurn said, with a sigh. "She is my life. I would do anything not to put her nose out of joint." Once again, I was captivated by a memory of her face. Aahz, too. He must have known what we were thinking, and gave us a fierce look. "You call yourselves problem-solvers. You are accepting that fool Samwise's capital to do it, but you spend your time up here feeling sorry for yourselves. I would call you frauds."

"Hey!" Aahz said. "Taking a little time off to recharge is not fraud."

"It is if you are failing to earn your commission," Gurn said. "I lay a second charge upon you: break the spell. *Now*. Her majesty must be freed of the affliction that causes her to lose the royal lunch almost as soon as it is consumed. If you figure out a way to solve the problem, she need never know. Otherwise, I will see you and that idiotic Imp locked in that dungeon until you have use for this invisible pyramid stone you keep visiting. My patience is not infinite. You must solve this problem quickly, or I will see to it that you suffer every punishment. I give you one week."

"Don't you think we have been working on it?" Aahz demanded.

"Perhaps without a sufficient goad to your back. Here is mine. I can have you imprisoned and tortured if you don't succeed. And I will enjoy it."

"Do you know how to undo the bad luck?" I asked.

Gurn looked up at me. "Why should I help you? Perhaps Diksen will change his mind and construct a pyramid fit for her majesty instead of this commercial monstrosity."

"And maybe pigs will go into investment banking," Aahz said. "I'd give the same odds to each event. This is the only stone triangle she's going to get, and you know it."

"Do I?" Gurn asked, aiming a pugnacious chin at him.

"We all want this to work," I said, getting between them. "Okay, maybe for different reasons, but we want it to be a big success. On a theoretical basis, how would you lift a curse that the maker refuses to undo?"

"Why, get him involved in it," Gurn said, with an innocent look. "Use your imagination."

Before I could ask him more, he vanished.

TWENTY-SEVEN

"Looking for love in all the wrong places."
—R. MONTAGUE

A week in Ghordon was seven days, the same as it was in Klah or Deva. That didn't give us much time to figure out how to get through to Diksen or find a means of breaking the curse without his help.

We went back to Deva for a brainstorming session with the rest of M.Y.T.H., Inc.

"Why don't we just back out of the project?" Bunny asked.

"No," Aahz said flatly. "We stay. Or if you all want to cut ties, I'll stay."

"I'll stay with him," I said.

"Then, what do we do?" our president asked.

"I could break into Diksen's office," Tananda said. "What if I went in through the top of the sphere and used a commercial freeze spell the way Markie did? If we knew when he goes out, I could search through his paperwork. If he found out I had been there, and he would, what could he do to me? We've already been affected by the curse."

"The answer to your second question is 'plenty,'" Aahz said. "The guy has some advanced ideas about privacy. We were only in his study for a few minutes. If he'll booby-trap plans he's throwing away, who knows what he's got on his permanent files? And as for the first question, useless. What if you did find a dogeared page in his 'Book of My Favorite Curses'? He still won't take it off."

"Bribery?" asked Spider. She and Pookie had come back for the current staff meeting to make sure I was still breathing, and offered their expertise. "There must be something the guy wants more than revenge."

"It might have worked before we confronted him, but I doubt his pride will let him accept anything now."

"Persuasion?" Pookie suggested. I knew what kind of persuasion she meant. The clingy jumpsuits that Aahz's cousin favored still managed to conceal a remarkable arsenal.

"It'd have to be psychological," Nunzio said. "I didn't see too many holes in security."

"That bubble is eminently defensible," Guido added. "He has the advantage of bein' able to see approaches from a long distance."

"Everyone's vulnerable somewhere," Pookie insisted.

"Again, he's pretty tough," I said. "I think the only reason he didn't start flinging all of us out of his office that night was because we were there under See-Ker's protection. He has no reason to hold back on intruders. Samwise said he didn't need to have other safeguards because of his reputation, but he earned it somehow."

"I am still upset with Samwise for bringing us in under false pretenses," Bunny said. Aahz flinched. "It's really not your fault, Aahz. There was only one person who could deny he had come by those plans legitimately, and we didn't ask him. We wouldn't have, considering that Diksen was running what we saw as a rival architectural concern. But it does us no good to continue to be associated with Samwise."

"I don't want to walk away from the project yet," Aahz said. "Samwise deserves it, but the rest of his people don't. In any case, it's still in our best interests to maintain contact until the curse is off."

"So, what's the best way forward?" Bunny asked. She didn't ask again if we insisted on staying on the job. Aahz aimed a talon at the ground.

"Gotta be Diksen himself. Find his weaknesses, and we find a way to persuade him to undo the problem."

"Research," Bunny sighed.

"I'll check into where he went to magik school, and where he lived before he settled in the Zyx Valley," Tananda said. "Maybe there's something in his records we can exploit."

"I'll make the rounds of magicians and wizards I know who've studied malicious magik," Aahz said. "Tweety said he'd ask around his colleagues, too. I don't have to be on site all the time. There's nothing much going wrong that can't be explained by the curse, and most of it is minor. I'll check in daily for progress reports from the department heads."

"I'll watch Diksen," I said. "See if he has any contacts that will be friendlier to us than he is."

"Or any nasty habits we can exploit," Pookie said.

"Good," Bunny said. "We'll compare notes tomorrow evening. Meeting adjourned."

With the help of a rotating group of volunteer Camels, I staked out Diksen's pavilion from various points out in the desert. The Ghord magician spent most of his time there. Through the translucent walls I could see him pacing around in his sphere-top office. His mother's apartments were curtained off to keep out most of the sunshine. In the evening, I saw her silhouette appear against the wall.

The second afternoon I was watching, a hole opened in the side of the sphere. I was so groggy after the vigil of a day and a night that I almost missed it. I slapped my own cheek to make myself wake up.

Diksen sailed out through the hole on a magik carpet. Even though the skies were empty and cloudless, I didn't dare lose him. Any chance to pick up information I could use to change his mind was worth taking.

"Follow that carpet," I instructed my Camel.

"Oh, that's easy," she said over her shoulder, nevertheless setting off behind the fast-disappearing figure. "Diksen always goes to the Kazbah in the afternoon."

She was right. We skimmed along the sands in time to see him set down on the edge of the crowded market. As Diksen stepped off the carpet, it rolled up into a tight cylinder. Diksen set it against a handy wall along with several others. He strode off into the crowd just as I got off my Camel.

I assumed a disguise as a Ghord with the head of a goat, as my normal appearance would excite too much comment. The merchants shouted about their wares, offered me tea or beer, but didn't try to insist when I politely foisted them off. I worried about losing Diksen in the huge crowds. People stopped abruptly in the middle of the street to gossip to one another, scream, complain or complete a speedy transaction. I felt a hand going for my belt pouch, and left the pickpocket stuck to a tent pole with a rope of magik. I didn't want to have to deal with the authorities. This might be my only chance to see where Diksen went.

We turned into the street past the wagons full of knick-knacks.

"Preserve your cultured milk solids! Keep your renneted comestibles safe from . . ." The seller of cheese plates called out to the magician, then stopped in mid-cry as he focused on who it was. Hastily, he covered the pyramid shapes with a length of faded cloth and held up a doll with the head of a dog. "Toys!" he shouted. "Toys for your precious children!"

Diksen stalked on, not even sparing a glance for the merchant. I scurried along behind him.

We were heading toward the oldest booths now. As he turned a corner I ducked behind a handy fold of cloth and changed my head for the face of a fish. My feet looked like silver fins now. I collected a few admiring glances for my natty appearance.

He strode onward through the street of food vendors. I dodged past My-Nah's booth, struggling to avoid a pig-headed female and her half-dozen or so offspring all clamoring to be fed first. An itinerant merchant with an open box slung around his neck followed a well-dressed Ghordess with a bird's head.

"You want this, dear lady! It will undo all the crow's-foot wrinkles that nature has wished upon you! It will wipe out all the signs of age that mar your loveliness!"

He sprayed a thin film into the air. Some of it landed on the lady. To my surprise, it did wipe out the lines next to her eyes. I got caught in the spray as well. It smelled like tangy fruit. I coughed and wiped my face.

Diksen's pace slowed. The sellers of antique documents were in the next section. I deduced that we had reached his destination. I kept close to the wall and peered around it cautiously to see what he was doing.

As I had guessed, he was talking closely with the nearer of the scroll sellers, the elderly female. Diksen thumbed through the piled charts on her shabby table as she exaggerated the wonders of each piece. As I watched, she looked both ways up the narrow corridor, and pulled a parcel wrapped in a length of cloth from below a table. Diksen unwrapped it to reveal a book. His eyes gleamed. I peered at it, trying to sound out the glyphs on the cover.

"Hello!" a voice said suddenly. Something brushed my leg. I jumped. "It is Master Skeeve, isn't it? Have you come to eat lunch?"

Startled, I turned around. Matt was looking up at me.

Bunny and Tananda had taken it upon themselves to continue to offer me further dating lessons whenever I came back to headquarters. "If a girl runs into you once, it's chance," Bunny had said. "Twice is deliberate."

"Oh, hi," I said, swallowing my shock. I realized that the spray the merchant had doused me with must have dispelled my disguise. I put my hand up against the wall and leaned against it, hoping I looked nonchalant. "I was just . . . yes, I thought I'd come back here for lunch. What a coincidence to run into you! Have you eaten? May I join you?"

"Why not? This is a good place to watch people." Matt led me to a narrow table up against a stone wall. My-Nah dropped off two bowls of food. I took a big spoonful. "The sellers of magikal texts are that way," she added conversationally, tilting her head toward the end of the alley. "But you know that already, don't you?"

I choked, spraying out my mouthful. The sacred cats underneath the table protested at the rain of green and brown granules. I hastily employed magik to remove the detritus. The cats were cleaned, but not amused. Matt went on as if I had not reacted.

"My employer is over there, examining a book on exotic plants. The last time I came this way to pick up a purchase that Diksen had ordered, they were most excited to tell me that a foreign magician had made inquiries of them, and did Diksen have any books or scrolls on placating the Ancients that he might choose to sell?"

"You don't say," I managed to sputter out. I kept my nose in my bowl. Matt ate with ladylike half-spoonfuls.

She smiled at me indulgently. "Oh, yes. They were eager to make a commission. It seemed to be most interesting that you want the very thing that would solve your problem."

"Matt, I . . ."

She twitched her fingertip at me, and the plumes on her head bobbed. "Go on, eat your lunch. People are watching."

I picked up my spoon, then dropped it again as Diksen appeared at the end of the food booths. Hastily, I reassumed my fish-faced disguise. I expected him to have a bundle under his arm, but he didn't. He glanced toward me with little interest, but only addressed Matt.

"Stop upstairs . . . dictation . . . association meeting. Oh, buy sweets . . . mother."

"Of course, sir," Matt said.

She pulled a feather from the top of her head and made a couple of notes on a parchment roll she took from her belt

pouch. Reading upside down, I saw her make a glyph of a
feather with an open mouth over it, and a picture of a Ghord
with the kind of swollen face I associated with toothache.
Diksen gave me a rough nod and started walking again.

"I had better go," she said. "Good luck. I won't tell him
I saw you."

She smiled at me and followed her boss. I began to think
she must really like me.

TWENTY-EIGHT

"You're supposed to have ulterior motives."
—CASANOVA

I didn't dare return to my place of concealment in the desert the rest of that day, knowing that Matt almost certainly knew I was out there. I was afraid that wittingly or unwittingly she might draw Diksen's attention to me. Instead, I left a Camel on duty with instructions to send me a glyph if Diksen emerged again.

I returned to the office. Samwise was seeing out a party of Gargoyles who obviously enjoyed their tour of the site.

"Matching corners will be no problem as long as you don't mind waiting for Phase Two," the Imp said, his arm around the wings of the granite-jawed male. He clutched a set of contracts to him with the kind of gleeful possessiveness that assured me they were signed. "It'll be just like looming over your favorite cathedral. Thanks for dropping by! Visit us any time. I'll be happy to see you."

I dragged him aside as soon as the Gargoyles had left. "How can you keep selling spots in these buildings knowing what could happen to those people?"

"I have faith in you," Samwise said. "I said to myself, it can't be too bad if M.Y.T.H., Inc., is still on the job. I know you'll get it all fixed up. My expenses don't stop just because you discovered the problem—and isn't that why I hired you in the first place? You'll make it better, and I can go on just as I planned." He slapped me on the back.

Gurn's cryptic statement that we should get Diksen 'involved' with the pyramid project left my mind a blank, but some of my partners had come up with creative ideas.

"It's obvious," Aahz had said. "If we manage to spread the curse back to him, he'll have to take it off."

Nunzio had made a suggestion that I was about to put into operation. If anyone who bought a tomb from Samwise was afflicted with the curse, then if we could get Diksen to accept one, he'd be cursed, too. Of course, we couldn't expect him to pay us for it, so it would have to be a gift. Samwise protested at offering up one of his prime locations for nothing, but I pointed out to him that he could end up with nothing. If Diksen felt like he was part of the project, he might be inclined to think more kindly of it. Either way, I doubted we could lose.

I had the deed etched onto a handsome slab of red marble, with the location picked out in gold, and a full sales brochure scribed onto the back.

"Now, I need a volunteer," I said, addressing the Ghord carvers at the water jug. "All you have to do is take this slab to Diksen. I'll supply transportation. Make sure you hand it to him personally."

Lol-Kit peered at me sideways. "It sounds dangerous. Why don't you take it to him?" she asked.

"It's a gesture of goodwill," I said. "I don't want it to carry more weight than just a simple gift. If I brought it, I might make him feel obligated, and that's not what we want. Right, Samwise?"

The Imp gulped nervously. "Right. Right, of course! It's just a present."

I could tell that most of the scribes were scared witless

at the thought of confronting the magician. To my surprise Pe-Kid, the green-faced Ghord, raised his hand.

"I'll do it," he said. "Maybe I can get a tour of that white pyramid."

"Idiot!" Lol-Kit said, shaking her head.

Before he could change his mind, I walked Pe-Kid down to the pier where Balu, our volunteer Camel was waiting. I saw them off, and hoped for the best. Either Diksen would accept it as a gift, or we'd manage to infest him with the curse. Either reaction should get the result we hoped for.

Unfortunately, we didn't have long to wait for the response. I heard the yell before I could see where it was coming from.

"Aaaaaa— AAAAAAGGGGGH!"

I looked up in time to see a figure hurtling down on me from the sky. I reached out with a net of magik, and intercepted Pe-Kid before he smashed into the ground. He landed on top of me. He got up and danced around in a circle, beating at the back of his kilt. It was on fire.

"Good will?" he sputtered. "He threw me out! With extreme prejudice!"

"Gee, I'm sorry," I said, sincerely. "I never guessed that Diksen would attack a messenger. Uh, where's the deed?"

Huffily, Pe-Kid held up a fist. He opened it, and red sand sifted down onto the flagstones. He stalked away without another word.

So the direct approach wasn't going to work. Subtler means were needed.

I tried leaving an interesting-looking document on the scroll-sellers' wagon with a deed to a slab written in small print in the corner. A passing thief picked it up and stuffed it into the front of his tunic. He was run over by a wagon full of cabbages at the next intersection.

I remembered from my shortened lunch with Matt that Diksen's mother liked sweets. I sought out the merchant that she favored, and had them send a box of the best dried fruits to the sphere. That afternoon, I watched them fall out of the bottom of the ball of water like a rain of pruny hailstones. They dropped into the sand, never to be seen again.

I was not optimistic when I returned to M.Y.T.H., Inc., that evening. None of my partners looked any more cheerful than I felt.

"I didn't find a thing," Tananda said, her legs curled under her in the exotic pouffe chair. "He was an honor student at M.I.T. Graduated at the top of his class."

I was impressed. The Magicians Institute of Thaumaturgy was the best school on the list maintained by the Council of Wizards. If I'd had the resources and, to be honest, the knowledge it had existed, I would have tried for it when I was starting out.

"Tweety said Diksen's a member in good standing of the Magicians' Club," Aahz said, though it looked as if it hurt to say so. "Never a single complaint. He's been in longer than I have . . . was."

I didn't say anything, but that statement filled in a blank for me.

"As far as I can tell, he's got no exotic hobbies, not much in the way of outside activities and if he has friends or lovers, he's amazingly discreet about all of them," Bunny said, referring to Bytina's screen. "He takes good care of his mother, and he minds his own business."

"We have no in," I said glumly. "Maul-De never goes out during daylight. Diksen goes to the Kazbah several afternoons a week. He visits a few shops in the capital, but never goes to the royal palace. None of the shopkeepers will tell me a thing."

"What about his secretary?" Bunny asked. "She seemed to like you."

"She won't say anything," I said. "She got upset when I asked her."

"All right," Bunny said, sitting upright in her chair. "We'll keep plugging away at our other prospects. Any other business we need to talk about?"

Bunny's question got me thinking. I hadn't really pushed Matt for information because it made both of us uncomfortable.

But there was more at stake now. I was worried about Gurn making good on his threat. I didn't want to spend any more time underneath the surface of Ghordon than I already had. I was also concerned about Aahz. He insisted on hanging on to Samwise's project in spite of the Imp's dishonesty. I, too, hated to leave the pyramids. It was one of the most fascinating things I had ever seen, watching the triangular buildings take shape from the ground up. The moment a stone was in place, it looked as if it had been there forever. I understood Aahz's attraction to them. But in the last few days, Aahz had lost his wallet once, gotten bashed by a falling hammer, had a Deveel woman slap him in the face because she thought he'd been the one to pinch her backside, and suffered several more papercuts, something that had never happened in his entire life. I just couldn't see him suffer any longer, if there was anything I could do about it.

I had to take a risk and see if I could get Matt to help me. Perhaps, if she came to think of me as a nice guy, she would sympathize with our position. I had been taking lessons from a couple of the smartest women I had ever known. It was time to put some of that knowledge to use. I would ask Matt on a real date.

"Don't make an invitation an all-or-nothing proposition," Bunny had warned me in one of our late evening sessions. "Make it easy for her to say yes, but leave it open for her to say no if she has to. Both of you will be less embarrassed. Make it friendly and casual."

To me, the best way not to provoke an instant "no" from her was not to invite her in person. I was too nervous to ask her face-to-face, and I really didn't want to take a chance on running into Diksen again. I would send her a glyph. Everybody in Ghordon used them. Why shouldn't I? Matt said she got messages all day, and her boss didn't mind.

But I had never sent a glyph. I needed help. I glanced around the office as I went in. Miss Tauret gave me a pleasant smile. I knew she sent and received plenty of glyphs, but she was the last person I could trust to keep confidence for me. None of the other clerks in the office were good candidates, since they all worked closely together. The curse was still more of a rumor than a reality, and I wanted to keep it that way. I also didn't want anybody teasing me about girls.

Ay-Talek was the obvious choice. The chief scribe was an older Ghordess who would understand that I didn't want a potential date to become news across Aegis.

I found Ay-Talek working on a stone with a dozen apprentices in front of her, all very young. The lion-headed boy Ghord at her feet was still missing one fang, and his mane hadn't grown in yet. The reptile-headed girl's teeth were rounded instead of pointed. But they were intent on the lesson.

I was fascinated, too, as Ay-Talek lectured, tapping out a careful glyph with her hammer and chisel. I started to read the engravings already on the huge stone block. I'd picked up a bit of the language, but not enough for the subtleties of an invitation. Still, I thought I could read some of the text. A thief, or so the picture of the male with hand in someone else's belt pouch indicated. I wasn't sure about the next image. From the rows of sharp teeth that had been etched in, it looked a little like a dragon, or maybe a lizard-headed Ghord. Ay-Talek was working on another glyph on a lower row. The patron who had purchased this stone was rich, or wanted the reader of this epitaph to think he was rich. Really rich. It was definitely a man's stone. He had won some kind of game that meant a lot to him. He had many people that looked up to him. He had two wives—no, girlfriends—no, female friends. In fact, he had lots of friends. I skimmed a few more glyphs. This man had had success in business. He was wise, lucky, liked playing cards, enjoyed good food and wine. I suddenly realized it seemed this person had led a life a lot like mine, except that I didn't have an ugly father. No names had yet been filled in, and no indicators were present to show what race the person came from.

"Who's this one for?" I asked curiously.

"All identities are confidential unless the client releases the information," Ay-Talek said crisply. She definitely was the person I needed to help me.

"Well, if the owner comes back to the site, will you tell him I'd like to meet him?" I asked. "He sounds like someone I'd like to know."

"Certainly," Ay-Talek said. She brushed stone grit off her lap and smiled at me. "What may I do for you?" I glanced at the children. She shooed them away. "Go play for a while! And don't get in the Scarabs' way!" The little ones ran off, and Ay-Talek tilted her head at me.

"I need a small favor," I said, once I was sure no one could overhear us. "How can I send a glyph to someone?"

"Is that all?" Ay-Talek asked. "Of course. Sit down."

She picked up a scrap of papyrus and tightened her skirts around her knees to form a desk. "What is it you want to say?"

"Uh, there's this young lady . . ."

"Say no more," the scribe said, a dimple showing in her feathered cheek. "And you wish to declare your heart?"

"Oh, no! I just want to take her out on a date. How do I write that?"

"It is very simple," Ay-Talek said. With a reed pen, she sketched a few lines that almost magically resolved into the figure of a male Ghord on his knees with a bouquet in one hand and a heart in the other.

"Not one knee?" I asked, frowning.

Ay-Talek laughed. "Not unless you are proposing marriage! Where do you wish to take her?" She held the pen poised.

"Uh, I don't know yet," I said. "First I want to find out if she's even interested."

"As you wish. But let us put it on a nicer papyrus, in your own handwriting, of course. I don't think we will try a hammer and chisel for your first attempt."

She handed me the pen and a clean square of paper. With some difficulty I copied the glyph.

"Now, fold it like this," she said. I followed her movements until the missive was tightly rolled up from one corner to the opposite corner and the ends twisted like tiny wings. "Think of your ladylove and send it off." When I hesitated, she patted my hand. "It's a very reliable system. Go ahead."

I let go of the tiny wad of papyrus. It lifted up and shot away, joining a stream of other little rapid-moving nuggets of information.

"Will you help me read the reply if she answers?" I asked.

"Certainly," Ay-Talek said. "Look, here it is now."

"It couldn't be," I said, disbelievingly, as a small knob of paper dropped into my hands, its wings crisp with heat.

"They only go to the person to whom they are addressed. Let's see what she said."

I unfolded it. All that was on the minute page was the image of a puzzled clock face. "She couldn't read it," I said, crestfallen.

Ay-Talek shook her head. "Not at all. She is asking where and when."

"You choose," I said.

"Not I," said the clerk. "This is your love life, not mine."

"No, I mean, how do I tell her, 'you choose'? Where would she like to go?"

Ay-Talek nodded understandingly. "Ah. You are a nice young man." I followed her quick scribbling on a new sheet. The answer was in my hands almost as soon as my papyrus ball flew out of sight.

The new message had two glyphs on it.

"She says," Ay-Talek told me, pointing at the pictograph of a smiling Ghord with a tweezer-like face under a half-sun, "'Come tomorrow at noon. We will visit the lair of Shan-Tun. It will be fun.'"

"And what does that one say?" I asked, pointing to the image of a man who wore a disheveled looking kilt.

"'Don't wear good clothes.' Good luck, young man!"

How odd, I thought, but it was Matt's choice.

TWENTY-NINE

"I was just stringing him along."
—ARACHNE

Bunny and Tananda were delighted that I had taken their suggestion to approach Matt. I took both of them with me shopping in the Bazaar to find a small present to give her along with the flowers that Tananda insisted I bring. I suggested a little enameled box that kept food fresh, so she didn't always have to trust My-Nah's not very delicious meals for her brief noon breaks.

"A first-date present should be useful but not practical," Bunny said. "If you brought her a lunchbox, she has every right, according to the universal women's charter, to hit you with it."

"Then what should I bring her?" I asked, replacing it on the display with regret.

"Nothing intoxicating, fattening, or intimate," Tananda added. "Just considerate."

"Then, you pick it out," I suggested.

"Oh, no!" they chorused. "This has to be your choice!"

I ended up with a miniature picture frame that captured the images of anything you pointed it at. I figured she could display a picture of the sacred cats. They also insisted I buy a little peach-colored silk bag to carry it in, instead of wrapping it in the heavy gray paper the Deveel merchant used. He gave me a sympathetic glance as we left.

The local Ghords assured me I couldn't get to Shan-Tun's on Camel-back, but they gave me good directions on how to get there by air.

I found Matt at the appointed hour on a cliff-top about forty miles to the east of the Zyx Valley. A lonely-sounding wind whistled around us, kicking up dust. There wasn't a single plant or a blade of grass for miles. It was the most unappealing site I could imagine for a date. Matt waved to me as I flew in. She had on a pleated white robe like those she wore to the office, but her skirts were divided into trousers. Her long, feathery black hair was braided under her headdress, which was held tightly to her forehead by a red band.

"Hi," I said. I cudgeled my brains to remember my lessons. "Uh, you look nice."

"This old thing?" she asked, looking down at her outfit. "It is comfortable. I am glad that you took my advice." She indicated my clothing. I had followed her instructions with regard to clothes, picking out garments that were good enough to be seen in but not dressy. Both Tananda and Bunny had verified my selection.

"Yes. I, uh . . ." My throat went tight. I thrust the small silk bag at her at arm's length. "Um, this is for you."

Her eyebrows went up in amusement. "For me? That is most kind of you, but unnecessary."

"It's not? I mean, it's just a little gift. I hope you like it. And these are for you, too." I handed her the flowers. She laughed. When she opened the bag and saw the frame, she laughed some more. This wasn't going as well as I hoped.

"Such formal presentations," she said, tucking the stems of the flowers into the bag on top of the little frame. "I hope that you are going to be able to relax!"

"Relax?" I echoed, my voice rising against my will. "What are we doing?"

"You have never heard of Shan-Tun?" she asked. When I shook my head, she smiled. "It is something that I have always wanted to do. And as you were so generous as to let me choose our activity, I thought you might like to share the experience."

"What is it?"

"Shan-Tun and his partner Bon-Jee have devised a most daring amusement," Matt said. "Come and see."

I followed her over the crest of the barren hill. The hilltop sloped down slightly toward a sheer drop at the far end. There, two enormous creatures like caterpillars but each about the size of a Sphinx hunkered, spinning shining white threads between their hands. I realized that each of them had five or six sets of limbs.

"They are Silkwyrms," Matt said. "Their people make all the clothing for the royal family, but some of them have gone into business for themselves. As here."

A dog-headed Ghord stood between them. The Silk-wyrms applied some of those thin white threads around his chest, down between his legs and up again. As soon as they withdrew their touch, the Ghord let out a wild yell.

"Yee-ah!"

With that, he leaped backwards off the cliff. I cried out and ran to try and help him.

"No," Matt said, running after me. She caught my arm to hold me back. "It is what he wanted to do."

"But . . ." I sputtered. "He came here to kill himself?"

"Not at all," Matt began.

Suddenly, the Ghord came catapulting up out of the void, high over our heads. "Whee-hee-hee-yeah!" he bellowed. He dropped down again. In a moment, he bounded back again, a little lower. I could hear his happy cries echoing down the ravine. When the bouncing stopped, the two Silk-wyrms started reeling in the nearly invisible threads until the Ghord's head reappeared. They grasped him by the shoulders and pulled him back onto the cliff's edge.

"It is wonderful!" he told us, ears flapping. "You will love it!"

He joined a knot of Ghords who stood laughing and chat-tering at a safe distance from the edge. They must all have gone before him, because their headcloths were disheveled and windblown.

"Come, come," the larger Silkwyrm, Shan-Tun, said, gesturing to us. "You must take your turn, so the others can go again."

"This is what you want to do?" I asked Matt, a trifle disbelievingly. "Jump off a cliff?"

"Yes," she said. "Head first. I have been looking forward to this for ages!"

"Why not go first?" Shan-Tun asked me.

I looked down over the edge of the precipice. It was a long way to the valley's bottom. A riverbed cut through the yellow-gray wasteland, but it must have been centuries since any water flowed through it.

"How does this work?" I asked.

The smaller worm, Bon-Jee, worked his mouth pincers. "We spin fresh silk for every leap," he said. "We wind it around you. You leap. You bounce. It is refreshing. Hold still, sir, while I measure you." He extended three pairs of arms and wrapped them around my chest, shoulders, and between my legs. It tickled, but I did my best not to flinch.

"That will be one silver piece each," said Shan-Tun. "Do you wish to pay for the lady, too?"

"Uh, yes," I said, taking the money out of my belt pouch. They expected me to attempt suicide, constrained only by threads narrower than a strand of my hair, and they wanted me to pay for it? In advance? But Matt was watching me. I smiled as I paid.

I was less than confident as I watched them spin. They pulled the lengths of white out of their backsides. It didn't look sturdy enough, even after they braided it into a triple thickness of cord. It could snap like the thread it was, catapulting me into the void. Had I told anyone where I was going? Would it hurt when I landed, or would falling on my head kill me instantly?

Then, I gave myself a mental slap in the forehead.

What was I afraid of? Was I a magician for nothing? I could soar off the precipice and float downward at my leisure,

perfectly safe and secure. I'd impress Matt with my courage
and nonchalance. Maybe I'd even turn a somersault as I
bounced upward. Maybe two.

I looked around for force lines. A nice, moderate power
source followed the line of the ridge we were standing on.
Plenty of magik. I absorbed an adequate supply. I stood at
the edge of the cliff hanging on only by my toes and held
my arms out straight in front of me. I'd leap head first, then
do a series of somersaults on my way up.

"Look at me!" I called to Matt.

I bent my knees and prepared to jump.

"Oh, no, sir!" Shan-Tun exclaimed, grabbing me around
the chest. "No magik!"

"What?" I asked.

"You must not do *magik*," said Bon-Jee.

"Why not?"

"Did you not see our sign?" asked Shan-Tun. He pointed
to a sign pounded into the windy plain that I had missed on
our way over. I peered at the line of pictograms painted in
red, each more alarming-looking than the next. "No glyphing, no flying, no magik. It weakens our silk. You don't want
to land on your head, do you?"

"No! I mean, not even a little magik?" I asked. Suddenly
my perch on the very lip of the cliff seemed too unsteady.
I took a step closer in. Matt called out to me.

"What is wrong?"

"Nothing's wrong," I said.

"You must release all magikal power," Shan-Tun said.
"Trust us. We have not lost any of our jumpers."

"Not in weeks," agreed Bon-Jee. The two of them
laughed, their mandibles quivering.

That didn't make me feel any better. But I had no choice.
I had to do the jump relying only on the Silkwyrms' silk,
or chicken out and maybe have Matt scorn me. I desperately
needed her approval. She was the only source I had left for
getting through to Diksen. This was for Aahz.

"Well . . . all right," I said, though my heart had moved
up to my throat. I hesitated.

"We can let someone else go until you are ready," Bon-Jee said.

"No! I mean, I'll go. Just give me a moment."

For the first time since I had started learning magik, I deliberately emptied my internal reserve of all the power I had. It left me with an uncomfortable hollow sensation inside. I looked down. The dry river bed seemed twice as far away as it had been before.

The Silkwyrms' mandibles separated in what I translated as a broad grin.

"That's right, good sir. Now, go ahead and jump!"

I held my breath and took a step backward.

I remembered when I was little that some of my family put me on a blanket they held among them and tossed me high into the air. I laughed and yelled and begged for more.

This was nothing like that. As I went over the edge, my hair flew upward, and my clothes flapped against my body, as if they wanted to free themselves from someone crazy enough to jump off a cliff. All the nerve endings in my body tingled against my skin. They'd be the first to know when I struck the ground. I was falling too fast to draw breath. It wasn't like being dragged underground by the slowsands. There was plenty of air up here—too much, in fact. I screwed my eyes shut, waiting for the inevitable impact.

Suddenly, giants grabbed me by the chest and dragged me upward, back into the air I had just fallen through. My eyes were forced open. The blue sky seemed to loom closer and closer. I heard a sharp, thin, agonized noise. Someone was screaming.

It was me.

I was flung up over the cliff's edge. Matt stood with the Silkwyrms, watching me fly up, up, up, until I hit the acme of my arc. Then I started dropping again.

It was no more fun the second time.

Or the third.

Or the fourth.

By the time I had bounced for the fifth time, I could feel my breakfast, and probably last night's dinner, fighting to get out of my stomach. I was no longer screaming, since that required breath, and I had none to spare. My heart banged against the inside of my throat, and my eyes were popping out of my head. This time as I passed the edge of the cliff, the Silkwyrms grabbed me and helped me back onto solid ground.

I could have kissed it. As soon as Shan-Tun and Bon-Jee disconnected me from their threads, I staggered down into the center of the hilltop and just stood, shaking.

Matt cheerfully took her place in between the Silkwyrms. They attached the ropes to her and helped her back to the edge. She gave me a jaunty wave and leaped out into the empty air.

The happy cries of excitement she emitted while catapulting up and down left me feeling resentful and more than a little foolish. When she returned at last to the starting point, I put on a pleasant smile and went to meet her.

THIRTY

"The end always justifies the means."
——D. VADER

I had arranged for a fine lunch in a restaurant that Chumley had recommended in the capital city. The waiter, a Ghord in a tall, conical hat, seated us with many bows and compliments. He took Matt's flowers away and returned them in a pottery vase with a ribbon around it, then left us to read the menu.

"This wasn't the first time you've done that jump, was it?" I asked, as soon as he was out of earshot.

"Well, no," Matt admitted, with a sly grin. "But I thought you would enjoy it more if you believed it was the first time for both of us."

"You knew I couldn't use magik out there, didn't you?"

"Oh, yes." The grin broadened out into a smile. "It was very amusing, watching the terror on your face. Shan-Tun let you bounce an extra time just for fun." She touched my cheek, then bent her head to examine the menu. "Now, what shall we try?"

The thought made my stomach roil. "I don't think I'll ever be able to eat again," I said.

"Nonsense," Matt said. "The food smells marvelous. Just take a deep breath."

I did. My stomach forgave me the abuse it had undergone. By the time the waiter came back with a slate and a stylus to take our order, I had lined up in my mind all the lessons that Bunny and Tananda had hammered into me. I was prepared to be charming at all costs.

"And what will the lady have?" the waiter inquired.

I nodded to her. "Whatever she would like."

What Matt liked, as it happened, was the rarest and most expensive item on the list. I kept my face straight, and ordered an entrée for myself.

"What about appetizers? Soup? Salad?" I asked.

"Why, yes," Matt said. She put a dainty finger on the list and ran down her choices of three more courses. "And essence of minnetango to drink, perhaps." The waiter gasped. "What do you think?" she asked me.

"I think that sounds good," I said. "Two."

"Two?" the server asked. His careful air of nonchalance dissolved into open delight. He scurried away into the back room, where I heard exclamations of disbelief and happy astonishment. I guessed that minnetango must be pretty pricey. I was determined not to react, whatever Matt did. It was only money.

I made determined small talk as we dined. Matt picked at her meal. I ate heartily. The food was as good as Chumley had said it would be. I commented on it, asked polite questions, and avoided the subject that was nagging at me as long as I possibly could.

The minnetango arrived in golden cups no taller than my little finger on a solid gold tray accompanied by every server in the restaurant and the manager, who bowed as the tray was presented to us. In a less fancy place, it would probably have been accompanied by a brass band and a robed choir. The fragrance hit me even before the waiter set my cup before me. The few ounces of bronze-golden liquid smelled like a combination of a whole hothouse of roses simmered together with marshmallows and fifteen kinds of fruit. One sip told me I should never judge anything in advance. It tasted like boiled spiders. Matt tasted hers. Her lips curled in a small, contented smile that wouldn't have been out of place on the face of one of her cats.

"Uh, that's pretty good," I managed to choke out.

"We are proud of it," the manager said. "It takes a hundred Ghords a hundred days to make a single bottle! Enjoy!"

"This is a special occasion," I said, holding up my cup to Matt. "I've never jumped head-first off a cliff on purpose."

She looked a little sad, but extended her cup to touch to mine. "Your continued good health."

"Yours, too," I said. I took my time finishing it. One sip at a time was about all I could gag down. Matt drank hers, but with little apparent pleasure.

"And, now, dessert?" the waiter asked, appearing at my elbow.

"What would you like?" I asked Matt. I refrained from suggesting that she probably had no room for one, since she had eaten very little of four previous courses and a sorbet (offered as a palate cleanser between the salad and the entrée), but I could just hear Tananda giving me a piece of her mind if I criticized my date to her face. I was determined to do this absolutely right.

"Nothing, thank you."

I was surprised. "Are you sure?" I turned to the waiter. "Why don't you give us some more time to decide? I'll call you when we make up our minds."

He withdrew to a distance where he could see us, but not hear us.

Matt leaned close and put her slender hand on mine.

"You must want this information very badly," she said.

"What?" I was taken aback. "No! I mean, I'm enjoying our time together. In fact, I'd be happy to see you again, any time."

She shook her head. "You don't really like me. You are being a gentleman in the face of my outright rudeness. I would have preferred it if you took me out because you wanted my company. The truth is that you're using me, or you would like to."

I was shocked. I shook my head. "But I liked having lunch with you the last couple of times, and I have really enjoyed being with you this time. Didn't you have a good time at all?"

"It was a nice date," she conceded. "You were brave to try the jump even though you were afraid. It shows how determined you are, and I can respect that. I've seen your women friends, the ones who accompanied you that evening to confront Diksen. I'm not under any illusions that I'm the sort of person you would choose for yourself, or that they would choose for you."

I grinned uneasily, picturing fire elementals or brassy Jahk women in filmy trousers. "I'd be concerned about the girls that either Massha or Markie would fix me up with."

Matt shook her head. "Don't be. They know you pretty well, and they care deeply about you. But that is not the whole story."

She was right.

"What is it you want?" I asked.

"Tell the truth," Matt said. "That's the only thing that means anything to me."

Up until then I hadn't realized how much of the truth I had been bending just to get my way. I was ashamed of myself. I'd given up my dreams of being a successful thief a long time ago. I shouldn't try to steal anything, let alone information.

I opened my hands. "Aahz is my best friend. He's been my mentor, my partner, my friend, the one I have trusted for years. I am scared for him." I told her about my concern that he was sick and not telling anybody. "But I refuse to let a *deal* kill him. I don't like him suffering to satisfy your boss's need for revenge on someone else. I do need your help, and I'll do anything to get it. Haven't you ever had anyone you cared about like that?"

Matt crossed her arms. "Maybe. You haven't earned the right to ask me personal questions."

"Sorry," I said. "We talked about a lot of things. I thought we were getting to know each other. But I guess we really didn't."

"We did," Matt said. "I learned you wanted to use me to get what you want and you can be ruthless, though in a nice way. You learned I'm not as dumb as I look. But I didn't think you were . . . ! She took the tallest feather out of her headpiece and touched it to my hand. The black feather glowed silver. She returned it to the top of her head. "The feather of truth never lies. And you are not lying, about this, anyhow. You mean what you just said."

I was determined to be straightforward from then on. "No. Not about Aahz. Will you help me?"

Matt raised her eyebrows. "You want me to incur a curse from my boss?"

"Well, yes," I said frankly. "I'd do anything for Aahz. And he'd do anything for me. That I'm certain of."

"If I help you, you will owe me. You already owe me one favor, for attempting to use me."

"Then I owe you two." I showed her an open, honest face. "I admit I took you out to get information about Diksen. I'm worried about my friend and I saw you as my last hope. I do owe you, and I don't deny my obligations. You can call on me any time, for any reason. You have my word on it."

Matt nodded. "Good. We will call it a debt against the future. Then what is it you wanted?"

I grimaced. "The problems my partner is suffering are getting worse. You won't believe it, because you've only seen him yell and carry on, but he's really a sensitive guy."

"He does not seem at all sensitive, from my experience with him."

I squirmed a little. Aahz did strike people as overbearing. "Well . . . you have to know him better."

"That I do not wish to do," Matt said. "But I see that you are sincere in one facet of your life. He likes books."

"Who?"

"Diksen. He will pay any price for an exotic book of wisdom. He has been looking for a good or excellent copy of the *Magus Sutra* for years. That is all."

"That's all?"

She smiled, a wintry little expression. "With your deter-mination, it should be more than enough. I am sorry I will not be getting to know you. I would have treasured having a friend like you. I hope your partner appreciates what he has."

"I think so," I said. "I hope so."

THIRTY-ONE

"Never judge a book by its cover."
—T. SUMMERBEE

"The *Magus Sutra*?" Bunny asked, calling a meeting in our secondary office suite across the Bazaar. Buttercup, delighted to have company during the day, ate sugar out of my palm. Gleep wound around my legs. "I've never heard of it."

"I have," Aahz said, with a wicked grin that spread across his face. "Back in magik school, we used to hide out in the rear staircase behind the library with the dean's personal copy." He rolled his eyes up, reminiscing.

"Aahz! Stay with us," Tananda said, tapping him on the knee. "I've read it, too. It's not as hot as some modern texts on Trollia, but you have to love the classics. It's got some amazing illustrations. If this is something that Diksen can't resist, then it sounds like the solution we've been looking for. Where can we get a copy of this book?"

Aahz shrugged. "I don't know. It's been out of print for over five hundred years."

"Can we, uh, liberate a volume from a collection?" Guido asked. "It sounds like you know of at least two."

"Not a good idea," I said. I was still feeling stung from

the hit my integrity had taken on my day out with Matt, and it was all my own fault. "I'd rather buy one. We'll get paid back for it. Matt said Diksen would pay any price to own it. By the way, why aren't we in M.Y.T.H., Inc.'s headquarters?"

Bunny shrugged. "Bytina picked up some buggy software. I think it came from a client who came into the office yesterday. I mean, there is nowhere you can sit without getting bytten! I'm having the place debugged by an expert. We should be able to get back in there tomorrow, next day at the latest."

Aahz made a face. "The curse must be spreading out."

"We'll get rid of it," Bunny assured him. "If tempting Diksen with the *Magus Sutra* will work, let's concentrate on tracking one down. As Skeeve says, it doesn't matter how much it costs if it works."

There's no more certain way to make the price of a commodity rise than to let it be known that you have to have it. We didn't spread the word, but somehow it got around that we were trying to find a mint copy of a rare book.

Deveels are masters of the hard bargain, and they are not above making a hasty fake in hopes of making a hasty profit. Before midnight, we had a line stretching from the door down the block and around the corner. About dawn, my turn to sit at the front desk and check out possibilities saw very little reduction in the number of sellers hoping to foist off their wares on us. Guido, Aahz, Bunny, Tananda and Nunzio had each had a shift.

"*Lusty Toasty Comics*?" I asked, eyeing the latest offering with distaste. A Deveel maiden cavorted on the cover, wearing nothing more than a smile.

"Well, that's kind of like *Magus Sutra*, isn't it?" asked the hopeful Deveel on the other side of the desk. He was about my height, possibly my age, skinny and pimply.

"This can't be five hundred years old," I said.

"Sure it is. It's issue number two! It's worth three hundred gold pieces!"

"No, thanks," I said, pushing it back again.

"How about five gold pieces?" the Deveel asked. "Look, I can buy a whole year's worth of *Zarzafan the Conqueror* with that!"

"No," I said firmly. "Next!"

The next would-be salesman barely came up to the level of the desk. I could just see his horns peeping over the edge. I leaned forward to look down into the spectacles of an elderly Deveel—or maybe he wasn't a Deveel. Something about him suggested he was wearing a disguise spell.

"I hear you want a copy of the *Magus Sutra*," he whispered, confidentially. He held up a cloth-wrapped bundle.

"Is it yours to sell?" I asked.

"Why," he said, blinking at me with the bemusement of someone who doesn't get out in daylight very often, "yes, of course it is. It has been in the family for a long time. I wouldn't like to sell a family treasure, but you know, times are hard."

I let him natter on, and took the bundle. I knew as soon as I opened the parcel that I was holding something rare and precious. It virtually crackled with potential magik. Even the title seemed to writhe sensuously across the cover.

"Hey, Aahz?" I called. My partner was snoozing on the couch in the president's office. "Aahz!"

He emerged, orange circles under his eyes. "This had better be worth it," he said. "You woke me out of the best dream I've had in . . . whoa."

He homed in on the book on my desk and lifted it with reverent hands.

"Is it real?" I asked.

"Page sixty-seven," he said, thumbing through it hastily. He held it at arm's length, then brought it close, then let out a deep chuckle. "Yes. It's real." I leaned up to look over his elbow at the page, but he slammed the book shut, and aimed his chin at my visitor. "What do you want for it?"

"Well, I was thinking . . ." the elderly Deveel began, polishing his glasses.

"Half," Aahz said, promptly.

"That is hardly a decent offer for a priceless old book," he protested.

"Tough," Aahz said. He took a handful of coins out of his pocket and spread them on the desk. "Take it or leave it."

"How do you know . . . ?"

"I know," Aahz said. "It's got a label for the Magicians' Club library on the flyleaf. Considering how we parted company, I don't mind borrowing their property for a good cause. How about it?" he asked.

"Done," the short Deveel said amiably. He scooped the coins off the desk and tucked them away. "Good morning to you."

"Send the rest of them away," Aahz said, glancing out the door at the line of would-be sellers. "We'll deal with this baby later. I need some sleep."

After a few cups of very strong coffee, I followed Aahz to the shop of a book dealer we knew in the Bazaar. Dewie stroked the book lovingly.

"I hate to do this to a nice old book like this one," he said. He was a lanky Deveel with a back hunched over from years of reading small print in poor light. His large, pale green eyes peered at us over half-glasses with gold frames. "Are you sure you wouldn't rather sell it instead? I'd be proud to have it, and so would a hundred of my most discerning patrons. I could set up an auction for you."

"Gotta do it, Dewie," Aahz said, with regret. "Just get it over with quickly, okay? I hate to hear a good book scream."

"All right," the bookseller said. He disappeared into his workshop. In a short time, he came back. To me, the book looked exactly the same, but it was supposed to. I paid him, and we transferred back to Ghordon.

It was my first visit to the royal palace, and I regretted the haste, but we were running out of time. With some persuasion and several hefty bribes that left Aahz muttering to himself, we were shown into a high-ceilinged room in which every available surface of the white-plastered walls was covered with incised and painted pictographs and glyphs. I amused myself for an hour trying to read them. As far as I could tell, the wall nearest the door was the serialized adventures of a married couple in the desert.

Aahz paced.

When our patience (and Aahz's feet) was nearly exhausted, a grandly dressed vizier appeared and looked down his ape-like nose at us.

"The minister will see you now," he intoned.

Gurn looked up from his desk. I wanted to smile, because it had obviously been built to scale for the little Ghord, but I didn't dare. We needed his help.

"What do you want?" he asked.

"Good to see you, too," Aahz said sourly.

"Never mind the niceties," Gurn said. "You haven't wasted them on me in the past, and I doubt you need them now."

"We need your help," I said.

Gurn shook his head. "I am not getting involved in your dispute with Diksen. I will not mediate or negotiate on your behalf."

"We don't need any of that," I said. "We just need you to make Diksen an offer."

Gurn narrowed an eye at us. "What kind of offer?"

"One he can't refuse," Aahz said.

"Do I look like I work for organized crime?" the minister asked.

"You work in government, don't you?"

"Go away," Gurn said, wearily. "Her majesty is not feeling well, and we have a state visit by an interdimensional monarch coming up."

"We didn't get any sleep either," Aahz said. He slammed the book on the desk. "This is it. All you need to do is to let

Diksen know that you have this, and that you are willing to sell it to him. As an overture of friendship, or whatever bogus excuse you can come up with, you are making it possible for him to buy this book."

Gurn raised an eyebrow. "Why?"

"Because there's a contract for a block in Samwise's pyramid sewn into the binding," I said. "If he buys it, he buys the contract, and his own curse rebounds on him. We can't just send it to him. He has to accept it, or it won't work. You said to use our imaginations, and I am."

"But in order to pass along the curse, I must pay you for the book, then I will be affected by it as well," Gurn said. "No, thank you. I can just barely stand the food in this palace to begin with."

"It's for the Pharaoh," I pointed out. "You want to help her. This ought to do it. If we could figure out another way, we would. This is our best shot."

"How about it?" Aahz asked.

Gurn rubbed his lower lip, thinking deeply. We waited, holding our breath.

"It's devious," said the minister. "I like it." He smiled, which did nothing for his misshapen face, and passed a coin across the table. Aahz took it. "Very well. Leave it with me."

THIRTY-TWO

"Be careful what you ask for."

—MIDAS

It took until early the next morning for a glyph to reach me, almost as soon as I transferred into Ghordon from the Bazaar. The small chunk of stone smacked into my chest and fell to the ground. I picked it up and read it. It had one pictograph on it. I let out the breath I'd been holding in a rush. I handed the pebble to Aahz. It showed a circle with pinpoint eyes and a curving smile.

"He did it," Aahz said, grinning. "Now we wait for the bad luck to begin."

Nothing seemed to happen for two more days. I kept finding myself glancing nervously at the sundial, willing the hours not to pass. Gurn's threat would come due in another day, and I had no doubt that he would make good on it. I looked frequently in the direction of Diksen's pavilion. The office bubble and the gleaming pyramid looked exactly the same.

Diksen might not be noticeably affected by the curse, but we heard from a lot of people who were. A few of Aahz's clients had to back out with one excuse or another. One Pervect had lost his job almost as soon as he had signed the contract. A Deveel lost all her money on a single bet in Vaygus and couldn't supply the down payment. Bendix came back with a writ to threaten Aahz with malfeasance, or some kind of feasance, because even though Aahz had let him out of the contract, the bad luck had persisted. His lawsuit demanded damages in amounts that made my eyes pop. Aahz was visibly pained at the idea of paying penalties on top of having made a full refund. We wondered whether he was just the first of angry clients that Aahz had personally signed up. Aahz had dug deep into his list of acquaintances and persuaded them to rope in their friends and relatives. I knew Bunny would help Aahz make up any shortfall, as this was an official M.Y.T.H., Inc., project, but I also knew he'd rather eat his own stone rather than have to ask.

Other customers without curse-detectors complained that their technology had stopped working, or that their magik had let them down when they needed it the most. Some had acquired body parasites or new allergies, had run-ins with inlaws, or said something unforgivable in the hearing of the one person who shouldn't have heard it in a million years. None of them could precisely lay the blame at our feet for their misfortunes, but I felt guilty about not being able to tell them the truth. Instead, I listened sympathetically to their woes and offered to take them out to the future sites of their stone blocks. After seeing them off, I returned to the office feeling miserable.

"This had better work," Aahz said gloomily.

Until it did, we kept looking for alternatives. So far, nothing promising had come to light. Aahz and I kept up our rounds of the site, fixing what we could and sounding sympathetic about what we couldn't.

"Make way for the Pharaoh!" bellowed a voice from the sky.

"That's all we need," Aahz groaned. But he pasted on a smile as Samwise rushed in to rally us for a royal welcome.

"Hail, in the name of all the Ghords of Ghordon, Eternal Ancestors Who Give Life and Light to All Creatures. Blessings upon Suzal, daughter of Geezer, she who is Pharaoh and Queen of Aegis from the Underworld to the Overheaven, etcetera, etcetera, and so forth!" shouted her herald, alighting on the flagstones. He held up a hand, and the Sphinxes brought the chariot in for a landing. This was another casual visit, with perhaps sixty attendants, a handful of dancing girls, two jugglers and fifteen court officials on hand.

"And how are you doing, gorgeous?" Aahz asked, as he helped her down from the golden staircase.

"Not well, O Sober-faced one," Suzal said. She looked thinner than she had since her last visit. "Things do not sit well with me lately."

"It's the heat," I offered sympathetically.

"It's always hot here," said Gurn. We looked down at him. I had to look twice. Instead of the miserable, twisted figure that we were accustomed to seeing, he was . . . handsome. Very handsome. His eyes were wide and brown under a noble brow, his nose was straight as mine but more aristocratic, his chin strong and square.

"I . . ." I began. What could I say?

"Say nothing," Gurn snapped. "Her majesty wants to view the progress you are making. I hope it is worthwhile."

"The fourth tier is doing really well, your majesty," Samwise said, bowing over and over. He had no wish to get closer to Gurn. "May I offer you a tour?"

"I would enjoy a tour," she said, but she smiled at Aahz. "But I would feel more cheerful if my trusted minister came with me."

"No!" Gurn exclaimed. "I mean, your majesty, I must check upon the business dealings of your architect's company."

"Oh," the queen said, deeply disappointed. She turned to Aahz. "Then, would you escort me, O Sober-faced one?"

"It would be a pleasure, doll," Aahz said, bowing over her hand with a lascivious look. He tucked her arm into his elbow as the Sphinxes came around with Suzal's mini-chariot. He helped her into it and sat on the lip near her feet. The Sphinxes bent their knees, opened their wings, and took off.

I turned to Gurn again.

"What happened?" I asked, unable to contain myself.

"It is your cursed curse!" he said. "I have been able to keep my distance all these years from her majesty because she could hardly bear to behold me, but now she looks at me with favor, even curiosity. I tell you, it is torture! If you do not defeat Diksen soon, my effectiveness as her minister is at an end, and I will not stand for that!"

"It could be your dream come true," I said, keeping my voice low so the other courtiers couldn't hear me. "You said she is your life."

"It is a nightmare! She is the daughter of kings and queens. I am a bureaucrat. That is the way it must remain. Has he capitulated yet?"

"Not yet," I said, with a glance toward the distant pavilion.

"You have only one day."

"I know, I know!"

Gurn stormed away. Chumley took advantage of the fact that everybody's eyes were on the sky to come and murmur down to me.

"No luck on this end so far," he said. "And I haven't been able to find a copy of that book you were looking for."

"Never mind," I said. "We found one. I don't know if it's going to work or not."

"If you need me to, I will speak to the Pharaoh on your behalf. Gurn's not the only advisor she listens to."

"Thanks."

The chariot returned. The queen's normally pale skin had a green cast to it, but not as bad as usual. No doubt Aahz's ongoing chatter had kept her mind off her nausea.

". . . Pretty soon we'll be taking bids for the shopping area surrounding this thing," Aahz was saying as the Sphinxes brought the sedan chair in for a landing. "Sacrifices by Nee-Ro wants a prime location. The rent-a-mourner service is already signed up. All the modern conveniences, but quality only. You'll be proud to say you own the top spot."

"You ease my mind, O noble Pervect," Suzal said, as he handed her down. Aahz tipped me a wink.

"And all at rock-bottom prices," Samwise cracked. "Get it? Rock . . . never mind," he said, as we all looked at him. He cringed.

"One more day," Gurn threatened, as the queen ascended her grand conveyance again.

THIRTY-THREE

"Curses! Foiled again."
—S. WHIPLASH

I didn't sleep well that night. I kept waking up from dreams of being locked in a tiny, dank, dark chamber with slime dripping down the walls onto me. Then I realized that Gleep was asleep with his long neck and head stretched out on the bed beside me. The slime and the damp breath belonged to him. I breathed in the familiar gagging aroma of sulphur and tried to get some rest.

We went back to the office on the morning of the seventh day, but not to stay.

"I see no reason to sit around waiting to go to prison," Aahz said. "I wouldn't have come back at all, but I want a copy of the list of my clients. Either I'll figure out a way to make it up to them, or keep out of their way until this all blows over. Gurn is going to have to chase us if he wants to catch us."

I concurred. We couldn't do anything locked up in a cell. Aahz and I might have to go on the run for a while, but we had plenty of places we could stay for a few days at a time. Gurn wouldn't be able to tell where we had gone. We would work on lifting the curse at a safe distance from Ghordon.

As we appeared in the Zyx Valley, I glanced nervously over at Diksen's pavilion, worrying about threats from that direction as well. Then I looked back again.

"Aahz, look!"

I pointed. He looked.

The bubble, normally clear and iridescent, was murky and sort of brownish-blue.

"Was it like that last night?"

"No," I said.

As we watched, the bubble stretched upward into an ovoid, then compressed into an oblate sphere. It sprang into its normal shape, but the murkiness darkened. Aahz grinned.

"Maybe there's hope, partner. Come on."

We opened the Crocofile and started through the papyri of all of Aahz's contacts. I wrote down the names as he read them off. It turned out to be a much longer list than I had ever dreamed. Aahz must have drawn in people he had met as long ago as childhood, or anyone he'd ever chatted with on a street-corner. Miss Tauret was a little miffed that Aahz paid her little attention when she came in frequently with beer, sandwiches, cookies, chili or any other delicacies she thought would tempt him.

"Not now, honey," he said, holding up a hand without looking up from his stack of papers. "We've got a problem. Maybe later, huh?"

"Later means never!" Bulbous gray nose in the air, Miss Tauret went sashaying out in a huff. Aahz groaned and rubbed his eyes.

Mid-morning, we were only halfway through the sheaves of documents, when Samwise came in to wring his hands at us.

"Has Diksen sent any word yet?" Samwise asked. He had paled from his usual bright pink to a faint shell color.

"No," Aahz said. "Looks like he's going to tough it out."

"But Gurn could be here at any moment!"

"When he is, we won't," Aahz said.

Samwise's eyes widened. "You're going to abandon me?"

"We're here under false pretences," Aahz pointed out. "Your false pretences. You want to make something of it?"

"Well, no, but I thought you would help me!"

"Here's my last and best piece of advice," Aahz said. "Leave. Now. We're about to."

"But, I can't!" Samwise wailed. "I thought you believed in my project!"

"I did. But I also believe in being free to practice my own beliefs. I can't do that if I'm locked in a cell, particularly not with you." He bared his teeth and leaned toward the Imp. "You don't want me reminding you day after day whose fault it is that we're in this situation, do you?"

"I . . . I'll let you know if I see him coming," Samwise said, retreating toward the door.

"Tell him now," Gurn said, peering up at us. We all jumped.

"Gurn's here," I said unnecessarily.

The cursedly handsome minister wasn't alone. Two or three dozen Ghord guards stood behind us, their spears drawn.

"Kid!" Aahz shouted.

That was my cue. I was holding a full load of power from the blue force line. I enveloped Aahz and the protesting Samwise in the spell and transferred us out toward one of Aahz's designated safe houses.

Bamf!

The architect's office vanished around us.

Bamf!

We were back where we started. I looked at my hands as if trying to figure out if I'd thrown one spell too many, and realized I was looking up toward the ceiling.

I was lying on the floor with two or three spears at my throat and more pointed at other parts of my anatomy. I held up my hands in surrender. Aahz and Samwise were similarly occupied with their own branches of the queen's guard.

"You fools," Gurn said, bending down to leer at us. "You

forget that I, too, am a magician. Bind them! We will take them to the palace!"

The Ghords must have been trained by experts in Necropolis, because they wound us all expertly in yards of linen bandages until we were firmly trussed up. I reached into my inner reserves for magik to cut the bands as I had in Necropolis, but they were empty. Gurn must have drained the magik from me when he dragged us back. I reached out to the force lines I could see in my mind's eye, but it was as if they were behind glass. I couldn't touch any of them.

"Aahz, he's blocking me."

"I know, kid. Don't worry."

The guards rolled us onto flying carpets and steered us out into the main office. The clerks followed, wringing their hands.

"Let us go," I said. "We'll figure out something else. Maybe you can even stay as you are now . . ."

"No!" Gurn shouted. "Don't even think about that! Take them to the chariot," he directed his force. "We will throw them into the depths of the dungeons. Her majesty is not used to being trifled with!"

"Who said I offered her trifles?" Aahz asked, as they carried us toward the soaring chariot. There, the Sphinxes stood pawing the ground. "Chocolate melts in this heat."

"Not truffles, trifles!" Gurn shrieked. "Say no more, or suffer the consequences!"

"Are you going to say this is going to turn *ugly?*" Aahz leered.

"Aahz!"

"I refuse to kowtow to this miserable gudgeon."

"That's Gurn," the small minister insisted furiously.

Aahz was unimpressed. "Whatever. If you're going to shut us up, do it. I don't care. You can't hold us. We're powerful magicians."

The small minister danced in fury. "*One* of you is a powerful magician! *One* of you has a big mouth! You will *all* suffer the vengeance of Gurn!"

"Do you guys get your speeches out of a script?" Aahz

asked. "I mean, every two-bit despot and tyrannical prime minister always uses the same syntax. I could almost recite it along with you . . . Yeow!"

Gurn shot a lightning bolt from his fingertip that burned the end of Aahz's nose, but it didn't wipe the grin off his face. The guards dumped us on the golden steps at the foot of the chariot. The sharp edges bruised my ribs. I tried to use magik to ease my position, but Gurn's spell kept me from reaching any power. The small minister mounted the steps. He pointed downward.

"Ghords, to your places!"

"Yeah, he wouldn't want to accidentally *overlook* you," Aahz added. "He *is* short-sighted."

"Why are you provoking him?" Samwise wailed, lying limply in his bandages.

Aahz looked smug. "Because it's fun, and because it can't last. Look."

I tilted my head backwards in the direction of Diksen's pavilion. The bubble was no longer round or remotely clear. It had turned completely black and was twisting and deforming into weird, ugly shapes. Fumes seemed to rise from its surface. Black clouds stained the sky overhead, and lightning crackled down, striking the roiling surface. And something came shooting toward us from its direction.

As it got closer, I could see that it was one Ghord standing on a carpet.

Diksen.

The carpet skidded to a halt at the foot of the chariot. Diksen staggered off and strode directly toward us.

"Get up!" he burbled, gesticulating in the direction of his pavilion. Rain had started pouring down on the shimmering white pyramid. ". . . Fix . . . terrible mess!"

"Go away, Diksen," Gurn said, dangerously. "They are prisoners of the Pharaoh Suzal, may she live forever surrounded by beauty, music, and perfume. May every step she takes be on silk and down. May her glorious features be praised . . ."

"Let them up!" Diksen interrupted him.

Gurn smiled. It was an ugly expression. "Never. They are my prisoners."

"Let . . . go! Undo . . . disgusting . . . misery!"

The small minister was unmoved. "Let the harm they've done resound upon you a thousandfold! I have every reason to dislike you. You insulted her most sacred majesty, she whose parents were touched by divine inspiration when they begot her, she who . . ."

Diksen wrung his hands. "My Dorsals! Skin disease . . . Ick!"

"Sorry to hear that," I said sympathetically. "They are fierce fighters. You ought to be proud of them."

"Algae! Books . . . rotting! My beautiful globe!" Diksen glared down on me, and in the only entire sentence I had ever heard him utter so far, demanded, "Take off the curse!"

I tried to arrange myself into a dignified position, wrapped as I was from neck to heels, but only succeeded in bumping down one more step.

"It's *your* curse," I said haughtily. "I am a powerful magician in my own right. The curse has rebounded on you, with a few little twists of my own."

"My curse? How . . . ?"

"You'll never know," Aahz said, grinning.

"What is it you want?" Diksen asked. In his fury, he was able to produce entire sentences.

"Samwise has offered his apology," I said. "Accept it. Take off the curse, or we all continue to suffer. Now that will include you. You can see what collateral damage you caused."

"Never!" Diksen's jowls flapped angrily.

"Oh, fine," I said. "Then I hope you like living in a hurricane."

Diksen looked back at the twisting, bounding wreck that had been his beautiful office building. In a plaintive little voice, he said, "Mumsy."

"What kind of a son are you if you let your mother sit in the dark like that?" Aahz asked.

"Very well!" Diksen declared. "I accept! But none of you ever dare come near me again!"

"We can handle that," I said evenly. "How about it? You take off your spell, and I'll take off mine."

Diksen reached down into the powerful black force line deep under the desert. He spread out his hands. I could feel a blanket of magik settle down over all of us. It sank through my body and seeped into the sands. As it dissipated, I felt cleaner and clearer of mind than I had in weeks. Samwise, tied like a roast a few steps up from me, let out a hefty sigh.

"Now you," Diksen said.

Gurn folded his arms. I reached out for magik and found the way clear. I cut myself out of the bandages and stood tall.

"Thanks," I said. "It's over."

"But the spell you added to mine . . . ? Undo it!"

"I didn't have to do anything to you," I said. "You did it all to yourself. I just made sure you felt what you did to other people. I didn't add any magik at all."

Diksen gave me a furious look, then stalked back to his carpet. It lifted off and sped back toward the globe. As Diksen's dispell spread outward, the ball of water gradually cleared until it was transparent as crystal.

"Nice job," Aahz said. "Now, get me out of this tourniquet."

I was happy to oblige, snipping the bandages away with one sweep of my magikal shears. I had help: Tweety shook off his harness to help his old friend to his feet. Samwise I left to the less expert but more eager ministrations of the USHEBTIs.

"Now, about a nonstandard activity requiring my Scarabs to leave their assigned tasks in favor of a rescue of a member of the management team, employing nonstandard construction materials . . ." Beltasar's shrill voice would have gone on and on, but Aahz glared fiercely at her and brought his forefinger and thumb together in a sharp gesture. "Perhaps later." She called her minions together, and they swarmed away.

"Well played," Gurn said. "I am obliged that you didn't mention her majesty's suffering that was tied up with that curse."

"No problem," I said. "No need to tell him he'd added injury to insult by refusing to build her a pyramid of her own. Samwise's will be fine, now. Won't it?" I asked the Imp.

"Absolutely!" Samwise declared. "From now on, everything will be on the up and up! Completely!"

"I shall be checking on you to make certain," Gurn said. He stalked up to the main seat of the chariot and sat down.

"Am I still . . ." He felt his face with one hand, and grimaced.

"Yes," I said. Even though the curse was gone, he was still handsome. "You'll get used to it. By the way, thanks for the copy of the *Magus Sutra.*"

"What? Why would you believe I owned a salacious volume like that and would give it away for a handful of gold?"

That detail just confirmed it for me. "You really didn't think I wouldn't figure out that the one legitimate copy would turn up just when we needed it?" I asked. "It had to hurt to let it go. Nice acting job, too."

"You are smarter than you look, Klahd." Gurn shook his head. "As I told you, I would do anything for the Pharaoh. But if you tell any of the others, I will visit a new curse on you. A terrible one from which there will be no recourse."

"Never," I said. "You have my word on it. You can carve it in stone."

THIRTY-FOUR

"All's well that ends well."
—HAMLET

I owed Gleep a thorough head-scratching for being away so much over the past weeks. He lolled on the floor of Bunny's office with his head in my lap, drooling a little as I attacked the scales around his ears with my fingernails.

Aahz had kicked back in his big easy chair, his feet on the extended rest.

"It was my fault," he said. "I should have investigated closer. I should have known better."

"Don't kick yourself," Bunny said. "A lot smarter people than you were tempted by the idea of a kind of immortality, and many of them fell into the trap."

"Smarter than me?" Aahz asked, his eyes narrowing. "No. *Smarter* people actually refused to invest in the pyramid to start with. Here's to getting out of the real estate business."

He raised his repaired goblet to us and took a drink.

"I'm done with oversized monuments and grand plans for the afterlife. Instead, when I go, I just want to disappear and leave people wondering." He bared those four-inch teeth in a grin that would make anyone cringe.

"If that's so," Bunny asked, "then why did I just get a bill of lading for having to warehouse two giant chunks of rock, F.O.B. Aegis?"

"*Two* chunks of rock?" I asked.

Aahz waved a hand. "Maybe Gurn broke my benben before he transported it here. I like to think of it as a souvenir. I don't intend to need it for a long time to come."

"So, M.Y.T.H., Inc., no longer has a problem with curses?" Guido asked. "We don't have to worry about unsatisfied customers comin' here lookin' for satisfaction?"

"No more curses, no more problems," I assured him. "All the stones Aahz sold for Phase Two have been worked into Phase One, giving it a 92% fill rate. Samwise is thrilled. He doesn't really need us any longer. He said he owes us."

"I already sent him his bill," Bunny said.

"He had better cough up in a timely fashion, or he is going to require one of his own tombs," Guido said, bringing his eyebrows down over his nose. "He caused us all to waste a lot of very valuable time."

"You sure gave Gurn a tough time when we were tied up," I said. "Were you really that confident that Diksen would have to ask for help getting rid of the curse?"

"No," Aahz admitted, "but what good would it have done to start panicking and pleading? Gurn would just have loved that. I keep telling you, kid, reputation is as much a part of being an effective magician as the actual chops."

"I know," I said.

"How's the Pharaoh feeling?" I asked Chumley, once again restored to his oversized chair beside that of his sister, Tananda.

"She is restored to her former glory, thanks to you and Aahz," the Troll said. He had cast aside his linen headdress with a grateful sigh. "Though she will miss seeing Aahz, she has come to insist that Gurn attend her nearly every waking moment."

"Poor Gurn," I said, "but it'll keep him from turning up when you least expect him."

"I am afraid the Pharaoh's fascination is going to halve

his efficiency," Chumley agreed. "But if it keeps his nose out of other people's business, it will be a good outcome of that curse."

"It's kind of a pretty nose now," I said, grinning.

"Looks aren't everything," Tananda said. "I think his devotion to Suzal is beautiful."

"Yeah," Aahz said. "You can't buy loyalty like that. Right, partner?" He raised his glass to me and took a healthy swig.

"Right," I said, happily, toasting him back. The others joined in.

Privately, I resolved to go looking for that warehouse where Aahz had had his stone delivered. I wanted a look inside. I had more than a slight suspicion that the papyrus I had signed was so Aahz could order a stone block for me. I didn't want to tell him what I guessed. He obviously wanted it to be a surprise. Moreover, I wanted to check and see if that block I had seen Ay-Talek working on with all the details that were so close to the story of my own life was being stored next to the big triangular monument that Aahz had selected for himself. It was nice to know he thought that much of me. But I wouldn't say anything. That's what loyalty meant to me.

"Next time, warn me when I start to get too emotionally involved in a project," Aahz said. "Anyone hungry? I'm in the mood to splurge."

"You?" Chumley asked, astonished.

"Yeah. Dinner's on . . . Samwise." Aahz held up a jingling purse. "I got my commissions out of him for the sales I made. How about it, Skeeve? Want to go out and get some food? It won't be as fancy as Le Mouton Suprisee, but it'll be edible."

"Gee, Aahz, I would love to, but I've got a date."

"A date?"

"Aaaahhhh!" my partners chorused. Bunny and Tananda looked pleased.

"With the pretty secretary with the black hair?" Aahz winked.

I was abashed. "Uh, no. She and I don't have anything in common." I didn't want to tell him how much I had humiliated myself with Matt. "I'm going to see Aswana. She's a lot of fun."

Aahz raised an eyebrow. "See-Ker's healer? I didn't think she was your type."

"She was really nice to me when I fell into Necropolis. I thought I'd go back and take her out for a great dinner."

Bunny and Tananda exchanged approving nods.

"Fine, kid," Aahz said, with a lazy wave. "Don't do anything I wouldn't do."

"Gee, Aahz," I said innocently. "I wouldn't think of it."

I *bamf*ed discreetly out of the room.

Afterword

Dear Readers,

I know. Ironic, isn't it?

Bob and I had a few different plots we ran by the publishers back in mid-2006 as to what would happen next in the Myth Adventures. The one we wanted to do first they considered too immediately topical, and wanted this one instead.

For those of you who don't know the backstory, Robert Asprin, creator of this series, and my writing partner on it for the last six books and an anthology, passed away suddenly on May 22, 2008, in his home in the French Quarter of New Orleans, Louisiana.

Bob was a remarkable person, who when he was inspired, strewed creativity broadcast. He had a lot of talents, all of which he was willing to share with others. His second ex-wife, Lynn Abbey, co-founder with him of the groundbreaking shared-world anthology Thieves' World (and now its sole proprietor/operator), said that he was the best first teacher that you could ever have. He gained new interests the way that a magpie picks up shiny things. His eclectic interests informed his literature, which is why you find the Myth Adventures full of references to the "Road" pictures featuring Bob Hope and Bing Crosby, the Marx Brothers, Hollywood musicals, gambling, game shows, *Star Wars*, and the writings of Poul Anderson, Gordon R. Dickson, Damon Runyon, and many others, on top of sly characterizations (we call them "tuckerizations" in American SF literature for their founder, Wilson "Bob" Tucker) of people he knew.

Several years ago, he and I began to work together. A lot of theories abound as to how and why we did. The truth is we thought it would be fun, and it would help break Bob out of the writer's block he had suffered for years. Our first collaboration was not a Myth book at all, but a stand-alone magical spy adventure called *License Invoked*. I can't say I was the reason Bob started writing again, but I feel I helped prime the pump, as did Peter Heck, who stepped in to give Bob a hand on the bestselling series Phule's Company. Most of the credit goes to a good friend of Bob's, Bill Fawcett, tuckerized by Bob in *Myth-ing Persons* as Vilhelm, the vampire with the desk full of telephones, and now my husband. Bill encouraged Bob to get back on the keyboard again. He helped Bob create other collaborative projects, such as with Linda Evans on the Time Scout novels, with Esther Friesner on *E. Godz*, and with Eric Del Carlo on *NO Quarter*.

At the time of his death, Bob had just published a new fantasy series, Dragons Wild. The first book, *Dragons Wild*, had gained rave reviews. The second book was complete and ready for copyediting. The publisher was prepared to offer a new and lucrative contract for two new Phules as well as more Myth Adventures. Our Hollywood agent was talking to a couple of producers who were interested in the series. The day he died Bob was just about to be picked up to attend a major SF convention in Columbus, Ohio, where he and I were slated as the literary guests of honor.

In my college pinball arcade, when you maxed out the score, loaded the machine with all the free games possible, racked up all the extra balls, then turned away from the machine, never to return, it was called the Boston walkaway. Bob just staged one of the greatest walkaways of all time. It was ironic because so much was going right, only a phule would leave at that moment, wouldn't he? Or someone who suffered the greatest of myth-fortunes.

All joking aside, Bob was my dear friend for many years. I will miss him. I'll miss working with him, hearing that staccato delivery he used when he was excited about something, or the bellowing laugh. I will miss the two of us breaking into song in the middle of hotel lobbies (to Bill's embarrassment). I'll miss the wisdom that informed the characters he created, and his absolute belief in the magik of that marvelous friendship between Aahz and Skeeve. We should all be so lucky to have a bond like that.

The series is in my hands now. I hope you will trust me to do right by it. I have learned at the master's knee (mostly what a bony knee looks like), and will do my best.

Thanks for supporting the series.

Best wishes,
Jody Lynn Nye

Robert Lynn Asprin

Robert (Lynn) Asprin, born in 1946, is best known for the Myth Adventures and Phule series. He also edited the groundbreaking Thieves' World anthologies with Lynn Abbey. He died at his home in New Orleans in May 2008.

Jody Lynn Nye

Jody Lynn Nye lists her main career activity as "spoiling cats." She has published thirty-five books, such as *Advanced Mythology*, fourth and most recent in her Mythology fantasy series (no relation); three SF novels; and four novels in collaboration with Anne McCaffrey, including *The Ship Who Won*. She has also edited a humorous anthology about mothers, *Don't Forget Your Spacesuit, Dear*, and written over a hundred short stories. Her latest books are *An Unexpected Apprentice*, an epic fantasy, and *Strong-Arm Tactics*, first in the Wolfe Pack series. She lives northwest of Chicago with two cats and her husband, author and packager Bill Fawcett.

New York Times **Bestselling Author**
ROBERT ASPRIN
and
JODY LYNN NYE

Dragons Deal

As head dragon and owner of a successful gambling operation in New Orleans, Griffen McCandles has a lot on his plate. Especially since the Krewe of Fafnir—a society of dragons—has asked him to be the king of its Mardi Gras parade. Being the king is a huge honor, and despite the extra responsibilities, Griffen can't resist the krewe's offer to lead the biggest party of the year.

But not everyone is happy with Griffen's new leadership status. A group of powerful dragons is conspiring to bankrupt his business, from the inside out. And when a young dragon in Griffen's employ is murdered, it becomes clear that certain dragons will stop at nothing to dethrone the new king . . .

penguin.com